RETRIBUTION

Acknowledgements

Many thanks to the people of Bradford for their help, knowingly or otherwise, in the creation of this novel. Without their input, interest, and encouragement it would not have been completed.

Special thanks are also due to Rick and staff at The Little Coffee House in Calverley, Rick ('Nick', in the story) being the man who encouraged me to write 'Premonition', the initial book in this series, without which the rest of the series would not have existed.

This is a work of fiction. Although many of the places referenced in the book are real, some characteristics have been changed to fit the story. The characters and events in this book are products of the author's imagination or are used fictitiously. Any resemblance to actual persons, living or dead, is entirely coincidental.

CHAPTER 1

Brian and Sarah were seated close to each other on the sofa, watching TV. The kids, Daniel and Samantha, were as usual expending as much energy as possible until it was time for bed. At the appointed time, Sarah stood up and made the expected announcement.

"Right kids, it's time for bed. Come on, let's get ready."

The usual sighs and protests ensued. It was their ritual. But Sarah was sticking to hers.

"If you don't go to bed now, the bogeyman will get you."

Daniel was unconvinced and did all he could to convince his little sister it was a ploy. Brian was more realistic in his bargaining.

"Go to bed now, or you'll get no pocket money this week."

They immediately complied, with Sarah ensuring they were washed properly and in their nightclothes before tucking them in and singing softly to lull them to sleep.

"I'll stand by you always, always…."

It was a beautiful, calming, emotional song she'd downloaded immediately after she first heard it. But there was one more ritual to be performed. Daniel and his father always played the same game.

"I'm not tired. I want to stay up and watch telly."
"If you don't go to sleep, the bogeyman will get you."
"I don't believe in bogeymen."
"You will when you wake up in the morning and look in the mirror and find you've turned into a pig."
"I like pigs."
"You won't say the same when I make you into a bacon sandwich and eat you."
"Night night."
"And sleep tight, or I'll arrest you and make you spend the night in chokey."

They were soon sound asleep, and Sarah and Brian returned to the lounge, Brian wincing as he sat.

"What's up, Brian?"
"Stomach ache."
"What's brought that on?"
"Must have been the stew you made for tea."
"Cheeky bugger. Are you OK?"
"It'll pass."

The following morning, they ate breakfast together after Brian had showered while Sarah was getting the kids up, washed and dressed. Then there was the usual discussion to determine how they were going to spend their day. Brian's routine varied very little. Unless he had other plans, or he got a phone call while having breakfast, he would make his way to Bradford CID's HQ. Sarah would drop Daniel at school before spending the day either doing housework and shopping or taking Samantha out to the park or some other activity. She would then pick Daniel up after school and find some way of helping the kids expend their boundless energy before Brian came home.

Brian said goodbye to the kids and kissed Sarah before driving to work after saying,

"See you all at tea-time."

He had no inkling what the day had in store for him.

****

It was late afternoon. The van had been parked for fifteen minutes before the driver got out and walked up the drive of number 14. He looked left and right, drew a deep breath, and rang the bell and waited, tensed and ready. Sarah opened the door, smiling. Until she saw the knife in his hand. In a panic, she tried to close the door, but he was too strong and pushed her inside. He plunged the knife deep into her stomach. She gasped and dropped to her knees. He turned quickly and closed the front door behind him, checking first if anybody was in sight. All clear. He turned back to his victim, but gathering all the strength she could muster, she was on her feet and staggering away from him, closing the kitchen door as she passed it on her way to the lounge, desperately trying to get to her mobile to raise the alarm. Too late. He was on her, beating her skull with a heavy metal bar. Her blood sprayed against the wall as she fell, helpless, to the floor, where further thrusts of his knife into her guts ended her resistance.

He caught his breath and listened. All was silent. He walked slowly towards the window, peeping round the curtain out into the street. No sign of alarm. He turned and walked towards the kitchen where he expected to find his other two victims. He stopped outside the door and listened. He could hear a muffled sobbing from inside. He pushed open the door and saw them, a young boy and a smaller girl, just a toddler, wide-eyed with fear, clinging to her older brother who was brandishing a plastic toy hammer. He walked towards them slowly, the knife behind his back. The young boy stood in front of his little sister, in an effort to protect her and, raising his hammer, struck the intruder on the arm. The man grabbed the hammer, pulling it from the boy's grasp, and threw it in a corner before grabbing the boy by the hair, pulling his head back and slicing his throat with the blade. Blood sprayed everywhere as the boy's life was ended. He turned to the wailing girl and quickly put an end to her terror with the knife severing her windpipe.

Again, he stopped, savouring the silence as he peeled off his bloody jacket, wiping the blood off his hands and folding it inside out before taking a replacement top out of the backpack he carried. He pulled it on and removed his sweatpants, pulling on a clean pair. He stuffed the bloody clothes into his backpack and moved to the back door, opened it just a little and peered out. No sounds of alarm. He stepped out and walked down the path to the gate, released the catch, opened it and strolled down the narrow path to the end of the block where his van was parked. He climbed in and drove away, smiling, mentally replaying the carnage he'd just left. He wasn't in the slightest concerned that he'd left his fingerprints on the toy hammer when he wrenched it from the boy's grasp.

He began to focus on his next intended victims as he drove towards Wrose, parking at the roadside on a quiet side street. He took a crumpled sheet of paper from his breast pocket, smoothed it out and looked at the names written on it, planning who would be his next victim.

CHAPTER 2

DI Brian Peters had had a long day and was ready to log off when the call came. It was from Teresa, CID's analyst and factotum. She sounded upset.

"Brian, I've just had a report. There's been some sort of incident at your home. You need to go immediately."
"What's happened Teresa?"
"I don't know, Brian. But it sounds serious. I'll come with you. I'll meet you in the car park. Please hurry."

He logged off, picked up his keys and jacket and ran towards the exit. Teresa was already waiting in the car park for him. They got into Brian's Vauxhall and drove off.

"Are you going to tell me what this is all about, Teresa?"
"I don't know, Brian. I just took the call from Forensics."

They both remained silent for the rest of the trip, though Brian was clearly worried, as different scenarios played through his mind. As they turned into his street, they could see a crowd had gathered on the pavements, held back by tape strung across the road. Three uniformed constables were on duty. Brian stopped the car further down the street and walked quickly towards the house, not even bothering to close the car door. Teresa hurried after him.

Reporters had gathered at the end of the drive. Brian brushed past them, ignoring their questions, and walked past the SOCO van parked on his drive. He was stopped by a uniformed officer on duty at the door. He recognised Brian and Teresa and asked them to wait a second until he checked they were allowed to enter.

"Just a moment, please, sir."
"What the hell's going on?"

Allen Greaves, the head of Forensics, came to the door, escorted them into the hall and stopped them from going any further.

"What's happened, Allen? Why are you here? Where's Sarah? Where are the kids?"
"Let's go into the living room, Brian."

Teresa guided him in the right direction. He could see blood, sprays and damp patches of blood. He seemed numb, unable to understand what might have happened. Or, if he understood, was unable to process it.

"Please sit down. Brian. I've some bad news. You've had a break-in…."
"Where is everybody?"
"Sarah's been taken to the hospital, Brian. I'm afraid she's critically ill."
"What about Daniel? Sam?"
"I'm afraid it's bad news, Brian. I'm afraid…. I'm sorry, Brian."
"No! Why? How? What happened?"
"We don't know yet, Brian. Sarah managed to call 999 and they were able to trace the address. A car and an ambulance were dispatched, and we got the call as soon as they arrived. The kids were already dead, Brian. Sarah was clinging on. But it's not looking good. Is there somewhere you can stay, Brian? We'll be here for some time."

Teresa took Brian's arm.

"I'll take you to BRI, Brian. There's nothing you can do here for now."

He allowed himself to be led out to the car and driven away. He didn't speak. He *couldn't* speak. Teresa drove in silence until they parked at the BRI. She led him to Reception where they were directed to the Operating Theatre and asked to wait in the corridor outside. The thirty-minute wait seemed endless. It was then that Brian put his hands to his face and sobbed while Teresa attempted to comfort him until they received the news they were dreading. Sarah was dead. She had never regained consciousness. She had been stabbed several times in the stomach and beaten about the head in a frenzied attack. There was nothing more they could have done.

Brian broke down.

"Take me back to the house, please, Teresa."
"Are you sure, Brian?"
"There's nothing I can do here. I've signed the forms. I need to visit the crime scene."

"Would you like me to phone your parents?"
"No. Thank you, but that's a job I need to do. The house first, please. I need to know what happened. Someone has to pay for this."

They drove in silence back to Idle. As they approached the house, they could see that word had already spread. There was a TV van, along with the technical staff setting up and testing the equipment in preparation for a live broadcast from the scene. The reporter, having seen Brian getting out of the car, was already walking towards him when Teresa stepped in front of him, stopping him dead with a stare, followed by the words,

"This is a live crime scene. We'd appreciate it if you'd just let us get on with our jobs. We'll issue a statement the moment we have some news for you. Now, please step aside. We have work to do."

With that, she brushed him aside as they walked to the front door where a constable, having recognised them, allowed them immediate access. They met Allen inside. Brian took a deep breath, trying to remain detached, before speaking calmly.

"What have we got, Allen?"
"Are you sure you're ready for this, Brian?"
"I'm sure."
"It appears that someone came to the front door. Sarah opened it and was stabbed once in the stomach. She was pushed backwards and, I think, stumbled into the front room. I believe she was trying to get to the phone, and also, to keep the intruder away from the kids who were in the kitchen. Sarah was stabbed again, four times, and beaten about the head before the intruder, probably believing her to be already dead, went into the kitchen and cut Daniel's throat first, and then Samantha's. They died almost instantly, Brian."
"OK, Allen. Any fingerprints? Other clues?"
"We have prints. We just have to eliminate those of the family members. We also have footprints in the blood in the hall. Oh, and by the way, it doesn't look like a robbery. Nothing has been disturbed, apart from damage during the attack. Whoever did this wasn't looking for money or items of value. The motive, to me, appears to be murder. Pure and simple."
"If that's the case, either we're looking for a psychopath, or it's a revenge attack by someone with a grudge, probably against me."

"That's possible, Brian. Anyway, we won't be long now, and we'll give it our full attention back at the lab. I'll let you know as soon as we have something."
"Thanks, Allen."
"I'm truly sorry, Brian. We'll do all we can. We're finished in this room but please don't go elsewhere just yet."
"OK."

He sat on the settee, Teresa by his side, holding his hand as his tears flowed.

"I never had chance to say goodbye, Teresa. I needed to tell Sarah how much I loved her. I needed to kiss the kids and give them a big cuddle. Someone will pay. I promise here and now. Someone will pay."
"We'll all be with you, Brian. We'll all do whatever it takes."
"Thank you, Teresa. Now, would you mind? I need to phone dad."

****

It was a difficult phone call. Brian's parents doted on their only grandchildren and were devastated. Brian was adamant that he didn't want them to come over. He needed time alone. He would see them the next day to discuss arrangements. Right now, he needed to be alone.

"Would you mind letting DCI Gardner know what's happened, Teresa? Tell him I need a couple of days off. I need to arrange funerals. And there's legal stuff."
"I'll tell the DCI, Brian. I'm guessing the team have got wind of it already, but do you want to tell them anything?"
"Just tell them I'll be leading this case. Anything they learn comes to me. OK?"
"OK. I'd best get back. Do you want me to call in later?"
"No, Teresa. Go home to your partner. Kiss her and tell her you love her. It's important."
"I understand. Try to get some rest."

As soon as the Forensics team had left, Brian took a bottle of malt whisky from the cupboard and poured himself a large glass. And then, another one. He stared at the bloodstained carpet and at the spatter on the wall by the door, imagining the horror and pain

Sarah must have endured, and her anguish at being unable to do anything to protect her innocent children.

His thoughts were interrupted by the buzz of his mobile. His closest friend and ex-boss, Don McArthur.

"Hello, Don."
"Brian, I've just heard. I'm so sorry. Is there anything I can do?"
"No, Don, thanks. I'm still just taking it all in."
"Is anybody with you?"
"No. Forensics have finished, and I've sent Teresa home. I'm just having a glass before I tidy up a bit."
"Do you want me to come over?"
"No, Don. Thanks, but I've things to organise. And I just need some time to digest what's happened. I need to be alone just now. I'm not very good company right now."
"OK, Brian. Please call me if you need anything."
"Will do, boss. 'Bye."

He'd instinctively called Don 'boss', though it was a couple of years since he'd officially retired. Old habits die hard. He poured another glass and thought about Sarah and their kids. He wished he'd just had a regular nine-to-five job so he could have spent more time with them instead of spending his life chasing criminals. The thought had fixed firmly in his mind that his family had been murdered, targeted by someone who had crossed his path as a policeman. It could only be a revenge attack by someone he'd brought to justice. If he was right, there would be a long list of suspects.

He took the family's laptop out of a drawer and opened the album of photographs, each one triggering a particular memory. He scrolled idly through them. Some made him smile, others brought him to the brink of tears, reminding him of what had been taken from him. He finished the glass and went up to their bedroom. He couldn't help himself peeking into the kids' room as he passed, then, overcome with grief, closing the door and going to the bathroom where he was violently sick. He staggered into the bedroom and lay, fully clothed on the bed, where he slept fitfully, dreaming of some of the horrors he'd encountered in his working life. None, though, matched the one he faced now.

He was woken by the sun streaming through the open curtains. He staggered to the bathroom where he threw up once again. He undressed and showered. Pulling on a bathrobe he walked hesitantly down to the kitchen, horrified to find he'd left it as it was when Forensics had examined it. He took a cup from the cupboard and made a strong coffee which he sipped as he walked slowly from room to room, hoping in vain to see the kids playing, or Sarah reading, or any sign of normality. But life would never be normal again. He was consumed with the desire for vengeance. He vowed not to stop until he'd brought the killers to justice or been killed himself in the quest.

He finished his coffee and hurled the empty cup at the wall where it smashed. He would clean up the mess later.

He sat in the kitchen for almost an hour until his mobile buzzed. The display indicated it was Teresa. He really didn't want to speak to anyone but understood that Teresa wouldn't interrupt his grieving unless she had something important to tell him.

"Brian, I've just been speaking to the DCI. He's asked me to tell you you've been given three months compassionate leave – more if you need it…."
"I need to work, Teresa. I can't sit here moping. I need to get this out of my system and move on. Sarah wouldn't want me to grieve forever."
"It takes time, Brian. You need the time off work. We can handle it. And if you need anything, we'll be here for you."
"Who's handling the case?"
"Lynn and Gary, initially."
"Ask them to keep me informed."
"Will do. Take care, Brian."

He closed the call and sat with his head in his hands. An hour or so later, when his parents arrived, he still hadn't moved.

****

The next few days passed in a blur of phone calls, filling in forms and organising the things he'd always taken for granted. Shopping, paying bills, emptying the kitchen waste bin. Dozens of jobs he'd delegated for years. Things which were always taken care of while he acted the part of breadwinner, but which now took on a sense of importance. The routine helped keep him sane, gave him a purpose to get out of bed every morning. His mother taught him how to operate the washing machine and how to iron. Things he'd forgotten over time. It all helped to keep him busy as the funerals approached.

Sarah had no living relatives. She was an only child whose parents had died in a car crash when she was only seven. She was raised by foster parents and had left home when she was twenty-one. She had few close friends but had nevertheless been content with her husband and the two children she adored. They were her life. She wanted nothing more. She had long ago expressed her wish to be cremated and her ashes to be thrown to the wind on Ilkley Moor. Brian would honour that wish and ensure the remains of her beloved children would be with her for all time. That was what she would have wanted.

Every time he picked up a card which dropped through the letterbox he wept, even before he opened it. Most were from Daniel's school friends. But some were from people he didn't even know. Local people, who felt his pain, his grief, his anger. The entire population of Bradford was united in sorrow at the outrage which had occurred in their city. Each card, each article in the T & A and on the TV news, each mention on social media, simply fuelled his desire for revenge.

****

Brian's wish for a quiet ceremony at Scholemoor cemetery was respected. TV and news teams remained outside the boundary, along with a crowd of citizens come to pay their respects. It was a simple ceremony, attended only by Brian, his parents, his close friend Don McArthur, and Teresa, and afterwards, they adjourned for a private gathering at the Idle Draper.

It was a long day at the end of which Brian and Don were left alone in the kitchen at Brian's, sipping whisky in silence. Eventually, Don said what was on his mind.

"I can imagine how you feel right now, Brian. But promise me you'll let CID handle it. It's the top priority for them and will remain top priority until they bring whoever is responsible to justice. But you

need to promise me you'll step back from it. You're too close. Too involved."
"I can't promise, Don. You'd be the same in my shoes. This is personal. I have to be involved. I have to catch the bastard. I have to. For the sake of Sarah and our kids. I won't rest until their killer is dead."

There was a brief silence before Don held out his hand.

"In that case, I'm with you."
"You don't have to get involved, Don."
"I think you'll find I'm not the only one, Brian. Every member of your team feels the same. We're all on your side. In fact, we've already started work. Teresa's compiling a list of every criminal you've put away, as well as all their associates and family. We all believe this was a revenge attack. We *will* find out who was responsible, Brian. As for what happens then…."
"What happens then is that I take my revenge."
"I can't sanction that, Brian. You know that. Even though I would want the same if I were in your shoes. We have to let justice take its course."
"The only justice I can see is an eye for an eye."

They looked each other in the eye until, eventually, Don held out his hand again.

"If that's the case, I'm with you. Legally, I oppose it, but morally I'm on your side."

They shook hands and toasted their alliance with a large glass of malt.

"The first thing you need to understand, Brian, is that you are on leave. Gary and Lynn are leading on this case officially. You can't be seen to be involved. You need to let me act as your proxy. I can gather intelligence from CID, and we can act on it. Agreed?"
"We'll see. As long as I'm in at the kill."
"Agreed."

They drank in silence for a while before Don spoke again.

"There's one thing we haven't considered, Brian."
"What's that?"

13

"That you might be the next target."
"I have considered that. Let them come."
"You'll need a weapon. Let me get you a pistol."
"Can you do that?"
"Of course. There are still people who owe me favours. No questions asked."

****

He woke and showered early the next morning, while Don slept on the sofa. He dressed and made coffee before waking Don.

"Come on, Don. Rouse yourself. Here's a coffee."
"What time is it?"
"10.30."
"Christ! That must have been a hell of a session."
"Do you want some breakfast?"
"No, thanks. I don't think I could stomach it. How about you?"
"I'm not hungry."
"So, what are your plans for today?"
"Taking Sarah and the kids to their favourite spot."
"Do you want me to come?"
"No, Don. Thanks, but I just want to be with them for a while. Say my goodbyes."
"OK. Let me get washed and I'll be off."

****

It was a damp morning and quite cold. He sat on a rock at the Cow and Calf, looking over Ilkley and beyond while cradling the urns containing the ashes. There were tears in his eyes as he took out his phone and selected the track. He pressed 'play', mouthing the lyrics to Sarah's favourite song, Bruce Springsteen's 'I'll Stand By You', the song she used to sing to the kids every night when she put them to bed.

"You wake me in the night with tears falling down, come let me dry them for you.
I wish I could tell a story, chase away all those ghosts you've got inside of you...."

He was still in tears when it ended, yet he felt compelled to play it again before opening the urns and releasing the ashes in the wind.

"'Bye, darling. 'Bye Danny. 'Bye Sam. I'm sorry I've brought this on you. I promise I'll make it up to you and then we can be together again."

He sat there for a further hour before walking to his car for the lonely drive back to his empty house, stopping only at a supermarket where he picked up a couple of pre-packed sandwiches and a bottle of malt whisky.

****

Even though he'd left the central heating on, the house felt cold. Rather than adjusting the temperature, he kept his jacket on, pouring himself a glass which he sipped while he played back the messages on his answerphone. Condolences mainly. Messages of sympathy and support. None of them really registered. He turned to the stack of post which had arrived while he was out. Much of the same. He closed his eyes and drifted off to sleep.

He slept fitfully, his dreams populated first by happy memories of time spent with his family, but then interrupted by malevolent and disturbing images of demons whose faces gradually morphed into people he recognised. Rapists, murderers, people smugglers, drug dealers. The dregs of humanity. And each one of them was laughing at him.

He woke suddenly. His phone was buzzing.

"Hello?"
"Brian, it's dad. Are you OK?"
"Oh, yes, dad. I'm OK. I was just sleeping."
"I've tried to call you but didn't get an answer."
"I was sleeping. Sorry. What did you want?"
"Just to see if you were OK. If you needed anything."
"No, dad. I'm fine. Thanks."
"Do you want us to come over?"
"No. I'm fine."
"OK. Just let us know if you need anything."
"Yeah. 'Bye for now."

He closed the call, thinking he'd been unnecessarily rude. But his mind was on his dreams. He made himself a coffee and sat at the kitchen table. He picked up his briefcase and extracted the file he needed. The post-mortem reports on Sarah and the kids. Until now he'd only read them superficially. Now they had his full attention. He picked up a pen and an A4 pad and made notes.

"Sarah: Answered knock at door? Stabbed in stomach in hall. Tried to get to phone. In living room, stabbed 4 more times in stomach and beaten about the head."

He flicked through the pathologist's notes until he found what he was looking for and added to his own notes.

"Head wounds inflicted by the 'claw' of a claw hammer."

He then added further forensic details from the report.

"The wounds to Sarah's stomach and to the kids were caused by the same implement – a knife with a curved blade approximately 7 inches long."

He thought for a moment before agreeing with the pathologist's conclusion that there was only one attacker, whose sole purpose was to kill the occupants of the house. There was no doubt in his mind it was a targeted attack which had been carefully planned and executed. He noted that a set of fingerprints had been found in the house, as well as shoeprints in the blood, but as yet no match had been found in the criminal database. He decided to call Teresa for an update.

"Teresa, is there any news on the prints found at the crime scene?"
"You know you shouldn't be asking me that, Brian. You're on compassionate leave."
"So, show me some compassion and answer the question."
"There's no match on the UK database, Brian. The prints have been sent to Europol but we've heard nothing yet."
"OK. Who gave the instruction not to speak to me?"
"It's from high up, Brian. Above DCI Gardner. He would rather have you on the team, but the top dogs are frightened you might go on a vendetta."
"They're probably right. But I'm not prepared to sit back and wait for something to happen. I want to know what's going on. I *need to know* what's going on."

"I agree. Call me at home in the evening and I'll tell you what I know."
"Thanks."

He ended the call.

****

Brian woke suddenly next morning. It was nine-thirty, much later than he would normally wake but nevertheless he was tired. He'd had a restless night. He made a mug of strong coffee and sat at the kitchen table, thinking over what Teresa had said when he called her the previous evening.

One of his neighbours had seen a black van, a Ford, on the street on the day of the incident. He was expecting a parcel from Amazon and assumed it was the delivery van, but it just sat, engine running, a couple of doors away from Brian's house. After fifteen minutes, it drove away, but returned in the afternoon. He went to answer a phone call and when he looked out of the window, the van had gone. When he was interviewed by Gary after the incident, the only details he could remember about the van was a partial number plate, YC18. They'd checked all local traffic cameras and spotted the van on Wrose Road shortly after the assumed time of the attack. After running the plate through the DVLA database, it was found to belong to a Vauxhall Astra whose owner had reported the theft of the plates two days earlier. His alibi checked out. Currently, they had no other leads and were pinning their hopes on finding the Ford van. Brian made a mental note to talk to his neighbour in the hope that he might remember something else about the incident.

He answered his phone.

"Brian, it's Gardner. How are you?"
"I guess you could say I'm as well as can be expected."
"Of course. I'm sorry. I thought you should know that Gary is leading the investigation and the entire team is working on it. Inevitably, some will have to be re-assigned if, when, other crimes are reported."
"I understand, sir. Thank you."
"I'm aware that you will be conducting your own inquiry, so please keep us in the picture, and use Teresa's skills wherever possible.

We all want to help wherever we can, Brian, but we can't ignore other cases."

"Of course not, sir."

"There is some other help available to you though."

"What's that, sir?"

"I had a call earlier this morning from PC Schofield, who was temporarily assigned to us for a while last year. You remember him?"

"Scoffer? Yes, sir."

"He called me to pass on his condolences, and to ask if we needed his help in any way. He feels he owes you."

"Are you taking him on?"

"No, Brian. But I wondered if you might."

"I'm not with you, sir."

"He's due three weeks leave. He'd like to offer his services to you free of charge. Do you want his number?"

"Please. I'll talk to him."

****

Scoffer was sincere in his desire to help. They met up at the Draper and sat outside around the back.

"So, what can I do to help, boss?"

"It will be no different to any other case, Scoffer. Someone out there has murdered my family. I want whoever was responsible to be brought to justice. And I'll use any means possible."

"When can I start?"

"You understand that working on this case could be the end of your career in the police?"

"Why? Because we're bringing a murderer to justice?"

"That would be the best outcome. But I'm quite prepared to kill for revenge."

"If I were in your position, I'd feel exactly the same, boss. I'll do whatever it takes. I owe you."

"You don't owe me anything, Scoffer. But welcome aboard."

"When do I start?"

"Tomorrow?"

"Tomorrow's the day my three-week annual leave starts."

They shook hands and finished their drinks as Brian outlined his plans.

18

"From the Forensics report, it was a cold-blooded murder. Nothing was stolen. Nothing was disturbed. The motive, pure and simple, was to get inside the house and murder the occupants. As far as we can tell, there was only one killer, who knew that only Sarah and our two kids were in the house. Therefore, the house has been under surveillance for some time. A neighbour saw a Ford van parked close by around the time of the incident. It had false plates. The only other hard evidence we have are fingerprints, which we're unable to match, and shoe size nine. The objects used in the attack were a knife and a claw hammer. I'll send you a copy of all my notes and tomorrow we'll go door-knocking on the neighbours to see if anyone remembers any other details."
"Do you have any suspects?"
"Loads. Practically everybody I've put away has a grudge against me. I'll be taking a fresh look at every case I've handled since I joined CID."
"Then the sooner we get started, the better."
"Just one word of advice. Bradford CID are also working on the case. We need to ensure we keep them in the loop regarding our investigation, and they'll do the same for us. We don't want to get in each other's way."
"Understood."
"The other thing to remember is that, officially, I'm not involved in this investigation. I'm on compassionate leave. So, if I screw it up, or you screw it up, our careers could be finished."
"I'll take the chance on that."
"OK, bring yourself up to date regarding what we've got, and we'll pick it up in the morning. And thanks, Scoffer. I appreciate what you're doing."

****

The noise woke him. He turned to check the clock. 08.30. He dragged himself out of bed and moved the curtains just enough to see who was ringing his doorbell. Scoffer was looking up at him, waving. He opened the window.

"Sorry, boss. Am I too early?"
"No, Scoffer. My fault. I had a late night. I'm coming down."

His head was pounding as he made his way down the stairs to let Scoffer in.

"Make yourself a cuppa. I'll just get a quick shower."
"Do you want me to call Teresa to find out what they have planned for the day?"
"Yeah. Good idea. I won't be long."

He showered and dressed quickly, taking a couple of aspirin before going downstairs. He had stomach ache again. He knew he'd had too much whisky before he went to bed. It was impossible to disguise the fact. He'd deal with it. He'd book some sessions with his counsellor. But that would have to wait. He'd a killer to catch first.

"Jesus, boss. You look crap. You should go back to bed."
"Too much to do, Scoffer. Let's get started. I'll just get a coffee while you tell me what CID have got planned."
"Teresa emailed me a list of the prime suspects. The names in red are the ones who are the priority. CID will be looking into those. They suggest we look at the not so obvious candidates – the names in black type. Teresa's appended notes regarding each one."
"Am I right in guessing they are all criminals I've put away?"
"They seem to be."
"OK. Who's top of our list?"
"Dean Donachie."
"Him? He wouldn't have the balls for this! Besides, we have his prints on file. Surely, they've been checked."
"Maybe he's behind it but someone's committed the murder at his request."
"It's a possibility, I suppose. We'll talk to him. You'd better drive."

Donachie was quickly ruled out. He hadn't taken drugs for over a couple of years now, had a steady job at the Co-op, and no longer had any contact with Danny Hardcastle, the man who murdered his mother, and who was still in prison for that and other criminal activity. As Brian explained,

"Hardcastle was a bent copper. A DI at Bradford. He was running a drug smuggling racket along with three other officers, plus a desk sergeant, Barlow, who drove for him, and with the knowledge and implicit consent of a previous Chief Inspector. Hardcastle would be top of my list. I put him away, and he has the contacts and influence to pay someone to get his revenge on me."

"Lynn and Gary are visiting him in Strangeways this afternoon."
"OK. Are the names Barlow, Schofield, Ward, and Tarkovics on the list? That's a different Schofield by the way. Not you. He was a bent DS."
"Yes. They're all on CID's list."
"OK. Who's next for us?"
"Laura Carberry."
"She's still in prison, isn't she?"
"Yes."
"I doubt whether she has any interest in pursuing me. Or whether she has the influence to persuade anyone else to kill for her. I think we're wasting our time there. Let's go back and talk to my neighbours. See if we can jog anybody's memory."

They spent the afternoon learning very little of use, apart from the fact that two other neighbours had seen the black Ford in the area at different times. Altogether, the sightings occurred on six different days, at different times. Nobody in the area had received a delivery at any of those times. That was the clincher for Brian. The van had been used purely for reconnaissance. After showing his neighbours images on his laptop of various models in the Ford range, he was able to establish it was a 4th generation Transit, post 2013. Unfortunately, no accurate description of the driver was provided. All he had was a generic description. Male, 40s-50s, white/tanned, medium height/weight, short dark hair, and, unfortunately, wearing a face mask. It was a long shot, but he passed the information to Teresa anyway. She, in turn, passed the information to Traffic and all mobile units.

****

The fact that he felt as if he was contributing something to the team's efforts to catch the killer had galvanised Brian. He had an early night, after a couple of large measures of whisky, and slept well. He was up, fed and dressed by the time Scoffer arrived, followed shortly after by Don McArthur. They were sorting out their plans for the day ahead when a phone call stopped them in their tracks. DCI Gardner.

"Brian, I'm sorry to have to tell you this, but there have been some developments we in CID need to address. I don't know whether you've seen the news this morning, but there was an arson attack late last night which resulted in five deaths. Orders from above mean we have to give priority to this case."

"Why?"

"It looks like a hate crime. The family have been targeted. They are Asian."

"I see."

"And on top of that, we have to investigate a missing person report."

"That won't take the entire team."

"I know, Brian. But we still have to commit resources to it. But more to the point, my bosses have asked me to ensure that any possible racism is nipped in the bud. They feel that we may be seen as institutionally racist if we don't fully investigate the arson attack on an Asian family, but instead put our resources into investigating an attack on one of our own. The situation is compounded by the fact that the shop is owned by the brother-in-law of a local councillor."

"Any chance of bringing in some temporary help?"

"You've already taken Scoffer. I'm waiting to hear if we can borrow Andy Thompson again for a while. But as it is, we're fully stretched."

"OK. I understand. Just promise that we'll have access to Teresa while we investigate our case."

"That's a given."

It was only when Brian had ended the call that it occurred to him that he had referred to 'our case'. He was doing his job dispassionately and objectively.

Those members of his team who had been reassigned to the new cases felt the same. Though disappointed and frustrated at being removed from Brian's case, they approached their new assignments calmly and professionally. Gary and Jo-Jo took the arson, and Lynn and Paula looked into the missing person case. Louise floated between the two, wherever she was needed.

****

Nonetheless, Brian had already planned his main task for the day. He had read Gary's report of his interview with Danny Hardcastle the previous afternoon and wanted to follow up. He reckoned that Hardcastle wouldn't be able to forgo the opportunity to gloat over his arch-enemy's misfortune and might let slip something valuable. Don and Scoffer, meanwhile, would be speaking to Hardcastle's underlings, apart from Schofield, whom Brian had always suspected was an unwilling partner in Hardcastle's illegal schemes.

****

Brian presented himself at HMP Manchester at the agreed time, was signed in and had his identity verified before being escorted to a private room where he sat patiently until Hardcastle was brought in. The two men stared silently at each other until Hardcastle eventually broke the silence.

"Long time, no see, Mr Peters. How've you been?"
"You know the answer to that, Hardcastle. Let's cut the crap. It's been about three years since we spoke."
"You're right. In fact, the last time I saw you was in court, when I was sent down. You had a great big grin on your face. You're not laughing now, though, are you?"
"You know all about it, then?"
"News travels fast round here. When we heard, there was a bit of a party. We were all so sad. Not."
"You know we're analysing every phone call you've made since you've been here."
"You won't find anything, Peters."
"Don't be too sure."
"You won't. Because it was nothing to do with me. Shame, really. I would have liked to have claimed responsibility, but I had planned to wait until I was released. And now someone's beaten me to it. You could do me a favour, though."
"What's that?"
"Send me copies of the crime scene photos. I need something stimulating to put on the cell walls."
"Well, I'm sorry I'll have to leave you here, but it's only for another fifteen years or so. But don't worry. As soon as you get out, I'll be in touch."
"I'll look forward to that, Peters."
"Not as much as I will, Hardcastle. Believe me, I can't wait to meet you somewhere quiet. Just you and me. And if I find out you had anything to do with my recent problems, you'll wish they'd kept you in here until you died, because your life outside won't be worth living."
"Just let me tell you this, Peters. I had nothing to do with your family's murder. That's God's honest truth. But I wish I had. It's what you deserve."

Brian saw no point in continuing the interview, so summoned the guard to escort Hardcastle back to his cell. He sincerely hoped that Don and Scoffer had better luck with the other ex-officers who were complicit in Hardcastle's crimes.

On his way out he called at the Governor's office. The Governor was in a meeting, but his secretary gave a guarded answer to his question regarding the use of mobile phones in the prison.

"No. They have access to a prison phone and are only allowed to call specific numbers for family and friends. The calls are recorded and monitored. However, mobiles frequently turn up in searches of prisoners' cells and communal areas. They are smuggled in by friends and it's a continuing battle. It's a criminal offence."
"Has Hardcastle ever been found with a mobile in his possession?"
"No. But that doesn't mean he can't access one. They'll always find a way. In the past we've sacked prison officers who have been bribed to provide a mobile phone. It happened occasionally. But now, they have to leave them in their locker when they come on duty. We've also found that occasionally a visitor would attempt to pass a phone to an inmate during visiting time."
"Thanks for your time."

It was the answer he expected. And without gaining access to the specific phone, he wouldn't be able to trace the calls made on that device. He got back in his car and drove to Armley, where ex-DS Schofield was serving his sentence.

CHAPTER 3

He parked up and presented himself at Reception. Having shown his ID, he was escorted to an Interview Room, where Schofield was waiting. Brian was a little taken aback when Schofield rose and extended his hand.

"Good to see you, sir. I was hoping to get the chance to apologise for bringing disgrace on the unit."
"Would you mind if I ask you a few questions first?"
"Go ahead."
"I'm sure you've read the papers and seen the news. You're aware that a mass murderer has killed family members of a serving officer?"
"Yes. I was sorry to hear it, honestly. But what does it have to do with me?"
"There's a theory that it was a revenge attack on a police officer who was involved in the arrest of some bent officers a while ago."
"If you're thinking it was me, can I point out that I've been in prison, under lock and key, for quite some time now. And so have the others who were tried at the same time."
"It's well known that being in prison hasn't stopped inmates from arranging for someone else to do the job for them."
"That's highly unlikely, don't you think?"
"To quote Sherlock Holmes: 'When you have eliminated the impossible, whatever remains, however improbable, must be the truth.' So, I'm here to ask what you know about it. I'm not saying you were responsible, but you may know who is."
"I can honestly state, hand on heart, I had nothing to do with these murders. I don't know who is responsible either."
"Have you kept in contact with Hardcastle?"
"Absolutely not! I want nothing to do with him. Look, I was stupid. I was naïve. I was struggling to pay the bills. He made it sound so easy to make loads of money, I fell for it. But I've learnt my lesson, and, believe me, it's not going to happen again. I'm really sorry for what's happened to your family, sir, but it was nothing to do with me. That's the honest truth. And I sincerely hope you catch whoever was responsible and make them pay."
"OK. Would you mind telling me exactly how you got involved in Hardcastle's criminal activities?"

Brian left an hour later and made his way back to Bradford to speak with ex-Sergeant Barlow, before returning home to prepare for his next day's work.

****

Late in the afternoon, back at Brian's house, they compared notes.

"We spoke to both Ward and Tarkovics. Both regret getting involved in Hardcastle's drugs business and both have been model prisoners. Neither of them has had any contact with Hardcastle since they were sentenced, according to them, anyway."
"Do you believe them?"
"Yes."
"OK. I spoke to Hardcastle and I can't rule him out. Schofield – that's ex-DS Schofield, by the way, Scoffer – also regrets getting involved. He was married, with two young kids and a large mortgage, struggling to make ends meet with a wife who wasn't exactly thrifty. Hardcastle offered him easy money. He told me if he'd known where it was leading, he would have got out. I believe him, too. I also spoke to ex-Sergeant Barlow. He's working as a security guard in the Broadway Shopping Centre, would you believe. He'd co-operated with the police in return for a lighter sentence. He told me he'd hadn't been in contact with the other offending officers nor ever intended to in the future. I believed him. He told me he only drove for Hardcastle on two occasions because he needed the money. He accepted the fact that he made a mistake and served his time. He's learnt his lesson and he's straight now. So as far as I'm concerned, we can rule them all out, except Hardcastle. Have we traced Muesli?"
"Emigrated."
"Where to?"
"The USA. Tarkovics said he thought Moseley's wife had some family there. But seriously, I don't think he could be involved in this. Getting thrown out of the Force was a wake-up call for him and losing his pension didn't help. I don't believe he'd ever get involved with Hardcastle again."

Brian smiled. It had been a big coup for him and his team. Bringing Hardcastle to justice convicted of running a large-scale drug importing business meant the end of service in the police force for DCI Moseley (AKA Muesli), DS Schofield, DS Ward, DC Tarkovics and Sergeant Barlow, as well as DI Hardcastle himself, of course.

He knew Hardcastle would never forgive him and would do anything possible for revenge, including murder. He needed to explore a little further. He was fully aware that Hardcastle had friends and business contacts in Albania, and, almost certainly, in other parts of the world. He decided to ask Teresa for a favour.

As Don and Scoffer were leaving, Don whispered to Brian.

"I've got something in the car for you. Don't open it until you get back inside, and then put it away somewhere safe."

They walked to the car, where Don duly passed him a carrier bag with a shoe box inside.

"Take care of it. You may need it one day."

Brian had guessed what it was.

"Thanks, boss."

Back in the house, he opened the box. It was as he expected. A Glock 17 pistol, along with a handwritten note.

"For emergency use only!"

Over a glass of malt that evening, he thought again about Hardcastle's criminal gang of officers. They all *seemed* to have turned over a new leaf, but could they actually be believed?

****

Meanwhile, members of Brian's team at HQ had commenced their inquiries into the newly emerged cases.

Gary and Jo-Jo had read the report from Forensics, which concluded with the opinion that the fire at the off-licence which killed an entire family was caused by a planned arson attack. Gary set up a whiteboard and listed the salient facts.

- Mr and Mrs Shah died from smoke inhalation. Their bodies were found downstairs near the rear exit door at the back of the storeroom.

- The door had been blocked from outside by a large refuse bin.
- The two youngest female children were found dead in the cellar, huddled up in a corner and covered with blankets. They had both suffered severe burns due to contact with the flames as they sought refuge in the cellar.
- The elder male child was found in the shop, near the front door which had been almost totally destroyed by the flames.
- The fire on the ground floor was caused by petrol having been poured through the letterbox and ignited by a 'molotov cocktail' thrown through the window.
- At the same time, further firebombs had been thrown through the upstairs windows, causing outbreaks of fire at four different points.
- The building was almost totally gutted by the time the fire was extinguished, and severe damage was caused to the adjacent buildings from which the occupants had to be evacuated.
- Clear evidence of arson was gathered at the scene, backing up anecdotal evidence that a group of white male adolescents had been causing problems for the shopkeeper and his family for a number of weeks prior to the attack and had been recently barred from entering the premises.

It was a real horror story. Jo-Jo shook her head in wonder.

"How can anybody do such a thing?"
"Let's get down to the area and collect some statements."

****

As they arrived at the premises near Whetley Lane, the burned-out building was being boarded up and made safe by a team of contractors. SOCO had completed their work and the Fire Brigade had finished damping down. High steel barrier fencing was being erected around the building and warning notices displayed. The buildings adjacent to the target site had been similarly treated.

"Let's go and talk to some of the neighbours."

The comments they received from local residents were all practically identical. The attack was the culmination of increasingly more aggressive behaviour by a group of white youths. For months, they had been breaking windows, damaging cars and daubing racist slogans on buildings. Many of the local residents were afraid to leave their homes after dark, and an unofficial vigilante group was formed as a result of the lack of action by the authorities. Last night, following a report that the local community centre was under attack, the vigilante group went en masse to that site, during which time the off licence was fire-bombed.

"A cleverly coordinated attack. These are not just kids out of control. Someone's pulling their strings."
"Any CCTV?"
"There was a system in the shop. Forensics took it away to see if they could salvage anything. Likewise with the backups which were kept upstairs. They didn't seem over-optimistic."

****

Teresa was invariably the last to leave the office at the end of the day, frequently staying an extra three or four hours, extrapolating data from various databases to provide names for Brian's team to follow up. When Brian started up his laptop in the morning, the first action he took was to check his emails, opening the one from Teresa first.

Today, there were only six names. The problem was his team was already behind with checking out the names on the previous lists. Including today's, there were now seventeen names to follow up. The task was becoming increasingly difficult. They had already eliminated all Hardcastle's known associates and were now working through the names of others who were imprisoned or *employed* at HMP Manchester at the same time. Still to come were the guns for hire, the mercenaries, who advertised their services on the Dark Web. And after that, there was a long line of people who for whatever reason held a grudge against him. This would include not only those who Brian had helped bring to justice, but also perhaps friends, lovers or partners of those people.

And finally, it was always possible, even though remotely, that the murders were completely motiveless and random.

Brian knew it was an impossible task without a great slice of good fortune. But he also knew that he would never stop looking for the killer until he found him and gained his revenge. That single objective was what kept him going.

When Don and Scoffer arrived, they quickly decided how they would approach the day's workload. Each took a separate geographical area and made initial contact with as many of the names on the list in that specific area, before setting off to speak to them in person. The names of those who refused to meet were underlined in red pen for further investigation.

Soon, Don was on his way to Lancashire to speak to four men who had worked at HMP Manchester while Hardcastle had been incarcerated there. None was still employed at the prison. The first man had quit his job about two months ago without serving notice. His name was one of those underlined in red.

Don pulled up outside a large house with electronically operated gates. He checked the address. It was correct. He switched off the engine and pressed the button on the gatepost, watching as the CCTV camera moved to focus on him. He smiled at it, holding up his old CID ID card.

"What do you want?"

The voice crackled through the speaker. He moved closer and answered.

"I'd like a word with Derek McGuire, please."
"And you are?"
"My name is McArthur. Don McArthur. I'd like to talk to you about your time working at Strangeways."
"What about it?"
"Can we possibly speak face to face about this?"

The gates slid open, and he walked into the paved courtyard. McGuire was standing in the doorway, eyeing his visitor. Another man, ugly and bulky, stood just behind him. His minder. Don ignored him and spoke directly to McGuire.

"I'm working on behalf of a client who is owed money by a man called Danny Hardcastle. I understand he was on your wing when you worked at Strangeways. What can you tell me about him?"
"He was a bent cop. Always wanted special treatment."
"What sort of treatment?"
"Access to a phone. That sort of thing?"
"And did you ever oblige?"
"Never."
"Do you know anybody who did?"
"There were rumours."
"Could you give me names?"
"No. Can't remember."
"You seem to have done well for yourself."
"What are you implying?"
"That anyone who did favours for Hardcastle was well paid for them."
"Look. It's none of your business but I'll tell you anyway. I never took a penny from Hardcastle. I've got no time for bent cops. And as far as my financial position is concerned, that's down to a big win on the lottery. You can check it out yourself. Nearly a year ago. I didn't tell anybody. I had this house built and when it was finished, I decided to retire, so I just went to work one day and told the boss I'd quit and wasn't going back. I don't need to work now. It's all legit. Check it out for yourself. Now, I'd like you to leave."

Don got back in his car and watched as the gates slowly closed and locked. He called Teresa and asked her to check McGuire's finances. She corroborated his lottery win. He scrubbed McGuire's name off his list and drove to the next address.

By the end of the day, when they convened back at Brian's, between them they had been able to cross eight names off their list of suspects. Yet they all felt they were losing ground. There must be a better way. Brian ordered a takeaway and opened a bottle of Nero D'Avola.

They discussed the situation, at times heatedly, as they ate their food and drank the wine, but they were in total agreement they had to persist. It was the only option.

They were sharing their second bottle of wine when Scoffer came up with a suggestion.

"There's something we haven't considered which might be of help."
"Let's hear it, then, Scoffer."
"Well, we're spending all this time investigating practically everybody who's ever come into contact with Hardcastle, but we're missing a trick."
"Go on."
"Well, it's just occurred to me, we've been investigating where McGuire's money came from, but shouldn't we be looking into Hardcastle's finances. We know he had an account at a bank in Malta, so, surely, he's got others in various countries where his drug business operated…."
"That's a good point, Scoffer, though, legally, I'm not sure we can get access to his accounts."
"But, if we could, we could see who he was paying, and then work out what he was paying them for."
"I bet Teresa could find a way of accessing his accounts. I'll call her now."

****

Lynn and Paula had also been kept busy. Their first call had been in Thackley, to interview a Mr Hartley, who had reported his wife missing. He let them into the kitchen.

"So, Mr Hartley, first of all, can I have your first name, and your wife's."
"My name's Simon. My wife's Andrea."
"Thank you. When was the last time you saw your wife?"
"Last Tuesday. Night."
"And what happened?"
"We'd had tea and sat in front of the telly. We had a glass of wine, then as usual it all kicked off."
"Can you be a bit more specific?"
"We started arguing. We argued a lot."
"About anything in particular?"
"Same thing all the time. She thought I was having an affair. I thought she was doing the same."
"And were you?"
"I wasn't doing anything. But I'm sure she was."
"OK, so then what happened?"
"She swore at me and just stormed out of the room. I heard her run upstairs, then, after a while I heard her come back down. I thought she'd calmed down, but then I heard the front door slam."

"What time was this?"
"About half past eleven."
"And then what?"
"I sat for a few minutes. I thought maybe she'd just gone outside to cool off. When she didn't come back, I went out and got in the car and drove around for a bit to see if I could see her. Then I came home. I sat watching TV for an hour or so, waiting for her to come back. Then I went to bed."
"And what time did you get up in the morning?"
"About half past nine."
"She'd not been home?"
"No. So, I eventually called her daughters to see if they knew where she was."
"*Her* daughters? Not yours?"
"No. We've both been married before. We've both got kids from a previous marriage."
"OK. We'll need the names, addresses and phone numbers of all the kids, please."
"OK. I'll get them for you."
"Another thing. Has she walked out on you before?"
"She's always doing it."
"For how long?"
"A couple of days at most. She's always gone to one of her daughters."
"But not this time?"
"No. Neither of them has seen or heard from her."
"Can you think of anywhere else she might have gone?"
"No."
"Her ex-husband?"
"Are you kidding? She hates him more than she hates me."
"So, it wasn't a happy marriage?"
"No. As soon as the honeymoon was over, that was it."
"And how long have you been married?"
"A couple of years. Seems like an eternity."
"Do you have a recent photo of Andrea?"
"No, but you'll get plenty from her Facebook account – all with a glass in her hand."
"Do you work, Mr Hartley?"
"Why do you ask?"
"I just wondered if you'd had to take time off work while your wife was missing."
"I'm chronically ill. Unfit to work."
"You're on benefits?"

"Yes. I don't know what that's got to do with it."
"Just wondered. Were you working when you married Andrea?"
"Yes. I was diagnosed with COPD and asthma soon afterwards."
"OK. We'll see what we can do. We'll be talking to her daughters and to yours. In the meantime, if you hear anything, let us know."
"OK."

They walked back to the car and, once inside, shared their views.

"Don't you think it odd that he didn't have a recent photo of his wife?"
"I do. He sounded really devastated. Not."
"Mm. Exactly what I was thinking. Makes me wonder why he bothered to report her as missing. He obviously doesn't want her back."
"I was thinking the same. I think we need to talk to their daughters. They might tell us more about the relationship."
"OK, ring the nearest one. Tell her we're on our way."

They drove down to Shipley where Andrea's younger daughter, Jayne, had a flat. She welcomed them in.

"I suppose this is about mum."
"Yes. I understand Simon Hartley called you."
"Yes. He asked if mum was here. I said 'no'. He asked if I knew where she was. I said 'no'. He asked if she'd been in touch. I said 'no'."
"Sounds as if you don't get along with Mr Hartley."
"I hate him. Always have. He's a layabout. He's been abusive towards mum."
"Physically?"
"He's hit her more than once. I told her to leave him. I wish she had."
"So, when did he call you?"
"Friday night. Straight after he'd called my sister."
"I take it she hasn't heard from your mum either."
"That's right. It's odd, because every time it's happened before, mum's gone straight to Maggie, her being older than me."
"So, I suppose neither of you have any idea where she might be? Her parents?"
"No. They're both dead. They lived in Spain. She hasn't got any really close friends that we know of."
"Any lovers?"

34

"None we know about."
"Thanks for your time. Please let us know if you hear from her. By the way, have you tried to call her at all?"
"Yes. No answer."
"Could we have her number, please?"
"Yes. Here it is."
"Thanks. We'll be in touch."

****

Their next call was at Maggie's – the elder sister. She gave almost exactly the same story as her sibling, and obviously disliked Simon Hartley with the same intensity. However, they did glean some new information, something they should have asked her sister as well.

"By the way, why did your mother and your father divorce?"
"She found out he'd been screwing a woman he used to work with and asked him to stop. He refused and made it obvious to all his mates. Mum was humiliated, so divorced him. Can't say I blame her."
"Was your mother ever unfaithful to him?"
"Not as far as I know."
"Was she ever unfaithful to Simon?"
"Only once, as far as we were aware. She had a short affair with a young man after she married that bastard, Simon. She said she only did it because Simon shagged anything in a skirt, and she wanted to get her own back."
"Did Simon know about it?"
"Yes. They had a blazing row once and she told him she hated him and that she'd had better sex with a younger man."
"How did he react?"
"How do you think? He battered her. Gave her a black eye and some other nasty bruises."
"Did she report it?"
"No. She said she was too scared of him."
"Why didn't she leave him?"
"She was going to. She'd been looking at some flats. She definitely thought about it. She just needed to get away from him."
"Did Simon know she intended to leave him?"
"I don't know. He was such an arrogant and idle prat, he probably thought she needed him too much to walk away."
"Does your mother work?"

"Yes. At Aldi, in Idle."
"Thanks for your time."

Before they finished for the day, they managed to get hold of Simon Hartley's daughter from his first marriage, Jean, and arranged to call at her house.

"We'd like to talk to you about your father, Jean."
"What's he been up to now?"
"He hasn't been in touch with you?"
"No. I haven't heard from him for a long time."
"Any particular reason? He's your father after all."
"I haven't spoken to him since mum left him."
"Would you mind telling us what happened?"
"It's a long time ago. I never liked him and was glad when I left home to go to college. But I kept in touch with mum. Then one day I called her at home, and he answered. He said she'd left him. She'd run away with her lover. I'd never heard anything about her having a lover and mum used to tell me everything. Anyway, I haven't seen or heard from her since, but he called me a few years later out of the blue and said she'd phoned him, and she was living in Australia. I didn't believe him. I couldn't believe that my mother left without telling me, at least to say goodbye, and hasn't written or phoned me since. It's just not like her. Anyway, the next thing I heard was that he had divorced her on grounds of desertion."
"Have you ever thought that she might simply have wanted to start a new life and sever all connections with the past?"
"She'd *never* just go and forget me totally. She was my mother, for Christ's sake!"
"Thank you, Jean. I'm sorry we've put you through this. You've been most helpful."
"That's OK. Can I ask, though, why you're asking me about him now?"
"I don't know whether you're aware, but he re-married and his second wife has recently gone missing."
"Oh, God! I'm so sorry to hear that! It can't be coincidence."
"You have a theory?"
"I always wondered if what he told me about mum was true, or if he'd done something to her. I wouldn't put it past him. He used to hit her, and shout at her. And at me. He was a nasty piece of work, particularly when he'd had a drink. I always wondered if he'd done something to her. I wish I'd spoken to the police at the time."
"She was never reported missing?"

"No. He said she'd left him. And that wouldn't have been a surprise. It was just the fact that she didn't get in touch with me that made me suspicious. And now you think he might have done it again?"
"We're looking into it. We'll let you know if we discover any new facts about your mother's disappearance."

****

During the next two days, Lynn and Paula interviewed Simon Hartley's friends, who were few and far between, and Andrea's workmates, before presenting their findings to DCI Gardner. There had still been no sightings of Andrea, nor any contact from her.

"We've had the same story from everyone we've spoken to. Her boss and colleagues at Aldi thought very highly of her. She was hard-working, pleasant, and sociable. But practically everyone who met her husband disliked him. He was variously described as lazy, arrogant, and bossy, and abusive, verbally and physically, to Andrea. He was a heavy drinker, and he was unfaithful to her. I'm not surprised she left him, if that's what really happened."

The DCI listened intently before asking.

"You think there may be more to it?"
"Well, yes, maybe. We spoke to Hartley's daughter by his first wife. Oddly enough, her mother, Margaret, went missing more than twenty years ago. He told his daughter he'd heard from her, and she'd moved to Australia. Then, he divorced her for desertion. Her daughter, Jean, is adamant that her mother wouldn't have left her without saying goodbye or contacting her since. She's heard nothing. No phone call, no letter. Nothing."

There was silence as Gardner considered.

"I think we have to consider the possibility that Andrea didn't leave him. It's possible she taunted him about the affair she'd had, and he lost it…."
"You mean, he killed her?"
"It's a definite possibility. Particularly in the light of the evidence which you've just turned up."
"Then, why would he tell us she was missing?"

Paula had the answer to that.

"Well, if he hadn't, and her daughters told us later, wouldn't we be immediately suspicious of him? It seems he's the last person who saw her. He has to be a suspect!"

"That's right, Paula. Well done."

"Sorry, sir. We should have considered that. It was only when we spoke to Jean that murder looked a real possibility."

"OK. The next thing to do is to talk to Mr Hartley's neighbours. Find out if they saw or heard anything on the night when she went missing. Let's see if they have the same version of events. See if anyone saw or heard him going out in his car late at night, as he said. If we get someone to corroborate his statement, it's possible we can find an image of his car on a road camera somewhere."

"Something else we missed, sir. We should have asked if she took anything with her. If she packed a bag. Unless she intended to go to one of her daughters, she would surely have taken at least a change of clothes."

"OK. Go check it out. And another thing – call Helen Moore at the T & A and ask her to print the story and appeal for help. Give her a photo."

CHAPTER 4

The same morning, Lynn and Paula were back in Thackley, speaking to some of Simon Hartley's neighbours. Only one of them was able to recall seeing or hearing anything unusual on the night in question. Mrs Williams, a retired widow who lived across the road had just let her dog into the front garden for a pee when she saw Mr Hartley's garage door open and his car drive away. She was unable to give any further details, apart from the fact that she was sure there was nobody in the car except the driver, who, she assumed, was Mr Hartley. She gave the time as being close to midnight but didn't see or hear the car return as she went to bed shortly afterwards. The officers discussed what they'd heard.

"In effect, she's corroborated what Simon Hartley told us. He'd gone out in the car to look for his wife. That's *his* version. It's also possible that he wasn't the only person in the car, despite what Mrs Williams said."
"So, you're thinking that maybe he killed his wife in the house, then carried her body into the garage through the back door, which, incidentally, is almost totally hidden from the road. He put the body in the car, drove off, and disposed of it, before driving back and going to bed."
"It's possible. Let's see if Traffic has any nearby cameras that we could look at."

She picked up the phone and made the call.

****

The T & A ran the story of Andrea Hartley in the Saturday edition. Within hours, the dedicated phone line for information was flooded with calls, most of which were of little or no use. As Gardner observed in a meeting with Lynn and Paula,

"This sort of thing always brings out the cranks, the idiots, as well as the well-meaning folk who imagine they know all about it, but then tell us only what's already been made public. Well, it was worth a try. So, what's our next move?"

The next move was a direct result of the one piece of useful information which the story in the T & A eventually elicited.

Lynn and Paula's first call was at the home of a lady who used to work with Andrea at Aldi. She told how Andrea's husband had once turned up at a night out for the shop staff, demanding that Andrea leave with him at once.

"There was no need for it. She wasn't drunk or anything like that. He just turned up and seemed to object to the fact she was enjoying herself without him. He was lucky one of the lads didn't slap him. He was just so abusive. He was just jealous she was enjoying herself without him, I think."
"And she left with him?"
"Yes. She was so embarrassed. And when she came into work a couple of days later, she had a black eye. She said she'd bumped into a door when she got home because she'd had too much to drink. We all knew better."
"Did she know you knew he was responsible for the black eye?"
"Oh, yes. It was common knowledge at work that he beat her up. But nobody liked to confront her with it to see if she could get help."

In the car afterwards, Lynn was angry. She phoned Gardner to update him.

"It's a shame when we spoke to staff at Aldi that nobody mentioned that specific event. The lady we've just seen doesn't work there now so without the T & A's article we wouldn't have known how bad things were. Now we have evidence of his capacity for physical abuse, we need to seriously consider this could be a murder case, or at least manslaughter."
"So, where's the body?"
"Do we have sufficient grounds for searching Hartley's home? There might be some forensic evidence. If not, we might at least be able to establish what she took with her. In other words, we can determine whether she planned to leave."
"It could have been a spontaneous decision. She might just have walked out and been picked up off the streets by a predator. We just don't know."
"So, let's find out."
"OK, ladies. Let's work at eliminating the possibilities. I'll organise a search warrant and we'll get Forensics to look around the house and grounds. It's a possible crime scene."

****

Next morning, at nine, Lynn and Paula arrived outside Simon Hartley's house, accompanied by Allen Greaves and members of his Forensics team. They had to wake Mr Hartley to gain entry. He was not pleased when the search warrant was handed to him as the officers pushed past him in the doorway and commenced their search. He sat silently in the kitchen with a uniformed officer for company, listening to the sound of people opening wardrobes and drawers, and rummaging through cupboards. Outside, in the garden, the contents of the refuse bin had been emptied onto a sheet laid on the drive. The garage was searched. His car's doors, bonnet and boot were open and being examined. Occasionally, a Forensics officer would call out to their boss to indicate an item of interest had been found. Each item was then bagged, tagged, and placed in a box in the back of the SOCO Transit van for further scrutiny at the lab. Allen Greaves took on the sole responsibility for gathering samples likely to contain Andrea Hartley's DNA. Her hairbrush was bagged, and other personal items were collected from the laundry basket in the bathroom. There was a shout when her handbag was located in the bottom of the wardrobe. It contained her purse, her bank card, and some cash. In a pouch inside, they found her mobile phone and her house keys. That was enough for Lynn. She asked Simon to accompany her to HQ for questioning regarding the disappearance of his wife. Head down, he complied. They left Forensics at the house to complete their business and drove off.

****

Gardner had been kept up to date with proceedings and was happy to let the ladies proceed with interviewing Simon Hartley, provided they took note of his word of caution.

"Remember, ladies. You're conducting an interview into the disappearance of this man's wife. Disregard all your preconceptions. His wife is missing, *presumed* dead. You and I, and most likely Forensics too, believe her husband has killed her, but until we extract a confession to that effect, or the evidence tells us conclusively that he has killed her, then we are acting on a presumption only. He is under suspicion. Follow the evidence."

Hartley stuck to his initial story. They'd had a row; she'd stormed out. He couldn't explain why she'd left without taking her handbag containing her money, bank card, house keys and phone. But, then again, he didn't have to explain.

Only when a call came through from Forensics that they'd found a kitchen knife bearing traces of blood, Andrea's blood, on the blade, did their hopes of a conviction rise. But only temporarily. Hartley had an explanation.

"She cut herself peeling potatoes for our dinner. She was always a bit clumsy when she'd had a drink."

They took a break during which they consulted Gardner.

"With a bit of luck, her phone might give us something. So far, Forensics have given us plenty circumstantial evidence, such as the fact that a piece of carpet from the spare bedroom has been roughly removed, possibly to wrap a body in. But, until we find the body, we've got nothing. We don't know where he went in his car that night. Road cameras haven't picked anything up, so we don't even have a rough idea about the area we could search. We have to let him go."

"Isn't there anything we can do?"

"Try to contact his daughter again. And find out if his parents are still alive. Even if we talk to them, all we'll probably get is background stuff. But the more we know about him, the better."

"We'll get on it, sir. There's always the chance that his laptop might give us more information about his sexual inclinations."

"Agreed. The internet is great for finding information, but it's also the repository of all the filth. Just a click away."

****

The search of files found on Simon Hartley's laptop took two days, but the results were unexpectedly disappointing. All those involved were amazed to find that he looked only at 'straight' porn. Nothing which would be classed as deviant could be found in his search history, even after the most exhaustive checks. More bad news followed. Both Simon's parents died within days of each other a few years ago, and his daughter hadn't spoken to him since their funerals. They had nothing.

Their spirits were lifted for a short while when the completed report arrived from Forensics. Among the items found at the house was a pair of Wellington boots, which Hartley claimed he wore to do the gardening. Soil embedded in the tread was examined and did not match the soil in the garden. Traces of the same soil were found in the car boot and on a spade found in the garage. Nevertheless, the decision was taken to let the cadaver dogs loose in the garden. As they expected, nothing was found. They were clutching at straws. Paula was the one who saw a possible way forward.

"I've had an idea."
"Go on."
"Well, when we searched Hartley's house, Forensics said they'd found mud on his wellies and on a spade and in the car, but that it didn't match the soil in his garden."
"So?"
"Well, I wonder if they can tell us where the soil actually came from."
"No harm in asking."

Forensics had also found two different types of fibre in the boot of Hartley's car. One type contained traces of paint and dust and was therefore believed to have come from a dustsheet of the type used by decorators. The other matched the carpet, part of which had been roughly removed from the spare bedroom of the house. Lynn questioned Hartley about these.

"Yes. I had a dustsheet. I used it when I decorated the house. I took it in the car to the Council Tip along with some other stuff a few weeks ago. I'd spilt paint on the carpet, so I cut the soiled piece out and took it to the tip as well. I've just never got round to replacing it yet."
"Can you explain the soil we found on a spade and on your wellies, and in the car?"
"Probably came from when I was gardening."
"Think again. The soil wasn't from your garden."
"Oh, that's right. I often wear the wellies if I go for a walk when it's raining. There are some lovely walks around this area."
"And you take a spade on your walks?"
"No. I lent it to a friend."
"Name?"
"I don't know. He wasn't that close a friend."
"You're a generous, trusting man."
"Always like to help if I can."

43

Lynn didn't believe a word of what Hartley had said, but it was difficult to disprove.

It took a while for Forensics to establish that the soil probably came from woodland, having carefully examined its composition, and acidity levels. They compared it against a database held by Askham Bryan college near York and went out to take samples from the local area. Buck Wood was a perfect match, but also a large area to search.

****

Before they had time to celebrate, Teresa took a call which shocked her to the core. She composed herself before calling DCI Gardner.

"Sorry to bother you, sir, but I've just taken a call from the emergency operator. It seems that DS Whitehead's mother has been attacked and killed in her home. I haven't got any other details yet, but SOCO are on their way to the address. Shall I break it to Lynn, sir?"
"No, Teresa, thanks. I'll do it straightaway. Please keep me informed of any further reports."
"Yes, sir."
"Come to think of it, would it be possible for you to accompany Lynn to my office? I think she'll need some support."
"Of course, sir. We'll be straight up."

Naturally, on hearing the news, Lynn broke down in tears. She was immediately allowed compassionate leave and escorted home. Gardner called Gary, gave him a quick appraisal of the case and asked him to cover it. Next, he called his boss, and was given permission to borrow DC Andy Thompson for an undetermined period with immediate effect.

****

SOCO officers were finishing their examination by the time Gary arrived at Lynn's house with Jo-Jo. After checking their ID, the constable on duty at the front door allowed them to enter after giving them a warning.

"Be careful where you tread."

They could clearly see a pool of blood in the hall, and spatter on the walls. Hearing the voice of Allen Greaves in the lounge they headed towards it, stopping at the door from where the full extent of the attack could be seen. Allen was on the phone and put up his hand before informing the caller.

"They've just arrived now. OK, I'll talk to you later after you've had time to read my report."

He closed the call, then outlined what appeared to have happened.

"Mrs Whitehead was in the house on her own. Her husband died a few years ago and she shared the house with her daughter, Lynn. We believe she answered a call at the door, opened it and was pushed inside where she faced a ferocious attack with a knife. She would have died very quickly as the first two blows, in the hall, were to the heart. She then staggered into the lounge where she suffered a further stab wound to the stomach before, finally, her throat was cut."
"How long before you can identify the type of weapon used?"
"I know what you're thinking. I'm almost certain it's the knife used to kill Mrs Peters and the kids. I'll be able to confirm that when I get to the lab. If I were you, Gary, I'd tell your workmates to be on their guard, because it looks to me like someone may be picking off your team's families. It's just a precaution, mind. But better to be safe than sorry."
"Where is Lynn? I understood she'd been brought home?"
"She broke down in tears as soon as she saw the bloodstains. She's been taken to her sister's. A female PC is staying with her for a while. I guess she'll need some time off."

Gary immediately called DCI Gardner and told him about Lynn and what Allen Greaves had suggested, before he and Jo-Jo did a quick door-to-door to establish whether anybody had noticed anything or anybody unusual in the neighbourhood within the last few days. They drew a blank.

****

That evening, the entire team were gathered in front of screens for a Zoom meeting held by DCI Gardner. By this time, they were all aware of the topic for discussion. Gardner started the conversation.

45

"Thank you all for making the time for this meeting. First, may I extend my heartfelt condolences to Brian and Lynn for the loss they have suffered. However, it's imperative that we now discuss these crimes as it appears they may be linked.
Forensics have now confirmed that the knife used to kill Mrs Whitehead was identical to the one used in the murder of Brian's family. Forensics believe the knife is a high-spec professional's weapon, and that the person who is using it has been trained in hand-to-hand combat and may be a mercenary.
To our knowledge, he has now claimed four victims, all of whom were related to members of this CID team, and it is possible there are further victims on his list. So far, the only link between the victims is the fact that they were related to our team. This fact should be, I believe, the starting point to use to identify whether there are any other persons at risk. With this in mind, I would suggest that all of you ensure that your relatives and loved ones are aware they may be at risk and take the necessary precautions. I would welcome any suggestions as to how we can achieve this."

Teresa was the first to speak.

"What's the possibility of getting armed protection for our loved ones?"
"Realistically, Teresa, round-the-clock protection is highly unlikely, unless, of course, we had them all in the same place at once. I would like you all to consider asking your loved ones if such an arrangement is acceptable. I'm sure that, in the short term, it would give us breathing space, knowing our loved ones were secure."

Jo-Jo made a valid point.

"How far along our family trees do we have to go? Are our cousins safe? Our in-laws? Grandparents?"
"We don't know, Jo-Jo. I suggest we start with those closest to us, both emotionally and geographically, until we turn up some more evidence. The hard fact is, at the moment, we know very little, and our knowledge only increases with each murder. All I ask is that we take all possible precautions, which, naturally, includes informing your loved ones that their lives may be at risk, without causing general panic. We need to keep this out of the papers for as long as we can."

There was silence for a moment before Brian spoke.

"I'd like to propose an alternative, sir. Let the papers have the full story. Let the public know a serial killer is out there. For all we know, he may evolve and start choosing victims at random."

"That's a valid point, Brian. But I don't want to panic the public at this time."

"It would make them more vigilant, sir. We would get more reports of suspicious behaviour."

"We could get overwhelmed, Brian. The conspiracy theorists would have a field day."

"At least get the NCA involved."

"I've already contacted them, Brian. They'll be with us tomorrow."

"Then let me give you my opinion. By all means tell your loved ones their lives may be at risk. But let them make the decision on how they want to be protected. Having been warned about the potential threat may be enough for some; others may require protection. Let them make their own decision. In the meantime, tell the papers a serial killer is at large and that everyone should be vigilant and report anything suspicious."

There was general agreement for Brian's proposal, and it was accepted. The T & A was informed, and the story appeared in the next day's issue.

CHAPTER 5

A grinning Simon Hartley had been released without charge and made a statement to the T & A alleging police harassment. Lynn, having just returned from a short period of Compassionate Leave, was furious and had a chat with Paula.

"In my opinion, he's picked a fight he can't win. He knows we can't charge him. He knows he's in the clear until we find the body. I want him watched. I want him to know he's being watched. And I want him stopped the second he commits any offence however trivial. I don't care if I personally have to work around the clock until he makes a mistake. I want him to be where he belongs. Behind bars."

Paula was of the same opinion, and agreed to work extra hours, unpaid. The plan was to be highly visible to Hartley, to put him under pressure, to unnerve him, in the hope that he would crack and give something away.

Lynn informed DCI Gardner of her plan and got the response she expected.

"Be very careful, Lynn. He'll accuse us of harassment. If the tabloids get hold of the story, we're in trouble and the Chief Constable will come down hard on us. I'm on your side, Lynn, but don't cross the line."
"Yes, sir. I'm fully prepared to take the blame for any 'indiscretions' we commit. I'll do my best to make sure you're not involved. But I'll put my job on the line for this."
"I admire your commitment, Lynn. Go ahead. And good luck."
"Thank you, sir."

****

At eight-thirty the next morning, Simon Hartley left his house, locking the door behind him. He got into his car, started it up and pulled out of his drive on to the road. He didn't see the police car behind him at first but heard the siren and saw the lights flash. He stopped the car at the roadside and wound down his window as a police officer got out of the car behind and approached.

"Good morning, sir. Do you realise you just pulled out of your drive into a main road right in front of us?"
"I looked. There was no traffic."
"So why did we have to brake hard to avoid running into you?"
"I don't know. Perhaps you were speeding."
"You, sir, were driving without due care and attention. Your name, please."
"Simon Hartley."
"Your address?"
"You know my address! You've been waiting for me to pull out."
"What are you insinuating, sir?"
"Never mind."
"Well, sir. I'll let you off with a warning this time. Make sure it doesn't happen again, eh?"
"It won't. Now do you mind if I go? I'll be late for an appointment with my solicitor."
"Off you go, then. But make sure you don't break the speed limit."

As he drove off, the policeman sent his message to his colleague on Leeds Road.

"He's on his way."

And then a text to Lynn.

"Job done. He's on his way to his solicitor."

The immediate reply –

"Thanks."

As he drove slowly in the queue of traffic inching its way down towards Shipley, Simon Hartley noticed a flashing blue light in his rear mirror. The car was overtaking the queueing cars before it slowed alongside him. He watched as the officer in the passenger seat wound down his window and gestured for him to do the same. He groaned and complied, only to be told to pull to the roadside and switch off his engine. Again, he complied. The police car parked behind him, its roof lights still flashing as the passenger got out and approached his car. The officer spoke calmly.

"Please get out of the car and come with me, sir."
"What's wrong? What's this all about?"

"Just do as I've asked, sir. And get into the back of the police car."

As he got out of the car, the officer put his hand on his arm and quietly warned him.

"Just do as we ask, sir, and you'll be back on the road in no time, once we've checked your identity."
"Why do you need to check my identity?"
"Just do as we ask, sir, or else you may find you're late for whatever it is you're in such a hurry for."
"Just make it quick."

Once in the car, he was asked to prove his identity. His driving licence was checked, as was his car tax, MOT, and insurance. All were in order.

"Why the hell did you stop me? I've done nothing wrong!"
"We had a report that this car had been stolen, sir. We're satisfied now that it must have been a hoax call. Have you any idea who might have done such a thing?"
"I can only think of one person."
"And who might that be, sir?"
"I can't tell you. But I'm sure you already know. I *will* be speaking to my MP about it."
"Good luck with that, sir. We're finished, now. You're free to continue your journey."

He could see the two officers laughing as he drove away.

Eventually, he reached Shipley and pulled into Asda's car park for the short walk to his solicitor's office. He was about to lock the car when it occurred to him that perhaps the police may have arranged for him to get a ticket for using Asda's car park without visiting the store. He had no change in his pocket. He checked his watch. He had ten minutes. He weighed up his options. He could make a purchase at Asda and hope there wasn't a long queue at the checkout. Or he could park elsewhere. But he knew from experience how difficult parking could be in Shipley. He could possibly drive around for fifteen minutes without finding a spot. He decided to leave the car in Asda's car park and risk a fine. He locked the car and walked briskly away, arriving at the solicitor's office with time to spare. However, a surprise awaited him when he reported to Reception.

"I'm sorry, Mr Hartley. Your appointment has been cancelled."
"What? Why?"
"It was cancelled about fifteen minutes ago, sir."
"Who by?"
"By your secretary, sir. She phoned to say you couldn't make it and would have to re-schedule it."
"I haven't got a secretary! Someone's been playing tricks. Is there any chance of an appointment today?"
"I'm sorry, sir. Can I book you in for another day?"
"Yes, please."

He left the office in a rage. He knew who was responsible, but he had no proof. He would have his revenge.

****

Simon Hartley was sitting at the table in his kitchen, a half-empty bottle of Spanish red wine at his side. He had been racking his brains trying to remember the names of the two detectives who came to his house to interview him. Eventually he remembered. One was DS Whitehead. He couldn't remember her first name though. The other one was Harris. Yes, that was it. DC Harris. The blonde one. Paula Harris. He powered up his laptop, opened Facebook and searched for the name. There were several entries, but only one in Bradford. He searched through the photos posted. She was an attractive blonde. It was her. No doubt.

He quickly set up a bogus account, inventing a name and some background, and 'borrowing' a photo from someone else's profile, he sent her a private message.

"Love to meet you. I think we may have things in common. Can we meet?"

****

Paula didn't notice the message until she had finished her shift. She opened it and was immediately suspicious. She resisted the temptation to block the sender, deciding instead to let Teresa look into it in the morning, and left her a note to that effect on her desk.

As soon as she started work, Teresa read Paula's note about the message, opened it, and immediately called Brian who, without fuss, had returned that morning to work from the office. He rushed to her desk.

"Paula's had an unusual communication, Brian. I think you should see it. The sender only created his profile yesterday. I suspect someone is looking for revenge. I would certainly be very wary of his motive for wanting to meet."

Brian read the message.

"There's no way Paula's meeting this perv, Teresa, without thinking this through. My money's on Hartley for this."
"That was my reaction, too, Brian, but perhaps we can lead him into a trap?"
"Too risky. I'm not putting an officer at risk. You should understand that, Teresa."
"I do, fully. But can we turn the opportunity down?"
"OK. Let's see what he's planning. If it gets too risky, we'll pull the plug. Teresa, you and Paula between you handle the conversation. Try to egg him on. But any time you don't like the direction it's taking, call me over. OK?"
"Yep."
"Any progress with Forensics?"
"Not yet. They're working their way through the woods closest to Hartley's home. It takes time. Once they get a close match, they'll take the cadaver dogs out."
"I'm assuming they're concentrating their efforts on sites which have easy access by road? I can't see him dragging a body any distance from his car."
"They're narrowing it down regarding access and privacy. They'll get there."
"Soon, I hope. I really want to nail this bugger."

****

At home in the evening, Lynn took a call on her mobile.

"Lynn, it's Allen Greaves. Sorry to bother you at home, but I think we may have found the site, or at least the area."
"Good work."
"We're knocking off now it's getting dark. I've asked for a car with two officers to keep watch overnight and we'll pick it up with the dogs in the morning. That OK with you?"

"That's fine, Allen. Which area are you searching?"
"Near Buck Wood, off Ainsbury Avenue."
"OK. Let me know the minute you find anything."
"Will do."

****

Early next morning, Lynn received a call on her mobile. Allen. She answered immediately.

"We've found two bodies, Lynn. Both female. One recently dead, the other badly decomposed. Maybe twenty years in the ground. We'll know more after we've got them on the slab."
"Good work, Allen. Anything else?"
"One was wrapped in a dust sheet and a piece of carpet. And there were boot marks at the site. We've taken a cast. Size ten. Judging by the tread pattern, I'm guessing they'll match the Wellingtons."
"That's great news. Thanks. We'll bring him in. Let me know as soon as you confirm the identity of either corpse."
"Will do."

She closed the call and summoned Paula.

"A nice little job for us this morning. We can go and arrest our friend Simon Hartley."
"That will be a pleasure."

****

Shortly afterwards, an elderly lady presented herself at the Reception Desk, introducing herself as Mrs Reynolds.

"Could I please speak to someone about Simon Hartley?"
"What exactly do you want to know?"
"I have some information about him. About something that happened years ago."
"Take a seat, please. I'll get someone to see you."

Since Lynn and Paula were out, Gary volunteered to interview the lady.

"Good morning. I'm Gary Ryan. I understand you have some information about Simon Hartley?"
"Yes. I'm sorry I haven't come forward earlier, but I've been in hospital."
"Oh, I'm sorry to hear that. Are you feeling OK now?"
"Yes, thank you."
"So, how can I help?"
"Well, a few days ago, I read an article in the T & A about Simon Hartley. It brought back a horrible memory for me. You see, I had a foster daughter. She'd had a difficult early life but seemed to be doing well. She'd settled with me. She attended school every day and when she left, she got a job in Sainsbury's. I was so proud of her. Then one day she came home and announced she'd got a boyfriend. I asked her about him, but she never told me much and eventually she stopped mentioning him at all though I knew she was still seeing him. She refused to talk about him. I knew she was having sex with him, because I did her washing, but she told me she was sixteen and it was none of my business. Then, without warning, she left home. She just disappeared. Didn't appear to have taken anything with her except I later noticed a jar I kept money in had been emptied. There was only about £30 in it, so I wasn't that bothered. I just expected her to come back, or at least call me to explain and tell me she was OK. But I never heard anything. After a week, I reported her missing to the police, and, initially, they called me to tell me how their investigation was proceeding, but really, they wanted to know if I'd heard anything. I guess they just wanted to close the case...."
"So, how does Simon Hartley come into it?"
"I recognised him from the photo in the T & A. He was a lot younger then, of course, but I was certain I'd seen Sharon, my foster daughter, getting out of his car outside our house once. When I asked who he was, she told me it was her boyfriend, Simon."
"And how long ago was this?"
"Eighteen years."

****

Lynn and Paula returned with the news that they were unable to find Hartley. His house was empty, and his car was missing. The news from Gary made finding him even more urgent, as Lynn was quick to point out.

"Sharon could possibly be one of his early victims. We need to look at the file from the initial investigation."

An alert was issued to all Forces in the north of England. Paula was still optimistic, though.

"Maybe he still wants to meet me. If I convince him I'm off work and don't know what's happened, he won't be able to resist an opportunity to meet up. It's worth a try."
"Assuming he hasn't disappeared from the area."
"I'm guessing he still wants revenge. Let's give it a shot."

She opened Messenger and typed.

"Sorry. Just seen your message. Been off sick. You look dishy! Love to meet.
P. xxx"

She turned to Lynn for approval.

"What do you think."
"Go for it. Send it."

The reply was almost instantaneous.

"Can we meet tonight? Somewhere quiet so we can sit and talk."

By now, Teresa had been alerted and was watching as the situation developed.

"Let him choose, Paula. But not Ainsbury Avenue. If he sees it's been dug up, he might become suspicious."

She typed again.

"Your choice. But looks like it might rain."

There was a pause, before Teresa made a suggestion.

"What about one of the safe houses?"
"Of course. Find out what's available, Teresa. Quick as you can."

Hartley's reply came through.

55

"What about yours? Do you live alone?"

Paula hesitated to reply until Teresa confirmed the status.

"We've got a flat in Shipley. Here's the address."

She passed a scribbled note to Paula. She read it and typed.

"OK. Come to mine. It's so lonely living here on my own. I'm in Shipley. Is that OK? Have you got transport?"
"Yes. What time? Send address."
"8pm? 4, The Court, Ashfield Road, Shipley, BD18 4LF for your Satnav."
"Can't wait. I'll bring wine. See you then."
"I'll have a nice surprise for you."

The conversation ended. Louise, seated at her desk, had been following proceedings and looked over at Lynn, hoping to be included in the anticipated arrest.

"OK, volunteers, please."

Louise's hand shot up.

"Well, I'm in and obviously Paula is in and now we have Louise as well. I want one more, inside, and two in a car in case he eludes us."

A quick call to DCI Gardner helped to recruit volunteers from the uniformed ranks. There was no shortage of volunteers. Unsurprisingly, Teresa also wanted to play a part.

Between them, they ironed out the details. It was decided that Louise would sit in an unmarked car with a PC out of uniform. A second PC in plain clothes would man a back-up vehicle along with Teresa. Gardner himself would be inside the flat with Paula and Lynn. Only once everyone was fully conversant with their role in the operation were they allowed to disperse.

****

That evening, DCI Gardner had a quick meal before heading back to Shipley where he parked on a side street and walked the half-mile to the flat, where Paula and Lynn were already waiting. He called Louise and received confirmation they were in place. Teresa confirmed the location of the second unmarked vehicle. Now, they all waited. Then a text came through from Louise.

"On his way. Car's just passed us. Moving to next position."

Gardner sent confirmation and turned to the officers waiting in the room.

"He's almost here. You know what you have to do?"

They both nodded and waited. Paula stood by the window, watching.

"His car's just pulled into the car park. Is everybody ready for this?"

She moved towards the intercom and waited until it buzzed. She answered.

"Hello."
"It's me. Can I come up?"
"'Course. I'll let you in."

She pressed the button to release the front door and smiled to Lynn. Seconds later the doorbell of the flat sounded. Paula stood back from the door and called out.

"Come in. It's open."

He walked in to see Paula and Lynn smiling at him. He looked puzzled until Paula spoke again.

"I thought you might like a threesome. With maybe a little bondage thrown in."

He smiled back and walked towards her, only stopping when he heard the door slam shut behind him and felt a strong arm grip his elbow. He froze as DCI Gardner approached him with handcuffs, then struggled to free himself as an arm locked around his throat.

"Don't resist, Mr Hartley. You're not the only one who can physically hurt people. You're under arrest."

Lynn handcuffed him just as Louise and her partner for the operation walked in. She was visibly disappointed.

"I was hoping he'd struggle so I could give him a good hiding. Instead, he's just a little lamb. Still, you can't win 'em all."
"At least he's brought a bottle of wine for us all to share. That's nice of him."
"Hey, it's a decent bottle as well. This isn't supermarket stuff. The man's got class."
"I can't wait to open it."

Paula stood directly in front of him.

"Well, you nasty little piece of shit, what do you think of the little surprise I set up for you?"

Gardner, who by this time had searched his prisoner, was not surprised by what he found: a knife, a kitchen knife.

"He had a not-so-nice surprise for you, too, Paula. Let's find him some lodgings for the night. Maybe, a nice comfy cell."

Teresa had already called the van, which pulled up in the car park, and quickly sped off with the prisoner in the back. A brief phone call to Forensics led to a member of their team coming over to collect the knife for immediate examination in their lab. Gardner thanked his team.

"Well done, everybody. That's another drink I owe you when they finally get around to opening the pubs again to large rowdy groups. See you all in the morning."

****

The report from Forensics was waiting for Lynn when she logged on next morning. It confirmed the identities of the two bodies with the help of dental and medical records. Hartley's two wives. Different people; same fate. Though not yet conclusive, it was thought highly likely that the knife taken from Simon Hartley was used as the murder weapon in both cases. Lynn worked most of the morning completing her report and checking the reports filed by the other members of the team, before submitting them to Teresa for copying, forwarding, and filing.

58

However, the case couldn't yet be closed, as the whereabouts of Sharon, possibly another victim, had still to be verified. A plea for her to come forward, and a second plea for information as to her whereabouts were both printed in the T & A but yielded no result. Lynn approached Jean, Simon's daughter, to ask for his previous address so she could speak to his neighbours at the time. It was a long shot, but eventually, in conversation with one of the few neighbours who lived there at the time, she learnt that he remembered Sharon.

"It was a long time ago. After his wife had left him and his daughter had moved out, he lived on his own for a while, but he kept bringing girls back to his house. Young girls, some of them underage, in my opinion. I know for a fact that at least one of them spent the night there, because I saw her leaving the following morning. I suppose I should have reported it, but then he moved out shortly afterwards. It surprised me a bit because he'd just started doing up the place."
"In what way?"
"He said he was having a garage built, or rather, he was building it himself. He'd dug out for the foundations and started laying the concrete, then changed his mind and decided to move so he filled it in again."
"Can you remember when this occurred?"
"I don't remember the exact year, but it was the same year he moved out. The couple who live there now will tell you. They bought it off him."
"You've been a great help. Thank you."

Lynn called on the couple who'd bought Hartley's house. They confirmed the year, which fit the timeframe perfectly. Lynn immediately called Allen, in Forensics.

"Allen, I might have another body for you in the Hartley case."
"Tell me more and give me the address."

****

After a brief court hearing, Simon Hartley was remanded in custody pending trial. He was escorted out of court and into the prison van wearing a broad grin much to the annoyance of the CID team.

****

Lynn was waiting when the Forensics van pulled up on the road outside and guided them to the area to be investigated, watching as they unloaded the ground-penetrating radar equipment and wheeled it towards her.

"Just over here, please. There may be a layer of concrete."
"Let's see what the display shows."

They passed the machine back and forward over the ground and looked at the display.

"It's possible there's something under here, Lynn, but we can't quite tell what it is."
"I thought you could see through walls with these."
"Modern ones, yes. But this is a bit of a museum piece. Our budget won't stretch to a new scanner and software. All we can see for certain is concrete, I'm afraid."
"So, the body's buried beneath the concrete."
"You'd better be right, Lynn. The lads are not going to be happy smashing through the concrete if there's just earth underneath."
"Just do it, please. If I'm wrong, I'll apologise for wasting your time."
"OK."

They unloaded picks and shovels and set to work. There was a foot of earth before they hit the concrete, then a layer of rough concrete a further foot thick and two feet wide. It took the best part of an hour to break through. At this point they put the picks aside and used smaller tools, hammers and chisels, to chip away at the concrete before eventually revealing woven fabric. They motioned Lynn to come forward.

"We've got something. It looks like old carpet. We'll just remove a bit more so we can look underneath."

They continued until they'd cleared a roughly circular patch so that Allen could pass a hand-held radar scanner over the exposed carpet. He inserted a sharp blade to cut out a small square so he could confirm Lynn's fear.

"It's a corpse, Lynn. It looks like it's wrapped in bin bags inside a roll of carpet. It's been in the ground for years, so we'll take it back to the lab for inspection."

Lynn, fighting the urge to vomit, nodded her approval and returned to her car. Once back at HQ, she informed the DCI of the latest discovery and updated the case notes while waiting for confirmation from Forensics.

****

The call came the following morning.

"Hi Lynn, it's Allen. We've examined the corpse. I can confirm it's a female, aged in her late teens, approximately five-seven. We're waiting for dental records, and I'll hopefully confirm her identity then."
"Thanks, Allen."

Shortly after lunch, Lynn answered her phone the second it rang.

"It's confirmed, Lynn. We've matched her dental records. There's no doubt it's Sharon."
"Thanks, Allen. Do you have cause of death yet?"
"Manual strangulation by a woollen scarf, which we found wrapped up with the body. I doubt we'll get any DNA from it, though. The other thing is she was pregnant. Maybe four months."
"Can you get DNA from the foetus?"
"It's possible, but not guaranteed that we'll get enough for a useable sample."
"OK. Do your best."
"Will do."

Lynn thought about the situation before deciding she would bluff when she confronted Simon Hartley with the evidence. She wanted to interview him as soon as possible.

She was at her desk when she took an intriguing call from Teresa.

"Lynn, I'm sorry to bother you with this, but I think it may be worth investigating."
"What is it, Teresa?"

"I've just taken a call from a Mr Anthony Sullivan. He's a freelance writer who provides stories for magazines, newspapers and the like. He specialises in crime. He's come up with some information which may be relevant in the case against Simon Hartley."

"Did he say what it was?"

"He thinks there may be another victim."

"What's your gut feeling? Is it worth following up? Or is he just some hack looking for a story?"

"I think we have to talk to him while we're still preparing for Hartley's trial."

"OK. Give me his details and I'll call him."

CHAPTER 6

Teresa took a call from Wakefield the following morning. The officer asked her to pass on the message to Don McArthur that the father of one of his former officers had been found murdered at his home. Don took the news badly. The dead man was identified as Arthur Lee. His son, David, had been in Don's team when he worked for the CTU, the Counter Terrorism Unit, for the Northeast of England.

Don drove to Wakefield immediately, having first informed Brian. Brian immediately made the connection and called Lynn at her home, where she was trying to sort out her mother's affairs.

"Lynn, it's Brian. How are you?"
"I'm coping, Brian. I've just about finished sorting out mum's stuff. The funeral's tomorrow, and I'm still working the Hartley case. I'm hoping to get tomorrow off and then take compassionate leave for a couple of days before I come back to work."
"Never mind that, Lynn. Please listen to me carefully. I believe your life may be in danger. Are you at home now?"
"Yes."
"Then please make sure the door is locked, and don't let anybody in. I'm sending you a minder. He will identify himself to you with the words 'Charlie Tango Uniform – All Together Now'. Have you got that?"
"Yes. What's going on?"
"I believe our murderer is taking his revenge on our old CTU team. Don't let anybody else in. Your minder will bring you here. Just pack a suitcase and we'll sort out some safe accommodation for you."
"OK."
"And if it's OK with you, he'll accompany you to the funeral as well."
"OK."
"I'll pick up any urgent cases you're working on."
"Thanks."

He closed the call before contacting Don.

"Boss, where are you?"
"Wakefield Police Station."

"Good. Stay there. Listen, I think I've discovered the connection between the murders. Remember the Bradford bombing? Well, all the victims of this current murderer were related to our team in CTU. Dave Lee, Lynn, myself. You could be the next target, Don. I think, once he's eliminated our closest relatives, he'll come for us."

"It's a valid theory, Brian. Let the DCI know and get Teresa on it. I'll be back as soon as I've spoken to David Lee's mother. She's in hospital recovering from a minor surgical procedure. Otherwise, she would most likely have been a victim too."

Don closed the call as the thought flashed through his mind that the last time he'd spoken to Mrs Lee, he'd told her that her son had been killed. And now he was on his way to inform her that her husband had suffered the same fate.

Later, driving back to Bradford, Don reflected on what had been an uncomfortable and emotional experience for both of them at the hospital. It made him all the more determined to catch the person responsible before there were more deaths.

****

By the time Don got back to HQ, the entire team had gathered in the Conference Room, including DCI Gardner and the officers nominally on compassionate leave. Alex Sinclair from the NCA was also present. This was to be a team effort, requiring input and total dedication from each and every member. Brian had already set up a whiteboard with the name Amy Winston – the Bradford Bomber – underlined at the top. Underneath were the names David Lee, Brian Peters, Lynn Whitehead and Don McArthur. Beneath those were the names of the recently murdered victims. And beneath them was a large question mark with a line in red leading back to Amy Winston.

Brian began to explain.

"For those of you who weren't with us in 2017, Lynn, David Lee and I all worked under Don at the CTU in Wakefield. We uncovered a terrorist plot to explode a bomb in Bradford city centre during the Half Marathon. We were all on duty in Bradford during the races. On that day, Dave Lee and the bomber Amy Winston were blown to pieces as Dave tackled her before she could

detonate the device as she intended to do. Consequently, he saved countless lives and avoided a catastrophe.
My theory is this: although we always believed Amy was working alone, it is possible she was acting on behalf of another individual or agency. It seems this 'agency' may be avenging Amy's death by killing people close to the members of CTU on duty on that day. So, I lost my dear wife and kids, Dave Lee's father was stabbed at his home yesterday – his wife would undoubtedly have been a victim too, but for the fact that she was in hospital – and Lynn lost her mother. I have no doubt that Don will also be on the victim's list as he has no surviving family. Now, the fact that our loved ones have been the targets suggests to me that the murderer was either related to Amy Winston or was her lover. Any questions? Comments?"
"Obviously, I wasn't part of the team at the time, but, as I recall, the subsequent inquiry decided that Amy acted alone. Are you saying that wasn't the case?"
"You're quite right, Teresa. That was the conclusion, but it's possible they weren't in possession of all the facts. I'd like us to dig a little deeper into Amy's history in case they've missed something. It may indicate she knew our current murderer."
"And what if you're wrong, Brian?"
"I'll accept the consequences. But it's all we've got for now. Unless anyone else has a feasible theory?"

There were no comments, so Brian continued.

"I suggest that you, Don, accept extra police protection, and that the same protection is arranged for Dave Lee's mother. All the rest of us should be aware that we are all potential targets, as are all those close to us.
I would suggest that we keep this information within our group. I don't want the killer to know what we know. Let's ensure the news agencies are only told what we want them to know. We may be able to wrong-foot the killer into committing an indiscretion if he's unaware we're closing in on him."

DCI Gardner had sat quietly, digesting the information, up to this point. Now, he spoke up.

"I don't want to give the impression that I'm ducking my responsibilities here, but I would like this operation to be run by the people who know the most about the situation. The people who were engaged in the initial operation. I propose that Don and Brian, jointly, will run the operation. I am not handing over responsibility for its success or failure. I will carry the can if things go wrong, but I feel that both Don and Brian, and also Lynn, have the required experience for what is in effect an act of terrorism, and will be better able to make decisions instinctively. As I have said, I will take full responsibility if it all goes tits up, as they say. I'd also like you to work from the office as much as possible from now. There's safety in numbers. We need to keep the whole team together even though some of the officers will have to work other cases at the same time."

Don looked at Brian quizzically and got a nod before responding.

"Thank you for having confidence in us, sir. We won't let you down. And you can rest assured that we'll consult you whenever possible regarding our strategy. Now, unless there is anything else?"

Teresa spoke up.

"If it's OK with you, I'll start by printing the key points from the Bradford incident, and everything we currently know about Amy Winston, and I'll contact GCHQ to establish a line of communication."
"OK, folks. Let's get to it."

DCI Gardner made calls to his counterparts in the surrounding areas. Having listened to his plea, all agreed to pick up any cases he wished to pass on in order to allow his team to focus on their priority case. NCA were in agreement that they would remain on the sidelines but ready to join the investigation when necessary. There would be no excuse for failure.

At 9pm, the entire team of Bradford CID were still at work. DCI Gardner had to ask each one to knock off for the day and thank them for their hard work and dedication. Reluctantly, they left, but were all back in early the next morning to pick up the tempo once more. They were not surprised to find DCI Gardner also at his desk when they came in. On his arrival, Brian made straight for his office.

"Sir, sorry to bother you so early, but on my way in this morning, I suddenly remembered something from the Amy Winston investigation."
"What is it, Brian?"
"We interviewed a young man who appeared to be her boyfriend. We let him go because we got the impression he was just a stooge to give some appearance of normality to her life. He certainly seemed to have no idea what she was up to, but it's worth having a chat with him. Trouble is, I can't remember his name, so I'll have to look through the case notes. It won't take long."
"OK, Brian. Go to it."
"Thank you, sir."

Back in the main office, the team were still examining paperwork from the Winston case.

"Can I have your attention for a second, please? I'm looking for a report of an interview with a man who said he was Amy Winston's boyfriend. It will be dated 2017. Anybody come across it yet?"
"I've got it here, boss. Just a second. Here. Kevin Hargreaves. Is that the man?"
"That's him. See if you can get a current address, please, Andy. But don't spook him."
"Will do."

****

Early in the evening, Brian and Andy drove to Saltaire to speak to Mr Hargreaves. They were a little surprised when the door was answered by a woman with a baby in her arms.

"We're sorry to bother you, madam, but we'd like a word with Kevin if he's available."
"Yes, come in. He's just washing up. I'll call him. If you just go into the lounge you can talk in there away from the kids."
"Thank you."

It was a brief interview. Kevin had had no contact with Amy since the time he was last interviewed and had been totally shocked when the news broke of her terrorist act.

"She just used me, Inspector. I've moved on, now. I live a normal life. As soon as I met Anne, I told her about Amy. She's never

doubted me. We married, we've got two kids and we're happy. Why are you asking me all this now?"
"Something's come up which may relate to the terrorist incident. We're just covering all the angles. So, nobody has contacted you, or mentioned Amy recently?"
"Not at all. If they had, believe me, I would have contacted you. I don't want to be associated with anything like that."
"OK. Here's my card. Call us if anything comes to mind."
"I will."

Brian and Andy were of the same opinion. Kevin had nothing whatsoever to do with recent events. All the same, Brian asked Teresa to check his phone records and seek permission to look at his bank account. Leaving no stone unturned, he organised covert surveillance by plain clothed officers for the next seven days.

At the same time, Teresa had contacted Europol, requesting access to their files on Amy Winston.

****

Brian was checking his diary to ensure he was on top of things when he realised that he had failed to follow up on a phone call Teresa had received from someone who may have information regarding another possible victim of Simon Hartley, who was still on remand in Armley awaiting trial. He pulled out the file and dialled the number.

"Hello?"
"Is that Mr Anthony Sullivan?"
"Yes. Who's calling?"
"My name is Brian Peters. I'm an Inspector in the CID in Bradford. I'm sorry it's taken so long to get back to you. I understand you have some information regarding one of Simon Hartley's victims."
"Yes. Can we discuss it?"
"I have to tell you, Mr Sullivan, we're extremely busy at the moment. I'm prepared to meet you to discuss it, but if it turns out you're wasting my time, you might find you get little cooperation from the police in future when you're researching your crime articles."
"I understand that. I think you'll find my information useful."
"Where can we meet?"
"I know you're busy, so I'll come to you, if that's OK."

"Are you free this afternoon?"
"Yes."
"Can you make 2pm at Bradford HQ?"
"Yes."
"Just ask for me at the desk."
"Thank you."

He closed the call and typed 'Anthony Sullivan' into Google, making notes. He then typed the name into the police database.

****

They sat in the Interview Room where Mr Sullivan was allowed to explain his interest in Simon Hartley.

"I'm sure you've done your research on me, Detective Inspector, and you will know I provide true crime stories for magazines, periodicals etc, as well as writing novels."
"Yes, I'm aware."
"I followed the reports regarding Hartley's murders with great interest, simply out of professional curiosity, and mentioned it in one of my Facebook posts. Not long afterwards, I got a private message from a woman who thought the photo of Hartley I'd included might possibly have been that of a man who was dating her daughter many years ago before she went missing. There's been no trace of her since. So, I arranged to meet the lady and got the full story from her. I haven't published it yet, but I'd like your opinion first."
"Do you have a copy for me?"
"Yes."
"OK. Tell me the story in brief. If I think it's worth investigating, I'll take it on."

Sullivan seemed happy to accept Brian's offer and started to relate his story.

"OK. This is what the lady had to say. Her name is Mary Phelan. She's in her early sixties and widowed. She had a daughter, Rose, who she described as loving, full of life, happy and beautiful. When Rose was sixteen, she had a night out in Halifax with some friends. They went in a few pubs and in one she met a young man who chatted her up. She told Mary about him when she came home and showed her a photo of him she'd had taken in one of those booths. She said he was really nice and polite and handsome. His name was Simon and he was about five years older than Rose. They started going out but soon her mood changed. She wouldn't talk about him. She still went out with him but wouldn't let her parents meet him. Her mother asked her to stop seeing him, but she said she couldn't. And one evening, she went out to meet him and they never saw her again. An investigation was opened, and it was all over the news, but nothing came of it, and the case was eventually dropped. Mary and her husband struggled to cope and eventually separated, then Mr Phelan died of a heart attack. But Mary never gave up hope and when she saw my Facebook post, it brought the nightmare back."

"So, her only evidence is the photo on Facebook and the name 'Simon'? It's hardly conclusive."

"I know. She's grasping at straws, but I promised her I'd look into it. I was wondering if you had any photographs of Simon Hartley when he was young, so I could show her. She might be able to state categorically whether he was her daughter's boyfriend when she disappeared."

Brian thought about it for a while before making his decision.

"OK. What I'll do is assign an officer to look through our file on Hartley. If she finds any old photos, she'll get in touch with you and arrange to show them to Rose's mother. By the way, when did she disappear?"

"April 1996. Please go easy on her. I know it's a long time ago, but she still hasn't got over it."

"Don't worry, I'm fully aware of what it's like to lose a child."

Brian immediately regretted what he'd just said. It was clear that Sullivan was embarrassed, and Brian did his best to apologise but Sullivan stopped him.

"Please accept my apologies. I know what's happened and I'm deeply sorry. Having seen the effect it had on Mrs Phelan, I should know better."

"It's still raw, but people shouldn't have to pussy-foot around the subject. It's happened. It's fact. I just have to learn to live with it. I'll do what I can for Mrs Phelan, and keep you informed. Thank you for bringing it to my attention."

They shook hands and Brian escorted Sullivan to the exit and stood there, thinking, until he was out of sight. Then he returned to his desk and called Lynn over.

"How are you feeling, Lynn?"
"Angry. Hurt. You know *exactly* how I'm feeling. You shouldn't need to ask."
"I know. I'm sorry. I seem to be coping most of the time, but it only takes one stupid or thoughtless comment to bring it all back. Just like I've done to you."
"I'll learn to cope, boss. If you can, so can I."
"I'm going to ask you to look at a cold case for me, and I want you to be totally honest. If you don't want to take it, just say so. OK?"
"OK. So, what is it?"
"It's a twenty-five-year-old case where a sixteen-year-old girl disappeared after she went out to meet her boyfriend."
"And why has it been resurrected now?"
"It's possible the boyfriend was Simon Hartley."
"Is this the one that was allocated to me. The one from the journalist?"
"Sullivan."
"Yes. I'm sorry. I forgot to follow it up."
"So did I."
"I'll take it. I hate that bastard!"
"Pick one of the team to partner you on this. Just let me know and I'll reorganise duties."
"Either Jo-Jo or Paula, please. I really enjoy working with them."
"OK. I'll sort it. Take the file and familiarise yourself with it. Look for any photos of Hartley when he was a young man – early twenties. It's possible the girl's mother will be able to recognise him from them. If she can't, we may have to drop the investigation. Anyway, do your best."
"Of course. Thanks, boss."

He'd made the right choice. He knew that pinning another murder on Hartley would prove therapeutic for Lynn, and whichever officer she chose as her partner would be up for it. He sincerely hoped they would be able to make a case before Hartley was brought to trial on the original charges. He made a note to speak to the DPP about delaying the process a little.

It had gradually dawned on him that not only was he back at HQ full time, working the murders of CTU officers' families, but he was also coordinating the Hartley case and overseeing the arson incidents at the same time. He was once again, flat-out leading his team. He was glad. It took his mind off his grief for much of the time and allowed him to function as a productive DI, rather than a grieving widower.

****

Lynn and Jo-Jo started working on the case the next morning, but despite all their efforts they were unable to locate any old photos of the younger Simon Hartley. In desperation, they asked Teresa for help, and by the end of the following day she'd come up with the goods, as she explained to the officers –

"It was simply a matter of going back in time. I tried his employers in reverse order from 2000, in case there were any works outings or memorable occasions he might have been a part of. But there was nothing, so I carried on going backwards until I got to the end of his school days. I was able to establish which school he attended and discovered he'd stayed on at Grammar School into the sixth form to take A-levels and won a prize in English which was presented to him at the end of the academic year. Guess what? The school keeps records going way back and when I contacted their administrator, she found me a photo and sent me a copy the same day. He's easily recognisable and she's kindly noted he's third from the left on the back row. He had that stupid grin all those years ago!"

Lynn called Sullivan who was delighted with the news. They arranged to meet at Mrs Phelan's house in Halifax the following morning.

****

Mrs Phelan was waiting for them and ushered them into the front room of her small, terraced house. After the introductions had been made, Lynn showed Mrs Phelan the photo. She picked him out immediately.

"That's him! I'm sure that's him! He had that smirk."
"OK, Mrs Phelan. I know it must be painful for you, but would you please go through what you remember about the last time you saw Rose."

She gathered her thoughts before beginning, her eyes damp as the tears started.

"He picked her up from the end of the street in a red Fiesta. I know it was a Fiesta, because my next-door neighbour had one."
"Do you remember what time it was?"
"About half-past seven."
"Thank you. Please continue."
"When she hadn't returned by eleven o'clock, I phoned the police. They said they couldn't come until next morning, and I'd to ring them if she was still missing. Harry, my husband, and I stayed up all night waiting for her. I had this awful feeling...."

She burst into tears. Lynn moved to sit next to her and put her arm round her shoulder, offering her a tissue. They waited in silence until Mrs Phelan was able to continue.

"The police came before lunch and took my statement. They took a photo of Rose – which I never got back, by the way. We didn't hear anything for a couple of weeks, though I rang them every day. They must have thought I was a right nuisance. Anyway, they kept saying they were investigating and then I got a call to say they'd traced Hartley and were questioning him. They later told me he agreed he'd taken her out that night, but said she felt ill so he took her home. He said she'd asked to be dropped at the end of the street so her parents didn't know she'd been out with a man, so he left her there. He said he was shocked to find she was missing. The police were unable to pin anything on him and eventually dropped the case. He told the police where they'd been that evening, but nobody could remember seeing them. And that was the end of the investigation. Nobody seemed to care. Harry and I had to suffer, not knowing what had happened to our dear daughter. Wondering if, one day, she'd just walk through the door as if nothing had happened. But she never did. And then, Harry left me and died a couple of years later. His heart was broken. He'd lost all hope, all will to live...."

Again, she burst into tears, before recovering her composure and continuing.

"There were times when I felt like just giving up and joining my dear husband, but I had to go on. I had to be there if she ever walked through the door. It was only the hope that kept me going.

But eventually I had to accept that she'd never come back. She couldn't come back. But I kept hanging on, just needing to know the truth. And then, I saw Mr Sullivan's post and it just gave me hope. Please, don't take that hope away from me. If she's dead, I can accept that, after all these years. I just want to know the truth. I just want closure."

She looked at her visitors, pleading.

"Please help me."
"We'll do everything we can, Mrs Phelan. I promise you."
"Thank you. I just need to know what happened. That's all."

Outside, Lynn shook Mr Sullivan's hand and asked him to refrain from posting any follow-up to the original item or mentioning Rose Phelan without prior permission from the police. He agreed. Before returning to HQ, Lynn called Halifax Police Station to ask that the case notes regarding Rose's disappearance be forwarded to Bradford.

Once back at HQ, Jo-Jo checked DVLA's records to verify that Hartley, or rather, his parents, had once owned a red Ford Fiesta, a MK IV model. She logged the details and added them to the information on the whiteboard while Lynn made arrangements to interview Hartley at Armley Jail that afternoon.

They arrived on time and were shown into the interview room where Hartley was waiting, sitting at the table in the centre of the room. They nodded to the prison officer, indicating they wished to talk to Hartley in private. He left them and stood in the corridor outside.

"So, Mr Hartley, how are they treating you?"
"Fine. They leave me in peace. They don't hassle me all the time like you lot did."
"Well, you'd better get used to being hassled, because you've just been accused of another murder."
"What murder?"
"A young girl you were dating when you were about twenty. You picked her up at the end of her street."
"Don't remember."

"Her mother does. She told us you picked up her daughter, Rose, at about 7.30pm on 7th April, 1996, and she hasn't been seen since."
"She's got a good memory."
"Parents don't forget things like that."
"So, what's it got to do with me?"
"She recognised you from an old photo we got hold of."
"She's mistaken."
"She remembers your car. The red Fiesta."
"There were thousands of them around."
"I know. Your parents had one of them."
"Coincidence."
"Well, you've got to admit, not many red Fiestas were seen at that time in that area being driven by a psychopathic murderer with a young, innocent girl in the passenger seat."
"You can't prove any of this."
"Not at the moment. But we will, given time."
"Good luck."
"You'll be seeing us again. We won't let this go."

The moment they left the Interview Room, Jo-Jo made her feelings felt.

"There's just something about him that makes me certain he did it. He's an arrogant bugger, for a start."
"We'll get him. Next, we update the boss, and I guess we'll be putting out an appeal in the local papers. Somebody out there knows something. They just need reminding."

Gardner listened to Lynn's account of the conversation she'd had with Mrs Phelan and the subsequent interview with Hartley. Without delay he sanctioned another appeal for information in the T & A.

CHAPTER 7

The following day, the T & A, the Yorkshire Post and the Halifax Courier all featured the 'cold case' appeal for information. Now all they could do was wait and hope.

It wasn't long before they had some success. Among the bogus calls, one stood out as possibly genuine and worth following up. It came from a man who had been on leave at home from the Army at the time of the attack but returned to his unit abroad the following day and so was unaware of the murder until now. The newspaper article mentioned the red Fiesta and he remembered having seen it on the night in question. When he called the hotline, the decision was immediately made to follow it up with an interview. Lynn and Jo-Jo went to his home the next morning.

"Mr Parkinson?"
"That's me. Stephen Parkinson."
"We're following up on your call to the hotline, Mr Parkinson. I understand you have some information relevant to our inquiry."
"Can I see your ID, please?"
"Of course. Whitehead and Johnson. Can we come in?"
"Certainly."

It was a small living room, but comfortable and tidy. He motioned for them to sit down. Lynn started the conversation.

"So, I believe you witnessed a young girl getting into a red Fiesta. Can you give me the date and time, please?"
"As I recall, it was around 7.30ish. I'm not absolutely certain. Let's say between 7 and 8pm. I was walking to the pub and arrived there before 8."
"OK. And the date?"
"I'm certain of that. 7th of April. It was the last day of my leave. I was in the Army and went back to my regiment on the 8th of April."
"Can you confirm the year?"
"1996. My last year at Catterick Barracks before I went overseas."
"Thank you. Where exactly did you see the girl get into the Fiesta?"
"At the end of Westfield Terrace, off Pellon Lane. I was walking down Pellon Lane to meet some mates in a pub near the town centre."
"Can you describe the girl?"

"Long straight blond hair. Slim. About five-eight, at a guess."
"Can you remember what she was wearing?"
"Jeans. High heels and a red coat. It was buttoned up, so I don't know what she wore underneath."
"Any other details you can give us?"
"She didn't look particularly happy."
"What gave you that impression?"
"Just the look on her face. Scowling. Angry."
"But she got in the car anyway?"
"Yes. And it drove straight off."
"Which direction?"
"Up Pellon Lane. Away from the town centre."
"I don't suppose you happened to get the car's registration?"
"No. It was in good nick, though. Fairly new. It was a Mk IV. I had one of those myself for a while."
"Anything else? Anything about the driver?"
"He never got out of the car, so I never got a good look at him. He was a smoker, though. I saw him flick a fag end out of the window as they drove off."

Jo-Jo looked through her notes to check that Simon Hartley was a smoker and nodded to Lynn in confirmation.

"Thank you, Stephen. You've been a great help. If anything else comes to mind, please let us know."
"I will. I hope the bastard goes down for a long time."
"He will."

****

They returned to HQ to write up their report but had only been in the office for a matter of minutes before a call came from Teresa.

"Sorry about this, Lynn. Another lead's come in. The DCI would like you to follow it up."
"OK, give us the details."
"Emailing them now."

The call was from a Mrs Scott, in Queensbury, whose daughter disappeared in 1997. They sat in her kitchen and listened to her story.

"Her name is Susan. She was a lovely girl until she turned eighteen and was working. She got into a group of girls at work – she worked at Grattan – and started going out with them at weekends. They went to pubs and clubs in Bradford. She'd started drinking, and often we'd get a call late at night to tell us she'd missed her last bus home and could she get a lift home. Well, Jack, my husband, used to go and pick her up but eventually he got fed up and we spoke to her about it, and she agreed to get a taxi in future. That was OK for a while and then one night she phoned to say she was staying overnight at a friend's house. Well, that soon became the norm. We didn't say anything as she seemed happy enough. Then, suddenly, everything changed. She became moody and argumentative. She wouldn't tell us what was wrong. She told us more or less to keep our noses out of her business. Then, one weekend, Jack asked her straight out if she was using drugs. She went mental! She said she was moving out. When we asked where she'd be staying, she said 'anywhere but here'."

She paused to wipe her eyes and blow her nose before continuing.

"A week later, she'd packed up her clothes and some personal things, and walked out of the door without saying a word. Jack was out in the back garden, so I shouted him, and he came in. We watched through the front window as a car pulled up just down the street and she piled her stuff in the back and got in. It drove off without her looking round to wave or anything. I just burst into tears."

Again, she paused to wipe her eyes.

"We never heard from her again. We called Grattan to ask if we could speak to her and they told us she'd left. She'd left before she moved out of the house, apparently. They could give no reason why she left. She just handed in her notice and wouldn't speak about it. They didn't have an address for her apart from ours. We couldn't contact her. She didn't have a mobile phone, obviously, in 1997. We didn't know any of her friends. There was nothing we could do except wait and hope she'd come back. But she never did. It broke Jack's heart and he died five years later. He was only forty-five."

Lynn held her hand as she cried, not knowing what to say. However, Mrs Scott recovered her composure and continued.

"I always hoped she'd turn up on the doorstep one day. We've kept her bedroom exactly as it was. That was the only thing that kept me going. Then I read the article the other day in the T & A. About the car. The Fiesta. It was a red Fiesta that picked Susan up when we last saw her!"
"Was it a MK IV?"
"I don't know."
"Let me show you a picture."

Lynn pulled out her phone and found an image of a MK IV Fiesta. She showed it to Mrs Scott.

"Was it this model?"
"Yes. That's the one."
"Did you get a look at the driver, Mrs Scott?"
"No. The car was facing away from us, and he stayed in the car."
"Thank you for bringing this to our attention. We'll do all we can to find out what happened to your daughter."
"If you find her, tell her she doesn't have to come home. I just need to know she's safe and OK."
"Do you have a photo of Susan. Mrs Scott?"
"Yes, but it's the only one I've got of her as a young woman."
"We don't need to take it. I'll just copy it to my phone."

****

Back in the car, Jo-Jo had spotted the coincidence.

"Did you notice that Susan had long, straight blonde hair?"
"Yes. Just like the girl Mr Parkinson described. Just like Rose Phelan."
"Let's check on the other known victims."
"I'll call Teresa now."

****

By the end of the shift, they'd checked all the known victims, and the additional information had been copied to the whiteboard. Lynn read out the conclusion.

"Of the victims we're aware of so far, Rose Phelan, Susan Scott, and Sharon Reynolds all had long, straight blond hair. We've also learnt that his first wife, Margaret, was blonde, although it appears she only changed her natural hair colour, and style, when she married Hartley. His second wife, Andrea, appears in photos with long blonde hair, although, again, blonde was not her natural colour. We also have another possible victim, as yet unidentified, who, when spotted, had blonde hair. The conclusion is that Hartley had a 'thing' about ladies with long blonde straight hair, which, I guess, is why he selected Paula as his next potential victim. I think it's time we had another word with Hartley."
"That will have to wait, I think."

Teresa had entered the room with some new information.

"I've taken three more calls in the last hour. I think they're all worth following up."
"OK, Teresa. Let's hear them."
"The first two involve missing people, both young girls, both with long, straight blonde hair. Both callers recognised Hartley from the picture that we published. Both incidents happened in 1999."
"OK. What about the other one?"
"This could be the strongest lead of them all. The sighting was in a quiet remote spot. A bit of a 'lover's lane'. The caller witnessed an argument where Hartley slapped the girl. This was in 1999 too."
"OK. Jo-Jo and I will talk to him first and then the other two."
"Here's all the information I got."

****

The following morning Lynn and Jo-Jo were on the road to follow up the leads. All three incidents took place in the Halifax area, though the first address was in Queensbury. They pulled up outside the house where a man was looking out of the front window and came to the door to meet them. They showed their ID and introduced themselves. The man, Jimmy Bateman, took them into the lounge to tell his story.

"It was in September 1999. I remember that because it was when my girlfriend and I got engaged and to celebrate, we had a couple of drinks early in the evening in Halifax where we both lived at the time. When we left the pub, we were both horny for each other, so I drove out of Halifax and up Old Lane. In those days it was a well-

known spot for sex. So, I was driving along looking for the right spot and I saw a car parked up at the roadside in front of us. A man and a woman were stood by it having a real argument. Then he slapped her, and she spat and swore at him. I didn't want to get involved so I drove on to find a quiet spot so we could have sex. And then I forgot about it until I heard about your appeal. They had a Fiesta, a red one."
"Do you remember the colour of the girl's hair?"
"Blonde."
"Long and straight?"
"That's right."
"Do you remember what model the Fiesta was?"
"It was a Mark IV."

Lynn put two images of Hartley, one old, one recent, on the table.

"Do you recognise either of these?"
"This old photo looks very much like a younger version of the man I saw."
"Have you ever seen either this man or his girlfriend since this incident?"
"No."
"If we showed you an aerial image of the area, would you be able to point out exactly where the Fiesta was parked?"
"I'm not so sure, but if I went there, I'd be able to pinpoint it, I'm fairly sure of that."
"Thank you, Mr Bateman. That's all we need to know for now. We'll be in touch to arrange a drive around the area."

They returned to the car for the journey into Halifax. Jo-Jo was sure she knew what Lynn was thinking.

"You reckon the argument could have escalated to something much worse?"
"It's possible. And it's possible there may be a body in the area."
"Let the dogs out?"
"Precisely."

****

They interviewed the two other women who had reported their daughters missing. It came as no surprise that they both were blondes, with long straight hair. Both women were able to recognise Hartley from the photos, and when shown an image of a MK IV Fiesta, both agreed it was the same model of car which Hartley drove.

They drove back to HQ pondering their next move and decided they'd share their findings with the DCI, before asking to deploy the cadaver dogs.

It was a short meeting at the end of which DCI Gardner was in total agreement that one of his officers should take Mr Bateman for a drive along Old Lane. Then, if he were able to recognise the exact spot with certainty where he witnessed Hartley arguing with the girl, they would deploy the cadaver dogs in that area. Jo-Jo took a car to pick up Bateman, while Lynn organised Allen Greaves' Forensics team with the dogs and handlers. Officers were placed at all access points to Old Lane to halt all civilian traffic while the operation took place. And by the time everyone was in place for the search to begin, the heavens opened. Tents were hurriedly erected while a backup catering wagon was summoned to provide shelter, snacks and hot drinks for the soaked officers. Nevertheless, Bateman was certain he'd located the exact spot where the incident took place and the search began. Less than an hour later, one of the Forensics team reported that his radar had indicated a possible corpse. Officers rushed to the spot and digging commenced. The badly-decomposed body of a young female was unearthed, wrapped in plastic sheeting. Photographs of the corpse and the site were taken before the body was removed for further examination in the Lab. The searchers resumed their work, gradually widening the area until one of the dogs located a second decomposed body, again female. As the rain continued to pour down, Allen felt compelled to ask the question.

"How long are we going to be here, Lynn? My lads are getting drenched."
"Let's give it another hour, Allen. Then if nothing else turns up, we'll call it a day and resume when the weather picks up."
"Fair enough."

The hour passed without further incident and the search was called off for the day.

"We'll have a chat with Hartley and tell him what we've found. Let's see his reaction before we decide whether to resume work on this site tomorrow."
"OK, Lynn. We'll give the dogs a well-earned rest. Give us a call if you want them again in the morning."

****

Lynn and Jo-Jo went to the canteen at HQ while they waited for Hartley's solicitor to arrive at Armley. While they were there, Lynn received a call from the mortuary which informed her that the girl whose corpse was the first one found was pregnant. Lynn decided to phone Brian to give him the news as he wasn't in the office, and nobody seemed to know where he was. A full minute passed before he answered his phone.

"Hello."

He sounded weary.

"Brian, it's Lynn. I'm not disturbing you, am I?"
"No, Lynn. What can I do for you?"
"I just wanted to give you the good news."
"What is it?"
"We've found two more bodies we believe are among Hartley's victims. One of them was pregnant. They're being examined in the mortuary. We're just going to interview Hartley about them."
"OK, well done. Keep me informed."
"Will do."
"'Bye."

He ended the call. Lynn turned to Jo-Jo, puzzled.

"That was odd. Brian didn't really seem interested. He seemed pre-occupied."
"Perhaps he's busy with something."
"Perhaps."

They drove to Armley and signed in before walking down to the Interview Room where Hartley and his solicitor were waiting impatiently. Having completed the formalities, Lynn got straight to the point.

"We've been out over Halifax way today. Your old stamping ground, I believe. We took the dogs for a walk along Old Lane. There we were throwing sticks for the dogs to fetch, and guess what happened?"
"No idea."
"They started bringing bones back. Human bones. Not sticks. So, we followed them, and they led us to a spot where someone had been burying bodies. Female bodies. So, we called Forensics and they took their photos and took the bodies away for further examination. It won't be long before they identify them and confirm our theory."
"What's all this got to do with me?"
"Don't you remember? You killed them. And then you buried them in the woodland along Old Lane. Oh, and one of them was pregnant. Did you know that? Is that why you killed her?"
"I don't know what you're talking about."
"That's odd, because you were seen with both girls. Witnesses have identified you. They saw you arguing. They saw you by the car. You remember? The Fiesta your parents let you use. I bet they would have stopped you borrowing it if they'd known what you were up to."
"I don't know what you're talking about."
"It's funny how all your victims shared the same hairstyle, isn't it? Was it a fetish of yours? Blondes with long, straight hair. Or did you kill brunettes as well? Or redheads, maybe, just for a change?"

They could see Hartley was becoming angry. The more they goaded him, the greater the chance he'd lose his composure. Lynn decided to push him further.

"Is that why you fancied Paula Harris? You knew she was in CID, but you couldn't resist it, could you? Right up your street. Blonde, long straight hair. Police. What a turn on, eh? Surely you must have realised it was a trap. Surely you didn't think an intelligent woman like Paula could possibly have fancied you. God, you are so stupid!"

He lost it, pulling against his restraints, his face puce with anger.

"She's a whore! She deserved what I'd planned for her!"
"And what exactly was that? Sit down and listen!"

Both officers stared at him in total contempt before he relaxed and sat down.

"Let me show you some pictures to jog your memory."

She placed the photos, one by one, in front of him, facing him, watching his reaction.

"Look at them, Simon. Pretty, aren't they? And so young. And innocent."

His reaction was unexpected, but nevertheless welcome.

"Innocent? They weren't innocent! None of them. They were all begging for it. They couldn't wait for it."
"Wait for what, Simon?"
"What do you think? A good shagging. That's what. They were begging for it."
"Did they tell you that?"
"They didn't have to. You could see it in their eyes."
"That was fear you could see, Simon. Pure terror."

He sat quietly, looking down at his hands on the table. Eventually, he mumbled something they didn't catch.

"What was that, Simon?"
"I said, it was an accident."
"What was an accident?"
"This one."

He pointed at one of the photographs.

"Tell me about it. What happened?"
"She wanted it, and then she refused and started struggling and screaming."
"Did she actually say she wanted it?"
"I could tell."
"OK, what happened when she started struggling?"
"She was shouting. She tried to hit me. I lost it. I slapped her hard. She started crying and lashing out and I grabbed her round the throat till she stopped."

Again, there was silence. Lynn waited before asking the inevitable question.

"Why did she stop crying?"
"She was dead. It took me a while to realise, but she was dead. She'd gone all limp and pale. I shook her but she was dead."

Again, a long silence, until Lynn prompted him again.

"What happened next?"
"I dragged her out of the car and into the woods. And covered her with leaves and dead branches and stuff. Then, I drove home. My parents were out, so I went into the cellar where there was some plastic sheeting Dad got from work. I took some and went back with a shovel. I dug a trench, wrapped her in the plastic and buried her. Then I went home. That was it."
"What was her name?"
"Rose."
"Rose Phelan?"
"Yes."
"OK. What about the next victim?"
"This one. She was a whore."
"Really? What was her name?"
"Becky."
"Oh, that's right. Becky. Go on."

Jo-Jo winked at Lynn as she noted the name."

"She let me shag her in the car and then asked for money. I coaxed her out of the car and went round to the back to open the boot. I told her that was where I kept the money. I said come and look. When she got close, I grabbed the shovel and hit her a few times. Then I buried her."
"You took the shovel with the intention of killing someone with it?"
"No. It was just in case."
"Really? To me it sounds like you had it all planned in advance."

Simon's solicitor stepped in.

"I'd like to have a private word with my client. Could you give me a few minutes?"

Lynn and Jo-Jo left the room. Immediately, Jo-Jo gave a sigh of relief.

"That was pretty horrific, Lynn."
"Let's have a coffee and wind down. There's a lot more of this to come, I guess. Better be prepared for it."

The rest of the interview went better than they had expected. Lynn remembered a ruse she'd witnessed Brian using during an interview, so gave it a try.

"You know, Simon, if you tell us the names of all your victims, you could turn out to be the most prolific murderer in British history. Won't that be an accolade? The famous Simon Hartley, Britain's most prolific murderer!"

His face lit up for a moment, but he didn't take the bait. Lynn tried another ploy.

"I'm not sure whether you've heard the news today about the five more bodies we found near Halifax. All blondes. No coincidence, that."
"That wasn't me."
"That's immaterial. You'll take the blame regardless. They were your type. Blonde victims. Come on, we know you did it. With all these charges, you'll never see daylight again. So, tell us about them."
"I told you! There's no way I'm taking the blame for five more in Halifax!"
"Doesn't matter. The jury won't believe you. Five more bodies. Adds a long time to your sentence."
"No. That's not fair! I never did them. OK, I did another two, but that's all. And I didn't bury them anywhere near Halifax!"
"Tell me about these two."

Realising he'd been tricked, Hartley put his head in his hands before looking pleadingly at his solicitor who simply sighed and nodded.

"OK. The first was called Susan."
"Susan Scott?"
"Yes."
"Go on."

"Nothing to tell, really. She wouldn't give me a blow job. She'd been getting me horny, you know, wanking me. But then she stopped. So, I killed her."
"Where did you bury her?"
"Judy Woods."
"Where exactly?"
"I can't describe it, really. But I could take you there."
"We'll hold you to that. And the other victim?"
"Anne."
"Anne who?"
"I don't know her surname. I'd just met her."
"You'd just met her, yet she got into your car? That's an unlikely story."
"She was a whore. I picked her up on Lumb Lane."
"When was this?"
"I'm not sure. 1999, maybe."
"OK. What happened?"
"She got in the car, and I drove her up to Heaton Woods. We had sex and then she tried to charge more than we agreed because I took so long to come."
"And what happened?"
"I slapped her and then I strangled her."
"Would you be able to identify the site?"
"Yes."
"So, when you went out with a woman in your car, did you always have a shovel in the boot?"
"Yes, after the first few. I got it out of the garage before I set off. My parents didn't know."
"So, you went equipped to kill and dispose of the bodies?"
"Not exactly. I didn't kill everyone who got in the car."
"Why not?"
"Well, they did what I wanted basically."
"They satisfied you sexually?"
"Yes."
"So, tell me, did you ever have an orgasm when you were strangling these girls?"
"Sometimes."
"OK. Were there any more victims?"
"I don't think so."
"You don't *know*? What about Sharon?"
"Sharon? I don't know anyone called Sharon."
"Of course, you do! You buried her in the garden of your previous house."

"I'd forgotten about her."
"Did you know she was pregnant?"
"No."
"Any more victims?"
"Well, I didn't count them. Apart from my wives, of course, but you already know about them."
"Yes. That's quite a tally. I bet you're really proud of yourself."
"They should have done what they were told."

Exhausted, Lynn and Jo-Jo returned to HQ, completed their reports and went for a drink together to relax after what had been a long and gruelling day.

****

Brian was still pre-occupied. He hadn't felt well all day and had informed the DCI he'd be working from home after he'd contacted his doctor. It was nothing serious, he insisted. He just had a stomach bug. He'd be OK by the next day.

Except he wasn't OK. He hadn't mentioned it at work, but he'd had stomach pain on and off for several weeks and had frequently passed blood when using the toilet. The following morning the pain was excruciating, so much so that he contemplated calling an ambulance. Instead, he phoned in sick and repeatedly called his surgery until he finally got through to a human being. He explained his problem, and its severity, persevering until the receptionist finally promised a doctor would call him for a telephone consultation. He sat and waited until the call came.

"Mr Peters, it's Doctor Bentley. I understand you've an urgent problem."
"Yes. I'm bleeding from the rectum."
"How long had this been going on?"
"A few weeks, on and off. I'm either bleeding or I've diarrhoea, or I'm constipated. It varies all the time. And I've frequent stomach pain. I can't remember the last time I had a normal crap."
"You'd better come in. When can you get here?"
"About ten minutes."
"OK. I'll see you then."

The surgery was only a short drive down the road. For the first time in as long as he could remember, he ignored his phone, which rang frequently as he drove. Only when he'd parked did he check for messages and missed calls as he walked the final yards to the surgery's reception. From there, he was shown straight to Dr Bentley's office where he explained his situation and answered questions before lying on his side while the doctor conducted a brief internal examination.

"There's nothing evident, Mr Peters. I think we ought to conduct a further investigation, though. I'd like to refer you for a thorough examination at the Infirmary, if that's OK with you."
"That's fine. The sooner the better."
"I'll contact them today and they'll be in touch with you directly. I'll indicate it's urgent."
"Thank you."
"There's nothing I can give you, really, until we know exactly what the problem is. The BRI will be better placed to advise you."
"OK. Anything I should or shouldn't eat?"
"Avoid spicy foods and alcohol. Otherwise, we'll see what the BRI examination turns up."
"Thanks."
"Good luck. It might be something and nothing, but it's best to find out quickly one way or the other."

He drove straight home and only returned his phone calls and messages once he was seated comfortably with a mug of coffee. Teresa had tried several times to call him. He called her back.

"Teresa, you've been calling me. Is it urgent?"
"Are you OK?"
"Fine. What's up?"
"Nothing, really. I just called to update you on the outstanding stuff. Then, when you didn't answer, or call back, I started to get concerned. Are you OK?"
"I've got stomach ache, that's all. Must have been something I ate. It'll pass. Nothing to worry about. So, what's the status?"

The call lasted around ten minutes, after which he hurriedly picked up a copy of the T & A and rushed to the toilet. He was just in time to avoid a highly embarrassing situation.

Afterwards, he lay on the sofa with a hot-water bottle clutched to his stomach until, finally, he drifted off to sleep.

90

****

Lynn knocked on the door and waited until Mrs Phelan answered.

"I'm sorry to bother you, Mrs Phelan. I have some news for you. Can I come in?"
"Of course. Come into the kitchen. Would you like a cup of tea?"
"That would be lovely, thank you."

Seated at the table, Mrs Phelan opened the conversation.

"Have you some news for me about Rose?"
"Yes, Mrs Phelan. I'm afraid we've found her body."
"Did she suffer?"
"She was strangled, Mrs Phelan, and buried in the woods. We have her murderer in custody. He's killed several young women. I'm sorry I've had to bring you this bad news."
"Thank you, dear. At least I know for sure what happened. I'm grateful for that."
"One other thing. The photo of Rose you gave to the police and never got back?"
"Yes?"
"Here it is. I was given permission to replace it in the case notes with a copy as the case is now closed. You can keep it now."
"Thank you, dear. It's the only one I have of her at that age."
"There is another matter to be dealt with, Mrs Phelan."
"What is it?"
"We have the body in the mortuary. Would you like us to pass it back to you to arrange for a proper burial? With an appropriate service?"
"Can you do that? That would be wonderful. We will both be at peace then."
"I'll arrange it. I'll call you when it's organised."

Mrs Phelan was in tears.

"Thank you, dear. You'll never know how much it means to me after all this time. Thank you… so much."

Lynn walked back to her car thinking it was moments like this which made the job fulfilling, but, at the same time, so emotionally draining.

CHAPTER 8

They seemed to be getting nowhere. Every time a flicker of light appeared it was quickly extinguished. Every lead they followed came to a dead end. It was Scoffer who made the breakthrough. He was reading a file from GCHQ where they realised a breach of protocol had occurred resulting in Amy Winston's file being incorrectly marked as clean before it was re-examined and classed as CODE RED. It was dated 2017.

Hurriedly, he thumbed forward through the sheets of paper until he came to the revised evaluation. He read it carefully.

"Amy Winston is to be regarded seriously as a potential threat. Her great-grandparents were German Jews and victims of the Holocaust. Her grandparents escaped Germany in 1936 and eventually made their way to the UK. They changed their family name from Weinstein to Winston in 1939. Amy's father was born in 1948 when the family moved to Bradford and married a local Jewish girl in 1970. Amy was born in 1973. Her mother was verbally abused and frequently physically assaulted by her husband. She bore it stoically until eventually she knifed him during a struggle. Amy was 11 at the time and was put into care and had to endure jibes and bullying at school. But she was strong-willed. Despite all the odds, she won a place at Hull University in 1991. We believe during this time she came into contact with a Syrian student, Sayid Abadi, and may have had a relationship with him. His name has appeared on the Watch List in recent months. Amy has never publicly expressed any extremist views but there is a record of her contributing to a radical Islamic website under a pseudonym which we are positive had been used by her previously when at university. Amy never married. Relationships somehow never quite worked out. She worked long hours and refused to be dominated by any man. It is also suspected that Amy Winston was at the heart of a proposed plot to blow up a statue in Bradford's Lister Park which came to our attention while she was at university, though nothing ever came of it. Among her friends, one name sticks out: Ellen Stevenson. It seems they shared a flat for some months and may even have been lovers."

He opened the database and typed the name 'Sayid Abadi'. After reading a brief introduction, he arrived at the words 'HIGHLY CLASSIFIED. Intrigued, he called Brian over to his desk.

"Do you remember this, Brian? A report from GCHQ concerning Amy Winston."

Brian read it quickly.

"Yes, I remember it vaguely. Ellen Stevenson was working for us, while unknown to us having a relationship with David Lee, one of the officers in CTU. As it happened, Ellen had not passed on any information of any significance, as far as we know, which might have compromised our plans."
"It's the other part which interests me. The part where it mentions Sayid Abadi. I've just tried to check him out on our system and it won't give me access. Can you get into it?"
"Let me pass it to Teresa."

By 3pm, Teresa had received authorisation from GCHQ to access the file on Sayid Abadi. Don and Brian were with her in her office when she logged into the database and scrolled through the report before discussing the details, while Teresa made notes. Don picked up the phone and asked for a quick meeting with DCI Gardner.

"We think we may have identified our murderer, sir. But there's a problem."
"Go on."
"He's been granted immunity from prosecution by the US government."
"That's absurd! It's possible that he's been granted immunity with regard to some historical crimes, but certainly not current ones."
"That's what we thought, sir. But the information we've got from GCHQ suggests otherwise. Can you get clarification, sir?"
"Give me the details."

****

It took two days of negotiation between the Home Office and the US government before a compromise was reached. UK officers were to be allowed to arrest the suspect in the UK for crimes committed in the UK only. That was all they needed. While the arguments had been ongoing, CID had already been making plans with the help of the NCA. Now the hunt was on to capture him.

They were of the opinion that Abadi would be living in the Yorkshire area, given that all the sightings had been local and that all his victims and intended victims were resident in the area. They circulated his image to all local forces, indicating also that he was probably known by an alias. The T & A and the Yorkshire Post also ran an appeal offering a substantial reward for information leading to his capture, and though there were many phone calls, none were of any use. Nevertheless, the CID team never gave up, following every potential sighting, every lead, though they knew they were getting nowhere.

****

It was late in the afternoon, and it had been a gruelling day. Most of the team were ready to pack up and go home when Brian's phone rang. Teresa.

"Brian. There's been an incident at your parents' house."
"What's happened? Are they OK?"
"They're fine, Brian, but the PC on duty was injured. Luckily, he was wearing a stab vest. He's been taken to the BRI for examination."
"Thanks, Teresa. I'm on my way."

He closed the call and addressed the team.

"There's been another attack. One of the uniformed officers who were guarding the likely targets has been stabbed."
"Who were the targets?"
"My parents."
"Are they OK, boss?"
"Yes, thankfully. I'm going now."
"Scoffer and I will come with you, Brian."
"I'd prefer if you went to take a statement from the officer, Don. Scoffer and I will take the scene."
"That's fine by me, Brian."
"Thanks, Don. But before we go, we get our stab vests on first. And that applies to all of you. Whenever you leave the safety of this office, you wear a stab vest. Is that clear?"

****

They dropped Don at the BRI and sped to Brian's parents' home in Wilsden, pulling up outside the house, and behind the SOCO van, where Allen Greaves was completing his notes.

"The officer did his job, Brian. He was in his car, parked just on the corner when he saw the van pull up. He got out of the car when the man started walking up the drive and challenged him. The man pulled a knife, stabbed him once and ran back to his van and sped off. The officer's stab vest did its job. He's bruised and winded, but OK. He's gone to the hospital as a precaution. And he got the van's registration. It's already been circulated."
"Thanks, Allen. Mind if I go inside?"
"We're finished. We've just taken a look at the doorbell camera. There's no footage. He didn't get close enough to the door to trigger the motion sensor because the officer challenged him. At least the officer gave a description, of sorts."
"What do you mean?"
"The man was wearing a face-mask, Brian."
"Of course. Thanks, Allen."

Once he was satisfied his parents were OK, Brian asked them if they would be prepared to leave the area for a while until the suspect was caught. They were undecided.

"We really think we should be here for you, Brian."
"I appreciate that, dad. I really do. But it makes my job harder because I'm having to worry about you. I'd much rather you were somewhere safer."
"We'll think about it."

He took a call on his mobile.

"Hi Brian. Are your parents OK?"
"They're fine, Teresa."
"Good. I've got some news from Forensics. The prints we found at your home belong to Sayid Abadi. But there's a problem."
"What is it?"
"Sayid Abadi died almost three years ago. He was a member of the Islamic State terrorist group, fighting in Homs. He was killed when a rocket was launched and exploded in the building where his group were hiding."

"So, how come he's still alive?"
"I'm waiting for more details to come through. There's obviously been a mistake somewhere."
"OK, Teresa. Keep me posted."
"Will do."

****

It took three days for confirmation to arrive regarding the circumstances surrounding the fate of Sayid Abadi. Brian read out the facts to his team during the morning briefing.

"Abadi left the UK to join the protests against the Government in Syria in 2011, and thereafter joined Al-Qaeda before eventually swearing allegiance to the Islamic State. In September 2018, a missile strike resulted in the death of IS fighters hiding in a cellar in Homs. The bodies were badly burned and many were identified by the ID documents they carried. One of these was Abadi."

He paused to let the implication sink in.

"It's possible that Abadi survived the attack and swapped his identity papers with one of the casualties. If we pursue that hypothesis, it's possible he has had plastic surgery to look like the man whose identity he assumed and has now come to England to settle the score with those who were responsible for the death of his lover, Amy Winston. If that's the case, he's going to be difficult to track down. We don't have a name; we don't have a description."

The sense of frustration was evident in his voice until Teresa spoke.

"Well, I'm not giving up. I'll trace his every move since he left Hull University, every contact he made, every place he visited. Something will turn up. Trust me."

Brian nodded.

"I trust you, Teresa. We'll follow up whatever you unearth."

Soon, Teresa was passing information to Brian to be followed up and immediately his team were making phone calls and scribbling relevant facts to be added to the whiteboards which had been wheeled out for use. Teresa was in constant contact with Hull University whose Admin department struggled to keep up with her requests for information. They had already been given details of Abadi's address while at Hull – a Hall of Residence – and a list of his roommates, and, when contacted, they were able to give names of his known friends. In turn, the CID team made contact with many of them who then disclosed further details of his interests and pastimes. Gradually a picture built up.

Abadi, who had arrived in the UK on a student visa, had been taking a degree course in Politics and was considered somewhat radical in his views. He attended and helped organise rallies condemning the regime of Bashir al-Assad in Syria and was arrested several times during the course of demonstrations he attended and helped organise. After leaving university, without completing his degree course, he seemed to have disappeared for years before eventually turning up in Syria as a member of Al-Qaeda and was on the security Watch List.

A few of his 'friends' were able to confirm he and Amy Winston were close, and that they believed she kept in touch with him after he left for Syria.

And then, Scoffer hit the jackpot. He had gone with Andy to Pontefract to interview a graduate of Hull University, and now a lecturer and political writer. In the course of their conversation, he told the officers that in 2016, he'd bumped into Amy in Sheffield. She'd told him she'd just returned from a holiday in Turkey where she'd met up with Abadi who'd asked her to marry him. He'd then taken her over the border into Syria to a training camp for Al-Qaeda. The interviewee was unable to say whether a wedding had taken place, but it was his opinion that she may have become radicalised. Scoffer had asked him if, in his opinion, she could have become an active terrorist. His response left Scoffer in no doubt.

"Yes. I thought at the time she could become a threat to the UK. During our conversation, she mentioned how easy it was to make a bomb. She evidently had some practical training."
"Didn't you inform the police about your concerns?"

"I thought about it, but then dismissed it as pure bravado. She was always out to impress at Uni. Always saying outrageous things just to get a reaction."

The following morning, Scoffer related details from the meeting to the rest of the team. They were all in agreement that Abadi was the Number One suspect, but so far, the only way they could trace him was by stopping every driver of a black Ford 4th generation Transit van.

****

In time, though, through careful research, Teresa found what would prove to be a useful contact on the internet. A Syrian national, he used to be a news blogger based in Homs and had to flee two years ago when President Assad put him on a hit list. She made contact with him via email and passed the information she acquired to Brian by phone.

"His name is Abdul Khaled, Brian. Most of what he wrote on the internet has been removed, but he has a hard copy of much of his work. He thinks he may have a list of those who were present when the missile attack which supposedly killed Abadi took place. What I'm thinking is that if we can get hold of a list of those who were present and match it against those who 'died' we may be able to trace the other names, one of which may have been adopted by Abadi."
"That makes sense. Where can I meet him?"
"In O'Neill's, a pub at the Great Marlborough Street end of Carnaby Street in London. I've sent him your image. He'll approach you."
"When?"
"Tomorrow, at 2pm."
"I'd better get a move on, then."
"I've already booked you train tickets for the 9.30am from Bradford Interchange. I'm printing the info now."
"Thanks, Teresa. Wish me luck."

****

He had an early night, which was just as well as his sleep was regularly disrupted by episodes of severe stomach pain. Nevertheless, he was up in time to have a shower, get dressed and have a light breakfast before the taxi appeared outside to take him to the station.

As soon as he arrived at Kings Cross, he made a courtesy visit to the local police station to inform them of his presence and his purpose. In return, they arranged for a couple of plain-clothed officers to be in the pub during his meeting to keep an eye on proceedings. Initially, Brian regarded it as overkill, but, on reflection, he thought it was probably a sound precaution, and thanked them.

He took a taxi to the Beak Street end and walked the length of Carnaby Street, wondering how it had looked in the late sixties when his dad had visited during his younger days. Finally, he reached O'Neill's and made his way to the bar, looking around at the customers until a man seated at a corner table held up his hand and waved him over.

"Mr Khaled, I presume?"
"Call me Abdul, please, Mr Peters."
"Brian."

They shook hands, Brian ordered drinks and they took some time making small talk before Brian came to the point.

"My colleague, Teresa, told me you had information regarding a missile attack in Homs in September 2018."
"Yes. I have the documents with me, in my briefcase. One moment, please."

He fumbled through his files before extracting the relevant documents.

"Ah, here they are. Now, what do you wish to know?"
"According to the information we have, a man called Sayid Abadi was among those killed."
"That is correct. Or at least; that is what was released to the public."
"You mean identities may have been switched?"
"I believe so."
"Do you have evidence?"

"I have a sworn statement from another of the survivors. There were four survivors; two were severely injured, two escaped uninjured. Abadi was uninjured."
"Do you have the names of all those who died?"
"Yes."
"Can you *swear* the names are correct?"
"Yes. Here."

He handed over a sheet of paper. Brian checked before asking.

"Abadi's name is not listed. So, you're saying he didn't die."
"That is what I was told by one of the survivors. Abadi switched identities with this man."

He pushed another A4 sheet across the table. It bore details of a man named Hasan Mohammed, along with an image. He then continued.

"They were friends. They were also the same height, age and build. They had similar facial features and could easily be mistaken for each other, especially among the rubble caused by a bomb blast."
"You're absolutely sure about this?"
"Absolutely. My friend – the other man who survived – was paid to confirm Abadi was among those killed but told me later that Abadi went to Turkey and had facial surgery to look more like his dead friend, and then got a passport in his name."
"Thank you, Abdul. You've been a great help."
"If you're looking for Abadi, be very careful. He is a dangerous man."
"I know. He murdered my family."
"I'm sorry to hear that. I hope you find him and bring him to justice."
"I hope to kill him."
"Then I wish you good luck."

They shook hands and parted, Brian carrying a sheaf of paper in an envelope. On his way out, he nodded to the two men seated near the door. They nodded in return and left the pub five minutes later to return to the police station.

****

100

Brian sat quietly in a bar close to the railway station, killing time and looking through the documents he'd received. He put them back in the envelope and pushed them into the inside pocket of his coat. He checked his watch then looked around the bar while drinking his pint. He felt a little uncomfortable. There was a man standing at the bar with a half pint in his hand. He had been cradling it, sipping occasionally, while Brian demolished two pints. He wasn't certain but had a feeling the man had been in O'Neill's while he was talking with Abdul. He checked his watch again then got up to go to the Gents. He pushed through the door to the corridor which housed the toilets. He was in luck. It also led to an exit to the street. He was outside in an instant, running towards the station entrance, hoping he wasn't being followed, and once he'd crossed the busy road he looked back. He was in the clear. He strode into the station and presented his ticket at the platform, before moving as far from the entrance as possible while still being able to keep an eye on it.

The fifteen minutes he waited to board his train seemed much longer and he didn't feel safe until the train pulled away on its journey north. He sent a text to Teresa listing the names he'd been given and received the reply that the team would be working on them immediately. He relaxed now, thinking he'd simply been paranoid about the man in the bar. It could just as easily have been a plain-clothed policeman keeping a protective eye on him. Still, you can't be too careful, he told himself.

****

The taxi dropped him off outside his house. It looked cold, unlit and unwelcoming. With a sigh he let himself in, picking up the post on his way to the kitchen where he dropped it on the table still uncleared from breakfast time. As he looked around, he could still see blood spatter on the walls even though they'd been re-painted. He could still smell death in the house and imagine the pools of blood on the hall and lounge carpets though new ones had been fitted. In his mind, he could still see the house as it was the day he'd come home to the scene of carnage. It would never leave him. The house was tainted. At that moment he made the decision to sell it and move away although he knew the ghosts would never leave him. The memory would always remain.

He took a bottle of malt from the cupboard and poured a large glass, carrying it wearily to the kitchen table where he sat reading his mail until, finally, he hauled himself off to bed to face another night of disrupted sleep.

****

There was chaos in the office when he walked in, late, and still severely hungover, his head pounding despite the handful of aspirin he'd swallowed. There was a message on his desk to report to DCI Gardner as soon as he arrived.

The DCI was not in a good mood and came straight to the point.

"I do not expect my senior officer to turn up for work incapable of functioning at the standard expected. You either work or you don't. At the moment, I'm giving you a choice. The next time, you'll be suspended. Is that clear?"
"Yes, sir. Perfectly."
"Good. Now, take the information you got from your trip to Teresa. Brief her and then go home. Get some sleep. Get something to eat. Lay off the booze. And come back tomorrow, refreshed and ready to contribute. Have I made myself clear?"
"Perfectly, sir."
"I know it's hard for you at the moment, Brian, but you were given the option of taking compassionate leave but chose instead to work. It was your choice to work this case. You're doing nobody any favours unless you're on top form. You're the one who should be setting the standard for the rest. You have to inspire *them*. You know you're capable. Nobody doubts that. Now, tomorrow, we start afresh. OK?"
"Yes, sir."
"And don't let me down."
"I won't, sir."

He took the envelope Abdul had given him to Teresa, apologised to her and left, unaware that CID's workload had suddenly increased due to another arson attack in the Girlington area.

****

He was sleeping on the sofa in the living room when he was woken by the sound of the doorbell ringing repeatedly. He got up,

102

went into the hall and was about to open the door when it suddenly occurred to him that such an action could spell danger, as it had for Sarah. Instead, he called out.

"Who is it?"
"It's Teresa, Brian. I've come to see if you're OK. Can I come in?"

He opened the door and let her in.

"How are you, Brian?"
"I've been better."
"DCI Gardner asked me to call on you. He's concerned about your health."
"Really?"
"Yes, honestly. I told him that apart from the trauma you've suffered, you also had some physical ailments you're waiting to have treated at hospital. He's worried you're going to lapse into depression, Brian. Have you eaten yet?"
"No. I've slept on and off all day."
"Then it's time you ate. I don't suppose there's anything edible in the fridge, is there?"
"I doubt it."
"What about the freezer?"
"There should be some chilli mum made a week or so ago."
"OK. Get yourself showered and changed, and I'll get this sorted."
"OK, boss."

Teresa had just finished cleaning and vacuuming the lounge when Brian came down. He looked much fresher and had shaved.

"When did you last clean the kitchen work surfaces, Brian?"
"Er, I think mum did them last weekend."
"You need to do them more often. It'll help you get back into a routine. I know it's hard, but you have to move on. The sooner you can get back to some sort of normality, the sooner you'll be able to concentrate on catching the killer. Now, get the cutlery out and lay the table, please."
"Yes, mum."
"And as soon as we've eaten, I'll bring you up to date on progress."

After their meal, they cleared up together, then sat at the table where Teresa informed Brian that a man named Hasan Mohammed had indeed entered the country three months ago on a tourist visa and had since vanished. All forces had been alerted to look out for him, but the general feeling was that he may have changed identity again.

"We're currently going through ownership of all black Transit vans with the help of DVLA, but it looks like someone may have bought it so Abadi could use it. Whether that person is aware of his criminal actions is unknown."

"He'll turn up. He's not finished yet. I'm sure I'm a prime target for him, and by association, you are probably on his list as well by now. I suggest you wear a stab vest as a matter of course."

"You really think I'm in danger?"

"I think everyone I associate with may be in danger."

"Anyway, there's some other news you need to be aware of."

"What's that?"

"There was another arson attack in Girlington last night. Thankfully, nobody died, but two adjacent businesses were damaged beyond repair."

"Who's on it?"

"Practically the entire team! The DCI's made it a priority - on orders from above. The force is under pressure from the local community demanding action, with the local councillor driving protests."

"That's all we need. So, it's just back to me, Don and Scoffer on Abadi's trail."

"Don't forget me!"

"Sorry, Teresa. I didn't mean to imply anything. I'm guessing you're snowed under."

"Your case is still *my* top priority; whatever DCI Gardner thinks."

"Thank you."

"And Don and Scoffer are still working their way through the pages of names to be checked out."

"While I sit at home getting drunk."

"Now don't start feeling sorry for yourself. Sarah wouldn't have wanted that. She would have wanted to see you fully focused on catching her killer."

"I know. It's just that I'm struggling to cope without her and the kids. I guess I took it for granted they'd always be there when I got home, to cheer me up after a lousy day. I just miss them so much."

"So, the best way to deal with it is to do all you possibly can to catch this bastard. That's the only way to get even. If you let yourself slip any further, he's won. And you don't want that."

There was silence as he let her words sink in. He knew it was true. He knew he was letting her down. He put his head in his hands and started to weep. Teresa spoke softly.

"You know, when you walked into the office on your first day, I knew instinctively what a wonderful man you were. The way you treated your colleagues. The way you helped everybody. The way you led by example. Your strength and resilience. If it weren't for the fact that I'm gay I would have fallen in love with you."
"And if it weren't for the fact I was happily married, I would have fallen in love with you."

They looked at each other as Teresa held his hand, squeezing it gently.

"Will you stay, please, Teresa?"
"I can't."
"Please. I just can't cope with being alone in this big empty house again tonight."
"I'll sleep down here."
"That's fine."

She went up to the bathroom while Brian made up a bed for her on the settee. They talked for a while, then said goodnight as Brian went up the stairs.

She woke during the night. She could hear Brian weeping. With a sigh, she went up to see if he was OK. He was lying on the far side of the bed, facing away from the door. She lay on top of the sheets and put her arm round him to comfort him until he fell asleep, then quietly climbed in next to him and cuddled up close. She was still there when he woke up next morning.

They ate a hastily prepared breakfast of scrambled eggs in the morning, there being no other options in the house, and talked about work, the weather; anything other than the fact they'd shared a bed.

Hurriedly, they got ready and drove off in separate cars.

****

He was watching as Teresa got into her car and followed her on his motorbike as she drove home to change. He stopped further down the road, keeping his helmet on and pretending to make a phone call. Then he dismounted and squatted by the side of the bike as if he were performing a minor repair of some description.

Minutes later, he watched as the front door opened and she came out of the house accompanied by a woman who walked with her to the car and kissed her before she drove off.

He mounted his motorbike and followed her into the city centre up to the point where she turned into a car park. He pulled into the roadside and watched her cross the road and enter police HQ.

"So that's another loved one to deal with."

CHAPTER 9

By the time Brian arrived at work, the office was empty apart from Teresa.

"Morning, Teresa. Where is everyone?"
"Girlington. Gary and Andy are at the scene of the arson attack. The others are going door to door gathering statements."
"Have Don and Scoffer been in?"
"No, Brian. I think they may have gone to Hull."
"Hull? OK, thanks."
"Oh, by the way, I'm not sure whether you're aware, but Scoffer has to return to his unit shortly. They've already allowed him to take more than his due holiday entitlement."
"Ok. Thanks."

He called Don.

"Where are you, Don?"
"Hull. In a café with Scoffer. We're just taking a break from following up some potential leads Teresa sent us."
"OK, let me know when you get back here, and I'll bring you up to date on my trip to London. And give my thanks to Scoffer."
"Will do."

****

Gary and Andy had met Allen Greaves at the scene where the fire officers were still hosing down and ensuring the shells of both buildings were safe and unlikely to collapse until the entire site could be bulldozed.

"What's the verdict, Allen?"
"Much like the last one, Gary. Petrol poured through the letter box, then petrol bombs thrown through the windows."
"I thought they had mesh screens."
"They did. They were ripped off. Cables attached to a vehicle, apparently. Witnesses said they'd seen it drive off down towards White Abbey."
"Did you get an address? Where it went to, I mean."
"No. All they would say was they were white youths and they drove off in a pick-up."
"That's not much use."

"Sorry. It seems that the locals don't want us involved. I've a feeling they know more than they're saying and want to sort it out themselves."
"A turf war is all we need at the moment."
"The thing is, I don't think it's a racist attack. I've a feeling there's a different motive."
"Such as?"
"I don't know. The only pattern is that both attacks have been on small businesses."
"OK. We'll see what the rest of the team have found out. Thanks, Allen. Let me know if it becomes definite that both attacks were made by the same people."
"Will do."

Lynn, Jo-Jo and Paula were getting nowhere. Nobody would admit to seeing or hearing anything.

"I can't believe nobody has any information to give us. They're deliberately concealing something."
"Do you think they're keeping it quiet while they plot a revenge attack on the perpetrators?"
"Either that or it's all been staged, maybe for insurance pay-outs?"
"That seems a bit far-fetched when people have been killed."
"I agree. But let's not rule it out for now."

****

They were making very little progress until Teresa took a call.

"It's Alex at NCA, Teresa. Sorry to bother you. I've been trying to get hold of Brian."
"He's officially on compassionate leave, Alex. Can I help you?"
"I've been looking at Bradford's caseload. It's something we do regularly, and I noticed the arson attacks."
"And?"
"Well, often we find similar cases in other areas. We look for patterns, and I may have found something. A couple of years ago, there was a spate of arson attacks in Wolverhampton, against immigrant shopkeepers. When we got to the bottom of it, it came down to a concerted effort to buy property in an area which the council had privately earmarked for redevelopment. In general, the shopkeepers were under-insured or not insured at all, and a consortium would pick up the burnt-out property on the cheap and

submit plans for rebuilding. The council had to turn the plans down and then had to pay a premium to buy the site back for their own planned redevelopment. It might be worth looking into with regard to your cases."
"Thanks, Alex. Will you send me all the information you have?"
"Will do."
"Thanks, 'Bye."

Teresa read the file as soon as it arrived. Two councillors had colluded in the enterprise with a criminal group who paid gangs of local teenagers to torch the properties earmarked for compulsory purchase. The criminals then bought the burnt-out properties for a song and submitted speculative plans to the council. The council was obliged to turn down these plans but then had to pay over the odds for the properties so that their redevelopment plans which were already in process could be finalised. They seemed to think that was the more cost-effective option rather than going to court over a compulsory purchase order.

As soon as she'd read the file, she took it to DCI Gardner. After reading it, he arranged a team meeting.

"Some information has been provided to us by our friends at the NCA which might have a bearing on the recent arson attacks. I want you to read the handouts and follow up with local residents to see if you can identify if they have had a similar experience. It seems feasible to me. The fact that the properties are close together may suggest a link. Lynn will lead the investigation. Any questions?"

Lynn allocated tasks to her team, and they were soon knocking on doors in the affected area. Lynn took on the task of interviewing relatives of those who had died in the first arson attack.

"Did the family have any warning prior to the attack? Any threats?"
"They had people inquiring if they would like to sell the shop, but they refused. It was a ridiculously low offer."
"Do you know who they were? Who they worked for?"
"No. They just told my uncle he would regret turning down the offer."
"Do you think they were responsible for the attack?"
"Most probably. I think it was kids who did it, but it wasn't a hooligan attack. They tried to make it look like a racist attack, but I

don't think it was. The kids round here are not generally racist. It's their parents who dislike us."
"So, why do you think they were attacked?"
"I don't know. They were honest, hard-working people. They never harmed anybody."
"Thank you for your time."

They visited most of the occupied properties in the area before meeting back at HQ where they compared notes before Lynn presented her summary to the rest of the team.

"We interviewed residents of properties in two blocks on either side of the first site. In all, about sixty properties. Most are owner-occupied; some are rented, short-term. Almost all of them told us they had been approached about selling their houses, but none could provide a name for the proposed buyer, only a mobile number. We've tried it but get a recorded message to reply to. We've left messages, but no response. Next, I propose we ask one of the residents to phone asking to meet to discuss a sale and see if we can trap them. Anybody have anything to add?"
"I spoke to the council about planning. They told me there had been one or two enquiries over the last few years, but no plans had been formally submitted."
"OK. Tomorrow, we check out the White Abbey area. Teresa has printed a list of youth offenders who are resident in the area. I want them all interviewed. OK?"

****

They were back on the streets the following day, in twos, by car and on foot. The youths split up and walked off in different directions as soon as they saw the police approaching. They could sense them, even though they were not in uniform. It was a skill they'd inherited from their parents. The police were used to the strategy and were able to herd them into dead ends. Still, they were uncooperative.

"Look, we know you lot have been involved. We've got witnesses who will identify you. And even if you weren't involved, they'll say you were. So, you'd better have a good alibi. Unless you'd like to tell us who's paying you? Who's buying you the Nike trainers?"

There was silence from the group. Lynn had a solution to break the deadlock.

"OK. We'll just pick one of you at random. And then we'll tell his parents the rest of you grassed him up. Or we'll just pick on one of you and tell everyone you cooperated with the police and grassed on the rest of you. So, who wants to be today's informer? No volunteers? OK, we'll call for a van and take the lot of you in. We'll keep you in overnight and tell the whole estate you've informed on them. You've told us about every little criminal act. We'll even get your photos in the papers and a little article telling the world how you've cooperated with us. That will do wonders for your street cred, won't it?"

There was no response. Lynn sighed and shrugged her shoulders.

"OK. Have it your own way. We'll start with you three. You look like the youngest. Get in the car. We're going for a ride. It's possible that we'll drop you back here when we've finished, but don't bank on it. We might just drop you one at a time in Girlington with a sign round your neck with 'I'm an arsonist' written on it. See what the locals make of that."

She stood in front of them, silently staring directly at the smallest and youngest of the group as he stood, looking at the ground. Lynn knew that he was aware of her gaze and continued to stare directly at him. Each time he looked up for a second, she was staring directly at him as his face coloured. She knew she had him and instructed Andy to take him to the car and sit in the back with him before telling the rest to clear off.

She got into the driver's seat and turned to the young lad, Ben.

"Right. Are you ready to talk to me?"

He nodded and began to speak.

"It wasn't my fault. I only went along for a bit of fun. I didn't know they were going to set fire to the shop."
"So, whose fault was it?"
"Josh's. He knew the men who took us."
"Took you where? To Girlington?"
"Yes. They picked us up by the flats. Josh told us to wait there."

111

"So, what happened next?"
"The van stopped by some garages, and we got out. Then they unloaded some cans, and bottles with rag stuffed in their neck. Then they gave us some big stones and some lighters. Then they told us what to do and drove off."
"Go on."
"We had to put a scarf over our face, and we went to this shop. Josh poured petrol through the letterbox. Then we smashed the windows with the rocks and lit the rag on the bottles and threw them through the broken windows and then it all went up in flames and we all ran away after Josh. He knew where to go and the van picked us up and dropped us back near home. Then we all went home."
"And how much did you get paid?"
"I got a fiver. I don't know about the others."
"Who paid you?"
"Josh."
"Where did he get the money?"
"The driver of the van gave him an envelope when he dropped us off near home."
"What can you tell us about the men in the van?"
"Not much. They wore suits."
"Did you get their names?"
"No."
"Age?"
"Dunno. 40?"
"Height? Weight?"
"One a bit fat, short. Curly black hair. The other tall and skinny. Bald."
"What sort of van was it?"
"A Vauxhall. White."
"Any idea what year?"
"No. New, I think. It smelt new."
"Anything else?"
"I'm sorry, that's all. It was just supposed to be a bit of fun."
"Would you like to explain that to the family of those who died?"
"We didn't know there was anybody inside."
"Right, Ben, you're going to sit in a cell until your parents come for you."
"Parent, you mean."
"Pardon?"
"Parent. There's only mum."
"OK. Give us Josh's full name and address."

Josh was picked up and brought to HQ where he sat in an Interview Room and waited for a legal representative to be assigned to his case. His customary bravado was lacking, and he looked on the point of tears. Lynn wasted no time in getting to the point.

"Right, Josh. You know why you're here, right? You're directly responsible for the deaths of five people in a fire which you and your mates started deliberately. That's not disputable. What I want to know is, why? Money? How much did they pay you?"

Josh didn't speak. He just lowered his head and sobbed.

"Cut out the crocodile tears, Josh. Don't give me any crap. It doesn't wash. Just tell me why you did it."

He looked up, tearful and speaking almost in a whisper.

"They said it was empty."
"Who said it was empty?"
"The men who said they were playing a joke."
"What were their names?"
"I don't know."
"Well, how did you meet them?"
"They drove up while we were messing about on the estate. They asked if we wanted to make some easy money by playing a joke on some Asian shopkeepers."
"Did you ask what you were supposed to do?"
"They said we were going to burn their shop because they overcharged white people."
"And how much did they pay you?"
"I got twenty quid."
"Another lad we spoke to said he only got a fiver."
"I got extra for being team leader."
"They made you team leader? What did you have to do?"
"I was in charge of the team."
"So, you told them what to do, and paid them for the part they played."
"Yeah."
"OK. Did you set fire to any other premises?"
"No."
"No? How about the one just down the next street?"
"That wasn't us. I had nothing to do with that!"

113

"I don't believe you. The attack was exactly the same. The same van was seen in the vicinity. The shop was fire-bombed. And you're trying to tell me it had nothing to do with you?"
"I didn't know anything about it until the day after. Some of my mates were asking me why they hadn't been asked to do it."
"So, who did it, then?"
"I've no idea. Honestly."
"OK, I'm going to let you have a rest in the cells for a short while to give you time to think about what else you're hiding from me. Think hard, lad. And when we talk again, I'll expect you to name all the other lads who were with you."

Lynn picked up her file and walked out, leaving Josh to be escorted to the cells. She returned to the office to speak to the DCI.

"I'd like you to authorize stop and search patrols in the area of the White Abbey estate, sir. We need to put some pressure on the gangs, make them feel uncomfortable, and disrupt their activities."
"What's the rationale behind this action, Lynn?"
"I've just interviewed a youth, Josh, from the estate. He's admitted responsibility for the first arson attack, where people died, but denies the second one. I find that odd, unless he genuinely was not involved. I would have expected it to be the other way round. I believe him. It seems someone is patrolling the White Abbey area looking for kids to carry out attacks for them, in exchange for a small payment. They get the recruits, drive them to the chosen site, give them the equipment, the petrol and the like, and tell them what to do. Then they drive off and let them get on with it."
"OK. We'll do it. I'll talk to Uniform and get them involved."

That evening, the streets around the estate were full of uniformed officers patrolling in pairs. Patrol cars drove slowly, stopping all the young males, questioning them, asking them to empty their pockets, and noting their name and address. Vehicles were stopped and searched, and the drivers questioned. And although they found no incendiary devices, they netted quite a haul of drugs and stolen goods, which were confiscated, and the owners charged.

By the weekend, the streets on the estate were empty after 8pm as the kids found somewhere else to congregate. The CID team spent their time collating all the information they'd gathered over the last few days and organised further raids designed to upset the routine of the local criminal fraternity. And eventually, as expected, the miscreants got fed up with the harassment and started leaking bits of information to the police in return for a relaxation of restrictions on their lifestyle.

Jo-Jo had brought a young man into custody, having caught him dealing drugs from his car, and was about to start a recorded interview, when he asked for clemency in return for information. She was intrigued enough to ask Gary to attend the interview.

"So, Matthew, what is it that you think is important enough for you to be allowed to sell drugs in the open while we turn a blind eye?"
"You have to promise you'll let me off in front of my solicitor."
"Sorry, lad. Can't do that. Not until you tell me what exactly this information will lead to."

Matthew looked at his solicitor and got the nod.

"OK. It's drugs."
"What about them?"
"There's a bunch of dealers cuckooing."

Gary leaned forward at the mention of the word. They knew it was happening, but the victims were often reluctant to come forward having been unwittingly tricked into the world of drugs.

"OK, I'm interested. Tell me more."
"It started with an old lady who lives in one of the flats. On her own. She doesn't get out much and has carers every day. I don't think she has any family who ever visit."

"A prime target", Gary thought.

"So, there's this girl. A heroin user who was one of her carers. She started doing extra stuff for the woman. Bringing her shopping and stuff like that. And after a while, she started calling at the woman's flat when she was off duty. Just for a chat, or to bring her a piece of cake or something. And eventually she gave the girl a key, so she didn't have to get up and open the door for her. But what she didn't know is that her boyfriend was coming in and hiding stuff in a cupboard which wasn't used."
"Drugs?"

"What do you think? 'Course it was drugs. And anyway, one day she told the old lady she'd been evicted, and she was desperate for somewhere to stay. And the old lady took pity on her and let her sleep in the living room...."
"And then her boyfriend moved in with her?"
"Exactly."
"You'd better give us the address."
"You drop the charges first."
"Done. Write down the address and the lady's name. And the name of the girl and her boyfriend."
"Of course. Nice doing business with you."

****

Gary and Jo-Jo kept watch on the entrance to the flats from a car parked down the street, photographing everyone who entered and left. Jo-Jo broke the silence.

"It's the first time I've come across a case of 'cuckooing'. We did an online course about it last year."
"It's far more common than people think. There are a lot of elderly, vulnerable people out there, and there are always plenty more chancers looking for opportunities to exploit people."
"Look. There she is."

They quickly identified the girl, Emma Horton, and her boyfriend, Des Bassett, from the photos on their criminal records. They were each carrying a bag. The officers sat in the car until the pair were out in the open and walking together down the street. Gary followed them on foot, issuing directions on his phone to Jo-Jo to follow. The pair stopped outside the New Beehive before Emma took the bags and Des went in. Gary followed him inside while Jo-Jo alerted HQ to send a backup car.

It wasn't long before the action started when Gary alerted Jo-Jo.

"We've got a deal. He's coming out with a scruffy-looking young woman."

Jo-Jo watched from her car as Des and the young woman approached Emma. She held out one of the carrier bags, the contents of which the woman inspected before nodding and reaching into her pocket. She pulled out a wad of banknotes,

116

handing them over in exchange for the carrier bag. At that point, Gary issued the order for Jo-Jo to join the fun as he emerged from the pub doorway from where he'd been watching. The two officers converged on the trio as a police car approached and screeched to a halt beside them. Two uniformed officers jumped out, handcuffed them and bundled them into the back of the car before speeding away.

"Job done, Jo-Jo."
"Let's go up and have a chat with Mrs Armitage. Better get SOCO to join us there. I guess there'll be some evidence to pick up."

****

As they had expected, Mrs Armitage was shocked when it was explained to her that she was an unwitting accomplice to criminal activity.

"But Emma seemed such a nice girl. She'd just been unlucky being evicted and that. I was happy to help her. She'd been so good to me, fetching shopping and things like that. She was such good company for me, the only person I got to speak to, really."
"I'm afraid she used you, Mrs Armitage. The story she told you about being evicted was a lie. She just used your flat to store drugs and to doss in."
"Will I go to jail?"
"No, Mrs Armitage. You're the innocent victim. We'd like to help you, so it doesn't happen again. Would you mind if we send a social worker round to talk to you?"
"If you think it would help."
"OK, we'll sort it all out for you, Mrs Armitage. We'll be in touch."

Before they left the flats, they knocked on a few doors to check on the welfare of some of the other residents and asked if they were aware of any of the recent goings-on. They were surprised to find that a further three residents were also being 'cuckooed' and gathered sufficient information to apprehend and prosecute the offenders.

Jo-Jo spent the rest of the week on the phone, speaking to various community groups and was delighted at the response she received.

"Hello. My name is Joanne Johnson. I work for Bradford CID. I wonder if you could help me?"

Soon, Mrs Armitage was contacted by members of the local church who arranged a weekly shop and clean, and welfare visits through the week. She was also invited to attend the local Community Day Centre, where twice a week she had lunch, with the company of people in similar circumstances, and was entertained. Within a short period of time, other lonely single people living locally also began to attend. Jo-Jo looked on it as one of the most rewarding weeks she had spent in the force.

It was not long before the T & A picked up the story and ran a feature. As a result, Jo-Jo was commended by DCI Gardner for her work. She was pleased and felt it was compensation for her failure to enlist residents for their help in identifying those who organised the arson attacks.

****

Brian was on his way home from Ilkley. He was deep in thought as was always the case when he'd been to the Cow and Calf and had taken a tortuous route home, paying scant attention to road signs. He found himself driving down towards Rodley roundabout when he came to his senses and turned towards Calverley. As he drove up the hill and passed the Calverley Arms, he remembered a café he'd visited with Sarah when they were looking for a house before they settled on the one at Idle. He turned off the main road and soon found it on Victoria Street. The Little Coffee House. He parked a short distance further on and walked back.

It had changed since he was last there and the staff were totally different, but he vaguely recognised the face behind the counter, though he couldn't remember where he'd seen him before. The man behind the counter smiled, realising *he'd* seen the customer before but was equally unsure where from.

"Good afternoon, sir. What can I get you?"

Brian recognised the voice.

"Just a cappuccino, please. I recognise you from somewhere, but I can't place you."

The man smiled, remembering.

"The Draper, Brian. I used to run the bar when it first opened."
"Ah, yes. Of course. Nick, isn't it?"
"That's right. How's things?"
"A lot's changed. How about you?"
"Same. Decided I didn't want the long hours anymore, so I bought this instead. It's much more civilized. Are you still in Counter-terrorism?"
"No, Nick. I switched to Bradford CID after the Bradford Bombing. I needed the change. But it's just as dangerous."
"I read about it. I'm sorry about your wife and kids."
"Yeah. Me too."
"So, what brings you here?"
"I've just been over in Ilkley and took a detour on the way home. Sarah and I came in here once a few years ago when we were looking to move house. I guess I was just reminiscing. Still, the coffee's good. Business OK?"
"Yeah. Some nice regular customers. And they don't shout and swear and throw up in the toilets."
"That has to be a bonus. Sometimes I often wish we had a better class of criminal, but that'll never change."

They spent a further ten minutes in conversation before Brian finished his cappuccino and took his leave, promising to return whenever he could find the time. Driving home, he thought back to the last time he'd seen Nick. It was after John Braden's funeral. John Braden, the brave civilian who'd had a premonition of impending disaster and convinced the CTU to act to foil a terrorist plot. But for him, hundreds of innocent people could have died. As it was, the body count was in single figures. Until recently, that is, when the bomber's ex-lover, Sayid Abadi, came back to wreak his revenge by murdering the innocent loved ones of the officers involved.

When he walked through the front door, there was a letter on the mat. He picked it up and opened it hurriedly, having realised it was from the BRI. His appointment was in two weeks' time. The letter informed him what to bring with him and left detailed instructions regarding what to eat and drink in the days before his appointment, and, more importantly, what *not* to eat and drink.

CHAPTER 10

There had been no further arson attacks in the Girlington area for a couple of weeks and as a result the regularity of police patrols had been inevitably cut back. Gradually, reports of acts of vandalism in the area increased to the point where police were once again being called out each night. The police patrols were immediately reinstated, though this had an unexpected consequence, in that a large group of Asian youths began to fight back by damaging property in White Abbey where at the time there was minimal police presence. Again, the onus to investigate fell on the CID team. They followed up on every reported incident, taking statements, logging times, dates, places, and collecting descriptions of the perpetrators.

****

Brian's investigation had lost impetus. Scoffer had already used up all his holiday entitlement and had to return to his previous role, pending authorisation for a temporary reassignment to Bradford CID. In addition, Don's availability was rapidly being restricted due to ill health and the need for regular hospital appointments. Up until now, he had kept the reason for the appointments to himself, and Brian had respected his right to privacy, but both knew it wouldn't be long before his illness became unbearable. He knew Don would fight to the death, but he would still want to be on the winning side. He'd been sitting in the kitchen, at the table, for much of the evening desperately hoping for a break in the case, but eventually had to concede they'd checked every lead thoroughly to no avail. He pulled the cork from the bottle of malt and poured himself a large glass which he raised before drinking.

"Cheers, Don."

****

Teresa called Brian in the morning, to pass on the good news that Scoffer was temporarily back in the Bradford team and would shortly be re-joining him in his hunt for Abadi. There was no answer. She left a message on his voicemail and also tried his landline but got no response. She tried again without success before driving up to his address in her lunch hour.

She parked outside and looked at the house. The curtains were open, and the kitchen light was on. She pressed the doorbell and waited. No answer. She walked over to the kitchen window and looked through. Her heart was racing. There was a body on the floor. Brian. She hammered on the window. He didn't move. She walked round to the back door and tried the handle. It was unlocked. She took a deep breath and walked in, first taking the pepper spray out of her pocket before moving silently and slowly towards the kitchen. She opened the door and looked around. Apart from the body on the floor, it was empty. She knelt at his side and felt for his pulse. He was alive! Then she saw the empty bottle beside him.

"Oh, Christ!"

She took out her phone and called for paramedic assistance, and while she waited took a cushion from the sofa in the lounge and put it under his head. His breathing was shallow but regular. She took off her coat and laid it over his body and waited as tears ran down her cheeks until the ambulance arrived.

****

He woke, blinking in the light as a face came into focus. Teresa, smiling.

"Welcome back, Brian."
"What's going on?"
"You're in hospital. I found you on the floor in your kitchen and called an ambulance."
"What happened?"
"The paramedics said you were pissed senseless. The doctor had a more technical term for it. Whatever the diagnosis, Brian, you need to get a grip."
"I know. I'm sorry."
"You don't need to apologise to me. You just need to stop it. Or you'll lose all the respect you've worked for these past years."
"I just feel so helpless."
"You're *not* helpless. You have it in you to lead this investigation with the same tenacity you've fronted every other case. You *can't* give up. Sarah wouldn't want you to give up. You owe her. You owe your kids. You *have* to get revenge for what's happened. And drinking isn't going to help."

"I know. I know."
"Well, then make me a promise you'll put your energy into catching the bastard who murdered Sarah, and Daniel and Samantha, and all the others. We need you on top of this, Brian. So, quit the self-pity and get back to work."
"Yes, boss."
"I'm serious, Brian. You've been the driving force in Bradford CID. We all rely on you. We need you. Don't desert us now. Please help us."

****

Two days later he was back at work. Teresa had taken him home from hospital and helped him clean up and empty all the bottles of alcohol down the sink before driving him to HQ where he'd had a meeting with DCI Gardner in which he'd fully committed himself to his job.

"I'm pleased you've made the decision, Brian. You're highly respected in the Force. We need your leadership, your dedication, your tenacity. So, welcome back."
"Thank you, sir."
"Your recent episode will not appear on record, Brian. It never happened."
"Thank you, sir."
"As long as it doesn't happen again."
"It won't, sir. I guarantee that. I have medication and I'm booked in for regular counselling. And in addition to that, I'm waiting for an appointment at the BRI for a surgical procedure which should bring me some clarity regarding some other worrying health issues I have."
"OK. Go talk to your team and bring yourself up to speed with what's been going on."

****

Don had phoned Brian to inform him he had a hospital appointment that morning and would be in after lunch. Brian was glad to have Scoffer back and between them they spent the morning reading once more through the mass of information they'd collected in the hope that they'd find something they'd previously missed. They were interrupted by a call from Teresa.

"Brian, there's a man at the front desk asking if he can talk to someone about the case you're working. He says he has information."
"Tell him I'll be right down."

He turned to Scoffer.

"I hope it's not another time-waster."
"Trouble is, even if it is a time waster, we still have to check it out. You just never know."
"Fingers crossed."

He took the man, Mr Wagstaffe, to an Interview Room and asked him why he wanted to talk about the case.

"We've never met, Mr Peters. I've seen you, and you may have seen me, but we've never been introduced. I live in the end house on your road. I live alone since my wife passed away."
"I'm sorry to hear that, Mr Wagstaffe, but what is it you wish to see me about? We're very busy at the moment...."
"I'm sorry. I'll get to the point. I think I might have a photograph of the man who murdered your family."
"Do you have it with you now?"
"Yes. On my phone."
"Please, show me."

Mr Wagstaffe took out his phone and flipped through the photos until he found the image he was looking for.

"Here. This is him."

It was quite a sharp image but, in Brian's opinion, would certainly benefit from enhancement in the lab.

"Could you send it to my phone, please?"

He checked the copied image before continuing the conversation.

"Why did you take a photo of this man, Mr Wagstaffe?"

"I'd seen him several times. At first, I thought he was a delivery man. Amazon, or something. But he rarely seemed to get out of the van. And when he did, with a parcel in his hand, he always seemed to return with the same parcel before driving off. I just thought it was odd. Anyway, on top of that, he always seemed to park half on the pavement, and that always annoys me because there are women on this road who struggle to get past with prams and such, and there are a couple of old chaps with electric mobility scooters who have to ride in the road. So, I took pictures of his van to send to the police."

"Can I have a look at those too, please?"

Brian noticed immediately that the number plate was different to the one previously reported.

"Can you tell me when these photos were taken?"
"The day before the murders."

Brian couldn't conceal his annoyance.

"Why didn't you come forward earlier? We've wasted nearly two months!"
"I'm sorry, but later that day I had to call for an ambulance. They took me to hospital, and I was admitted immediately. I had Covid. I spent nearly six weeks in hospital and then a couple of weeks in a care home."
"I'm so sorry. I didn't realise. Please accept my apology."
"I didn't know anything about the murder until I was in the care home, so as soon as I was sent home, I got my phone out and checked the dates and read about the case in the papers and on the internet. As soon as I realised what I had, I came here."
"Thank you. You've been a great help. I'll see you out."

Brian looked again at the image of the Ford van. A previous report by a neighbour had stated its number plate began YC18, yet it was quite clear in the image. It read FD16 TXG. He picked up the phone.

"Teresa, could you please trace a number plate for me? FD16 TXG. It was seen on a black Ford van on my road on the day before the attack."
"Will do."

Two minutes later, she called back.

"According to DVLC records, it belonged to a pale blue Kia Picanto, which was written off in January."
"Who was the owner?"
"A chap called Arthur Metcalfe. He'd had it from new. He was killed in a crash in Rawdon and the car went to a scrap yard for parts. I'm sending you the address."
"Thanks."

It immediately dawned on Brian that the killer was buying, or stealing, number plates to use on his van to avoid detection.

"Get your coat, Scoffer. We're off to a scrap yard."
"Good. I fancy a scrap."

The owner of the yard wasn't really much help. As he explained to the police.

"We sell anything and everything to do with motors. No questions asked. Some people buy number plates in the hope that someone will want them. Perhaps their initials are the same as the plate. We just sell 'em. It's up to them what they do with them."

"Do you keep a record of each individual number sold?".
"No."
"Do you know who bought this particular number?"
"No. "
"Do you recognise this man?"
"Yes. I think he might have bought number plates from us."
"How did he pay?"
"Cash."
"He didn't leave an address or phone number?"
"Nope."
"Wait a minute. You must have a record of all the cars you've bought for scrap."
"Well, no. Sometimes we buy 'em from a third party. We don't necessarily get all the documents."
"Do you have the registration documents for *any* of the cars which have passed through your hands in the last six months?"
"Some."
"Get them, please."

They made a note of all the registration numbers available and left.

"Thanks for your help."

They sat in the car for a while, thinking.

"I suppose we could pass the numbers to Traffic. Ask them to let us know if they see a black 4th Generation Transit."
"I guess that's all we can do, Scoffer. Hope for a bit of luck for a change."
"Well, at least it's something. Nobody's going to buy plates without the registration documents unless there's a criminal motive or unless they're distinctive."

The following afternoon Brian received a call from Traffic. They'd stopped a car bearing one of the suspect plates on Rooley Lane and brought the driver and passenger, two males in their early twenties, in for questioning.

"So, which one of you owns the car?"
"Neither of us. We just borrowed it."
"You nicked it?"
"Not really."
"Do you know the owner?"
"Yeah."
"What's his name?"
"I'm not sure."
"You're not sure?"
"I can't remember."
"OK. Did you put the false plates on?"
"False plates? No. We haven't done anything."
"Apart from stealing the car?"
"Well, we just borrowed it. We were going to take it back."
"After a bit of joyriding?"
"Yeah. We didn't mean any harm."
"You'll be charged with TWOCing."
"What's that?"
"Taking without consent. Don't worry. You'll be released on bail and a date set to appear in court. In the meantime, keep your noses clean. OK?"
"OK."
"The constable will take all the details. By the way, where did you nick the car from?"
"Canterbury Avenue. It was parked up with the keys in the ignition and nobody about."

****

Forensics collected the car to dust for prints and called Brian the next morning.

"We've got prints, Brian, They're a match to Abadi."
"That's what I was hoping. I think we can assume that the other numberplates in the batch sold are in Abadi's possession. We can ask all officers to look out for a black Ford Transit with one of those plates. It's progress, at least."

****

The time had arrived for his hospital appointment. He had arranged to have just the one day off, and took a taxi to the BRI, arriving a little early for his 08.45 appointment. Although not looking forward to the op, he was relaxed about it, although he had found it difficult to stick rigidly to the pre-op dietary restrictions, particularly the bit where it stated 'you must refrain from alcohol'. But at least he'd managed to keep his intake to a minimum.

Once on the table, anaesthetised, he felt more relaxed than at any time in his police career, only vaguely aware of the tube entering his rectum.

Three hours later, fully recovered, he was informed his lift home had arrived and he was allowed to leave. He was delighted to find Teresa waiting in Reception. She approached him with a smile and the words:

"Taxi for Peters."

She drove him home and made sure he was comfortable before returning to work.

"See you on Monday."

****

True to his word, Brian Peters was back at his desk on Monday morning and was quickly up to date with progress on the hunt for Abadi. Unfortunately, it turned out not to be the progress they had hoped for. Over the course of the next few days, five cars were stopped, and the drivers questioned. All were driving stolen cars. Three had bought them knowing they had been stolen and had false plates; the other two bought the false plates on the internet to fix on cars they had themselves stolen. They were unable to trace the seller of the plates, nor were there any sightings of the black Transit. After much discussion, they decided to try a different strategy. They decided to go public and by the next day the local papers, radio stations and TV news all featured details of the hunt for Abadi, along with the latest image they had.

Despite a flood of calls to the phone line they'd set up, they made little progress until a pensioner called at HQ asking to speak to DI Peters. Hoping it wasn't yet another hoax, Brian went to Reception to meet the man and introduced himself.

"I believe you have some information regarding Abadi. Would you like to come with me to discuss it?"
"Thank you, yes."

They sat opposite each other at the table in Interview Room 2 where the interviewee introduced himself.

"My name is Griffiths. Alexander Griffiths. I was a professor at Hull University until I retired."
"So, you knew Abadi all those years ago? What have you got to tell me?"
"I'm sure you've already got his background, and the fact that he and Amy Winston had a relationship."
"Yes."
"Were you aware that he had another lover?"
"No."
"He did. It was another student. A male student."
"Do you have his name?"
"His name was Youssef Ahmad."
"Do you happen to know his address?"
"Sorry, no. I don't even know if he still lives in England. I have an old photograph if that's of any use."
"That would help, yes."
"One other thing. They, along with a number of other Muslim students, communicated on a website. I don't know if it's still active, but I've written down the address here."
"Thank you. Is there anything else?"

"Youssef was thrown out of Hull Uni for distributing propaganda relating to extremism. That's all I have. I hope it's some help."
"We'll certainly look into it. Thanks for your help. I'll see you out, and if anything else comes to mind, please get in touch."
"I will."

They shook hands at the door. Brian rushed upstairs to find Teresa.

"Urgent job, Teresa. I want to find a man called Youssef Ahmad. He was at Hull University at the same time as Abadi. They were lovers. Please do all you can."
"I'll be straight on it. Oh, by the way, Don rang in. He needs to speak to you urgently."
"OK. I'll call him. Oh, and another thing. While Abadi and Youssef were at Hull, they and other Muslim students ran a website. This is the address. Look into it, please."
"Will do."

He dialled Don's number.

"Hello, Brian. I'm sorry I can't come in today."
"Are you OK?"
"I've had some bad news, Brian. I'd rather tell you face to face, but I'm in hospital at the moment."
"What's the problem, Don?"
"I got the results of my latest tests this morning and I'm afraid to tell you I've got cancer."
"Oh God! I'm sorry to hear that, Don. Is it bad?"
"It's terminal."

Brian was stunned. He was lost for words for a while until he composed himself.

"How long have you got, Don?"
"They won't be specific. It could be months; it could be days. All they'll say is don't make any arrangements for Christmas."
"Can I come to see you?"
"All being well, I'll be home tomorrow morning. I'll call you then. Is that OK?"
"Of course. I'll talk to you later."

He closed the call, closed his eyes and prayed silently. He made himself a promise. He would catch Abadi and make him pay while Don was still alive.

Meanwhile, despite the fact that the latest image of Abadi had been widely circulated, there were no reports of any sightings.

CHAPTER 11

He picked up the phone on the first ring. He knew it was Teresa.

"Hello."
"Good news, Brian. Youssef Ahmad is in York, or at least, that's the address we've got."
"Send me everything you've got, Teresa, and a photo, please. And thank you. That was quick work."
"That's what I'm paid to do. It's on its way. I'll update you as soon as anything else comes in. You should be aware, though, he's on the Watch List."
"Terrorism?"
"In Germany, a few years ago. Part of a group suspected of bombing a synagogue."
"Thanks."
"And the website you signposted for me. It's just general propaganda, but there's a pointer to more pages which require a password. I'm working on it now."

He snatched the paper from the printer tray and called Scoffer.

"Get your coat. We're off to York."
"Business or pleasure?"
"What do you think?"
"I'll put my body armour on, then."

On the way, Brian called the CID in York, and agreed to speak to an officer before they called on Youssef. The officer, DI Milnes, took them into a private office.

"Before you go upsetting Youssef, you need to know he's a nark."
"That's a surprise. Has he given you any information about a man called Sayid Abadi?"
"Is that the guy who's been killing families of Bradford officers?"
"Yes. He killed mine. I want to find him, and we've been informed he knows Youssef. We were hoping to question Youssef."
"To my knowledge, he's never mentioned Sayid Abadi. Would you mind if I joined you when you speak to him?"
"Not at all. We've no interest in anything Youssef does. We just want to know if he can help us locate Abadi."
"OK. Come on, I'll arrange a meeting."

****

They met in the park near York Museum and walked slowly while they talked. Youssef acknowledged the fact that he knew Abadi, and that they were once lovers, but stated categorically that he'd had no contact with him for several years.

"I've read the papers. I've seen the news on TV. If I knew his whereabouts, I would have told the police immediately."
"Do you know if he has been involved with any terrorist groups or committed any acts of violence?"
"No. Don't you think I would have told the police if I knew anything like that?"

After a fruitless conversation, Brian and Scoffer returned to the car having thanked DI Milnes for his cooperation.

"What do you think, Scoffer?"
"It's possible he's lying, and DI Milnes knows it but doesn't want to lose an asset."
"So, how do we prove it?"
"Keep him under observation?"
"That would be practically impossible. I've a better idea. Let's see if Teresa can hack into his online activities."
"Sounds like a plan. Do you think the DCI will approve it?"
"He won't know if I don't tell him."
"If you don't tell him and he finds out later, that could be the end of your career."
"I know. It's worth the risk."
"OK, call Teresa. I'll drive."

As expected, Teresa was happy to take on the assignment, whatever the outcome, and soon was able to call on her skills, with some assistance from her friends at NCA, to acquire Youssef's email address and send a phishing email containing a virus giving her remote access to his PC without his knowledge. She called Brian as soon as it was activated.

"Come up and see, Brian. He's online now, and we can see whatever he's doing already. If that's harmless, we'll have a look at his address book."
"And he's got no idea we're monitoring him?"

"None at all. Oh, wait. He's initiated a Zoom call. He'll have to switch his camera on. We could watch his screen and see who he's talking to."
"Without his knowledge?"
"Yep."
"You can hack his screen?"
"Yep."

Brian sounded incredulous.

"Without his knowledge?"
"That depends. Some PCs have anti-spyware software which indicates if there are unauthorised users."
"It's worth a shot. He might be Zooming with Abadi. If so, I want to know what he looks like now. He seems to keep changing his appearance."
"You want me to try?"
"Let's get whatever information he has on his computer first. Can you copy his files?"
"Doing it now."

It took a mere five minutes before Teresa pronounced the operation successful.

"Let's have a look at the bugger he's talking to, then. Let's see his face."
"OK, here goes."

She typed in a few commands and hit enter. Her screen immediately showed Abadi's face. She took a screen shot, then switched off access to Youssef's screen.

"That's done. I'm going to disconnect before Youssef suspects anything."

It was too late. He'd noticed the screen flicker just as Teresa switched off access. He calmly closed the applications he'd been using and shut down the computer. He called Abadi and told him what had happened.

Abadi was angry. He would show them what he was capable of. It was time to select another victim. From his covert observations of Teresa, he'd realised she was close to Brian Peters and also to an unknown woman. By his calculation, that woman would be the easier target.

He immediately started making his plans, and by late afternoon he had parked his newly acquired white Vauxhall Corsa along the road from the house where he'd previously seen Teresa's girlfriend. He parked facing away from the house so that he could observe through the rear-view mirror and drive quickly away if necessary. He settled down, waiting patiently.

She arrived home on foot shortly after six. He watched her approach the house, unlock the door and enter. He decided to waste no time, getting out of the car and walking briskly towards the house. Taking a final look around, he opened the gate and walked up the path to the door. He rang the bell and heard the voice from inside.

"Just a minute."

As she was about to leave the kitchen, her mobile rang. She glanced at the screen, saw it was Teresa who was calling and instinctively answered as she walked towards the door.

"Nikki, where are you?"
"Home."
"Don't let anyone in. We're sending two uniformed officers to guard you. It's possible you're in danger, so just sit tight until they get there. OK?"
"Yes. There's someone at the door now. I was just about to answer...."
"Don't open the door! Whatever you do, don't open the door. Just do as I say and you'll be OK. Right?"
"OK"
"Right, just lock yourself in the toilet and wait until I call you back."
"OK."
"Stay silent and don't move. Understand?"
"Yes."
"I'll get back to you as soon as I can. Just sit tight."

Nikki did as Teresa requested. Teresa turned to Brian, a worried look on her face. He had heard the conversation.

"They'll be there in a couple of minutes, Teresa. Don't worry."

"Lucky I was able to decrypt some of the files on Youssef's PC in time."
"That wasn't luck. That was skill."

****

Abadi realised something was wrong, turned and walked swiftly back to his car. He could hear a siren, distant, but becoming louder, quickly, as a squad car approached, and he had just enough time to get in his car and duck out of sight as it raced past him and stopped outside Nikki's house. He started the engine and drove away as the officers checked the exterior while calling HQ to arrange access. Teresa breathed a sigh of relief and called Nikki to let them in. She stayed on the phone until Nikki confirmed she was safe.

****

Late that night, a car drove up towards Girlington, turned off the main road and parked at the end of the side road where it was darker. The driver switched off the engine and the car's lights. The two occupants sat in silence in the car for five minutes before the driver nodded to the passenger. They both got out and went round to the hatchback. The driver opened it and took out a rucksack, carefully picking it up while willing his hands to stop shaking. The pair walked to the back of the house, stopping for a while under the cover of a high stone wall before entering the small back yard through the broken gate. At the side of the door was an iron grate covering the small cellar window. The driver put the rucksack carefully on the ground and helped his passenger lift the grate clear, placing it quietly alongside the path. Holding his breath, he broke the cellar window with a blow from a hammer wrapped in thick cloth to deaden the sound. They crouched silently in the dark. No-one had stirred. No lights had come on. The passenger picked up the rucksack, attached a length of rope to it and lowered it carefully into the cellar, dropping the rope inside once the rucksack was safely on the cellar floor. They walked quietly back to the car, got in and drove slowly to the end of the road, the headlights still switched off. The driver looked at his accomplice, grinned and took out his phone. He dialled the number, took a deep breath and pressed 'Call'.

The explosion shattered the night silence. The driver put his foot hard on the accelerator, switched on the headlights and raced up the road as lights came on in houses all around them. They laughed and joked as they headed up Toller Lane, their spirits high until they saw the blue flashing light in the rear-view mirror.

****

The moment Gary walked into the office in the morning he was met with bad news. There had been an explosion in Girlington in the early hours of the morning. The Fire Brigade had put out the flames and made sure the area was safe before calling in SOCO to examine the premises affected, two adjacent terraced houses which, thankfully, were unoccupied at the time.

As soon as Andy arrived, they set off together to the scene, but on the way a call came through from Teresa. There had been a serious traffic accident on the B6269 Bingley Road close to Nab Wood. Two youths died after their car failed to negotiate a bend at high speed and overturned. At the time they were being followed by police after the car had been seen leaving a crime scene in Girlington. A second SOCO team was still at the scene of the crash, and Jo-Jo and Lynn were attending.

****

Gary and Andy pulled up as close as they could to the scene of the explosion and made their way through a crowd of onlookers and representatives of the local media. Gary recognised Helen Moore and nodded but had no time to comment and headed straight towards Allen Greaves who was leading the Forensics team.

"Morning, Allen. What have we got?"
"Morning. At about 4am an explosive device demolished these two adjacent unoccupied buildings. We have found the device, or what's left of it, and it's gone back to the Lab for analysis. One thing I can tell you is it wasn't a professional job. The device used was an IED – an improvised explosive device, possibly triggered by a radio wave. We'll know more when we've examined what's left of it."
"Did anyone in the area see anything?"
"A number of people were woken by the explosion and saw a car driving away. The general consensus was that it was a dark

hatchback, probably a Ford, containing two Asian males. I believe the car has been located, wrecked."
"So I understand. Two young Asian males. That's interesting. It wasn't a racist attack, then."
"Apparently not."
"Thanks, Allen. We'll let you get on with your job."

They interviewed as many witnesses as possible but got only sketchy information. Dark hatchback, maybe Ford. Driver and one passenger, both male. Asian youths. Gary relayed the information to Lynn who had arrived at the crash scene. She confirmed the information.

"So, let's see who the car belongs to."

A quick search of the DVLA database established the name of the driver, confirmed by the accompanying photo which bore more than a passing resemblance to the bruised, bloodied and battered face of the man pulled from the driver's seat of the wrecked car. The database showed a Keighley address.

"Let's break the news to his family."
"Whose turn is it?"
"Unless you want to volunteer, Jo-Jo, I'll do it, since I'm the senior officer."
"I was hoping you'd say that. It's a part of the job I dislike most, unless I'm dealing with some real villains."
"Well, let's not assume the parents are totally innocent until we've spoken to them."

****

Meanwhile, back in Girlington, Gary and Andy had established that both properties were owned by Asians. Number 33 belonged to a family who were now resident in Keighley. Number 35 was owned by a family whose daughter was engaged to the son of their neighbours. Both houses were for sale, the occupants having moved out a few months earlier. Gary's immediate assumption was that the properties had been destroyed for a specific reason. The insurance company would pay out. He quickly called Lynn.

"Where are you?"

"On our way to Keighley, to break the news to the family of the driver of the crashed car."
"Keighley? Stop the car for a minute. We need to talk before you see the family."

She pulled to a halt in a layby before continuing the discussion.

"First of all, Lynn, I assume you've got the driver's name?"
"Yes. We got it from DVLA, along with an image. His name is Deepak Bhatti."
"Bhatti is the name of the owners of one of the bombed houses in Girlington. Could you send me the image so I can show it to the neighbours and confirm it's him?"
"Doing it now."
"Thanks. Wait where you are until I get back to you."
"OK."

As soon as the image came through, Gary showed it to some of the neighbours who confirmed it was Deepak, who used to live at 33.

Gary asked Andy the question to confirm his suspicions.

"It's odd that these properties are so close to those which were deliberately set on fire recently. Do you think they're connected?"
"Not sure. The others were fire-bombed by outsiders and were occupied. These were destroyed by someone who was a resident until recently and were empty. We'll have to keep an open mind for now."

He called Lynn.

"Lynn. At the moment, I'm not sure this incident is linked to the cases of arson in this area. But keep an open mind when you talk to Deepak's parents. There may be a different motive, such as insurance fraud, here."
"I'll bear that in mind. Thanks."

When they arrived at the Bhatti's house in Keighley, Deepak's parents were already aware of the explosion and insisted it was a 'hate crime', committed, like other attacks in the area, by youths from White Abbey.

"What brings you to that conclusion, Mr Bhatti?"
"Obvious, innit. They set fire to the others, didn't they? They've just moved to bombing now. They're always hanging round. That's why we moved."
"Were you ever threatened?"
"Well, no. Not in person. But they were always hanging around the street corners. They made us feel uncomfortable."
"When did you move out?"
"Six months ago."
"What about your neighbours?"
"About the same time. They felt threatened as well."
"You were friends?"
"Yes."
"Your son was going to marry their daughter?"
"Yes. What has that got to do with it?"
"Probably nothing. I'm just looking to link the two properties. Why they were both attacked. It can't be a grudge against both of you, surely?"
"I don't know. These white youths hate us all. But maybe they just meant to blow up one house, not both."
"Perhaps. Is your son here, Mr Bhatti?"
"Deepak? No."
"When did you last see him?"
"Last night. He said he was going to see a friend."
"Who was the friend?"
"He didn't say."
"Did he say where he was going?"
"No."
"Did he say when to expect him back?"
"No."

Lynn hesitated for a moment before deciding to tell him.

"Mr Bhatti, I'm sorry to inform you that Deepak died in a car accident in the early hours of this morning."
"How did this happen? Deepak was a careful driver."
"He was speeding, sir, and failed to negotiate a bend in the road."
"I want you to leave now."
"OK, sir. But before we do, could you tell us why Deepak and a male Asian friend would be in the Girlington area at the time that your house and the one next door were blown up?"
"I have no idea."

"Do you happen to know the address where your ex-neighbours live now?"
"No. Please leave now."

Outside, the officers were puzzled.

"What do you make of that, Jo-Jo?"
"I don't know. He didn't exactly dissolve in tears, did he?"
"No. He seemed angry rather than upset. I think he knew exactly where Deepak was, who was with him, and what they were up to."
"I find it hard to believe he doesn't know where his ex-neighbours are living, particularly when his son was about to marry their daughter. He's lying."
"I agree. Let's go back to base and see if his accomplice has been identified."

While Teresa was trying all available databases to get identification of Deepak's colleague, which was proving difficult due to the extent of damage to his features caused by the car accident, Lynn suggested trying a different tack.

"Why not see if Brian's old mate, Kenny Collins, has any idea who he might be?"

She called Kenny, who worked at the Probation Office in Bradford.

"Hi Kenny. I'm not sure if you remember me. I'm DS Lynn Whitehead at Bradford CID. I work with Brian Peters."
"Oh, hello. How is Brian? I haven't heard from him recently. His family's murder must have hit him badly."
"He's doing his best to cope with it, Kenny, but it means he hasn't time to look into all our cases. Anyway, we're desperately trying to identify a young Asian who's just died in a car accident. The driver was a young man called Deepak Bhatti."
"Oh, I know him. Breaking and entering, theft, possession of stolen goods, drugs offences, to name but a few...."
"Would it be possible to see if any of his male friends are in your files? I can send details, height, weight and so on, but the image we have is post-mortem so may be difficult to recognise."
"Send what you've got, and I'll have a look."
"Thanks, Kenny. Brian always said you were a good guy."

Kenny called back early in the afternoon.

"I think I might be able to help you. I've got three names worth checking, but the most likely is a guy called Dev Patel. They went to the same school and have been close mates for years. They lived next door to each other…"
"In Girlington?"
"That's right."
"Dev lived at number 35?"
"Yes."
"Do you know if he had a sister?"
"Yes. I can't remember her name. She wasn't on my register, but she was Deepak's girlfriend."
"Thanks, Kenny. That's all I need for now. You've been a great help."
"A pleasure. Call me any time, Lynn."

****

Brian took the call from Don he'd been expecting.

"It's not good, Brian. I'm OK for the moment, but the prognosis is poor. I need to make good use of my time. I have some personal stuff to sort out with my solicitor – bring my Will up to date, funeral arrangements, that sort of stuff."
"I understand, boss. If there's anything I can do to help, just ask."
"You've got enough on your plate. I'll continue to help your investigations whenever I have a good day, but I don't expect too many of them."
"Use the time you've left to do the things *you* want to do. Don't worry about us."
"Just keep me informed. I'll join you whenever I can. 'Bye."

****

Once they had an address for the Patels, Lynn and Andy paid them a visit to inform them they believed their son had died in a car accident. Not surprisingly, they too had moved to Keighley, and lived less than a mile away from the Bhattis. Mr Patel answered the door.

"Sorry to bother you, sir. I'm DS Whitehead, this is DC Thompson. We're from Bradford CID. Could you tell us, please, if your son, Dev, is here?"
"No. He's not here."

"Could you tell us where he is?"
"No."
"When did you last see him, sir?"
"Yesterday."
"I'm sorry to tell you this, sir, but we believe your son was involved in a car crash this morning."

At this point, he grew angry.

"Yes, I know. He died because the police were chasing them. They were frightened. The police were always harassing them. They were trying to get away. They haven't done anything."
"I think we should go inside, sir."
"No. Go away. It's your fault. You police. You harass my son."

At that point a young woman emerged from within the house and took his arm.

"Go inside, father. I'll deal with this."

He flashed a look of pure contempt at Lynn before retreating into the house. The young woman apologised.

"I'm sorry for my father's behaviour. He's in shock. We only heard a few hours ago."
"May I ask who told you?"
"Mr Bhatti. He used to live next door to us."
"Yes, we know. How much did he tell you?"
"Only that my fiancé and my brother, Dev, were killed after a high-speed pursuit by the police, when their car crashed."
"Do you know why the police were chasing them?"
"No. Dad says they were always being harassed by the police. I'm not sure I believe him."
"They were seen driving away from the scene of an explosion in Girlington and followed by the police. They crashed because they were going too fast, and Deepak lost control of the car."
"I believe you. I understand. Deepak did not like the police."
"I understand you were next-door neighbours in Girlington."
"Yes."
"Do you know why they were there last night?"
"No."

"It's odd that both your family and the Bhattis moved out of your houses within weeks of each other, and neither house has been sold."

"Coincidence, I suppose. All I knew was that they decided to move, having found a better house, and my father thought he'd do the same."

"It must have been awkward financially for you."

"I don't know anything about that."

"Have you any idea why anyone would blow up your houses?"

"No. No idea. Unless it was one of the groups who hate us Asians. They tend to cause much of the trouble in that area. I believe they've been setting fire to some other properties in Girlington."

"But not empty properties."

"I'm sorry. I can't help you any further. We have funerals to plan."

"Thank you for your time."

Back in the car, they aired their opinions.

"So, Mr Bhatti lied to us. He *did* know where the Patels lived."

"And I find it too much of a coincidence that both families moved out within a couple of weeks of each other about six months ago without either of them having a sale lined up for the Girlington properties."

"Driven out by fascist hooligans?"

"Somehow, I think there's more to it than that. I think we need to see the Forensics reports, and also have a word with the Estate Agents handling the sales."

"It will have to wait until the morning. It's time to knock off for the day. We've just time to get back to the office to file our reports.

****

A phone call the next morning informed Lynn that Forensics hadn't yet completed their report. Lynn and Andy drove up Toller Lane to visit the Estate Agents who were handling the sales of both numbers 33 and 35. They were asked to sit and wait for a few minutes until they could speak to one of the partners, so entertained themselves by looking through the magazine featuring the properties on sale.

"These prices are ridiculous."

"They reckon prices have gone up all over the country, due to the pandemic and people moving away from the cities since many of them took to working from home."
"You reckon there's a rush of viewings of properties in Girlington?"
"It's the knock-on effect."
"Mmm."

They were eventually allowed to enter the office where Mr Allen was seated behind a desk overflowing with documents. He stood up to greet them with his broad Estate Agent smile.

"So, what sort of property are you looking for?"

Lynn and Andy looked at each other, bemused, before Lynn spoke.

"I think there's been a misunderstanding. We're not looking for property. We're from Bradford CID. DI Whitehead and DC Thompson. We'd like to ask you a few questions."
"Oh, I'm sorry. Yes, of course. How can I help?"
"We understand you were acting as agent for the sale of the two houses which were bombed the other night. 33 and 35 Whitby Road. Is that true?"
"Let me see. Numbers 33 and 35 Whitby Road. Mr Bhatti and Mr Patel?"
"Yes. I believe they were both put up for sale within a couple of weeks of each other."
"That's correct."
"And neither has yet sold?"
"Correct, although there was some initial interest from prospective buyers, the offers were withdrawn following the surveys."
"There were offers for both properties?"
"Yes, initially."
"So, what exactly was the problem?"
"It seems there was a problem with the party wall. Some damage in the cellar, I believe. They are quite old houses. Anyway, as I said, the offers were withdrawn and despite the fact that the price on both properties has been reduced, there have been no further offers."
"Do you have a copy of the surveyor's report?"
"No, but I can let you have their details."
"That would be very helpful. Thank you. I suppose the houses are no longer for sale?"

"They're no longer inhabitable. They'll be knocked down and the land sold for redevelopment."
"Were they freehold properties?"
"They were. They'll probably do quite well from the sale."

Discussing what they'd learned as they drove to the surveyors, both detectives were of the same opinion. Both the Bhattis and the Patels would benefit substantially from the insurance pay-out and the subsequent sale of the land.

"It's sounding more like a family enterprise. Two unsellable houses. Blow them up, collect the pay-out and sell the land. Quids in."

The surveyors more or less confirmed their theory.

"The Bhattis had started some work in the cellar. They said they were turning it into another bedroom but stopped when they noticed some cracks in the party wall. They had them repaired and put the house up for sale. Then the Patels next door put theirs on the market. Our surveyor took a quick look at both houses, noted the damage and mentioned some work was required in the cellars and the properties were priced accordingly. Initially, there was quite a lot of interest, but when an offer was made, and the prospective buyers asked us to perform a detailed survey so they could get a mortgage, it was then we discovered the extent of the damage to the party wall."
"And what exactly did you find?"
"There were deep cracks which had simply been plastered over and were already opening up again, and evidence of subsidence. In my opinion it would take a lot of work and expense to cure the problem. The Bhattis said they had intended to convert the cellar into a bedroom, but by the looks of the marks on the walls, and the debris on the ground, they'd been trying to install some heavy-duty equipment down there."
"Could you be more specific?"
"They'd run electric cables down the walls. Heavy-duty cables. Not what you would normally use for domestic purposes. At that point, we informed other interested parties, and had no further dealings with the sellers."
"Thanks for your help."

Outside, they concurred. The Bhattis were trying to set up heavy machinery of some description in the cellar of number 33 and either caused, or worsened, the existing damage to the party wall. Damage was apparent in the cellar of number 35, possibly as a result of the work next door, but maybe just due to the age of the properties. Either way, as a result, the two houses were unlikely to sell without extensive and expensive reparation being completed.

"So, they decided to blow them up."
"And blame it on Muslim haters."

CHAPTER 12

Lynn and Andy sat in DCI Gardner's office outlining their theory while he listened attentively and made notes before making the decision.

"OK. Talk to Forensics. They should have enough evidence to support or dismiss your theory. Personally, I believe you have come to the correct conclusion. If they confirm, we'll take it from there."

At the lab, they discussed the situation and Allen supported their theory.

"When we sifted through the debris, we found lengths of heavy-duty electrical wire and industrial fittings for power supply. They'd also coupled up a water supply. I very much doubt it was a bedroom conversion. It was the sort of set-up you would typically find in a small factory rather than a domestic location."
"Any guesses what type of industry they were interested in?"
"A wild guess would be a cannabis farm. It's only a guess, but the evidence supports it."

Lynn thought about the situation before proposing her theory.

"OK. So, they were thinking of starting up a farm. They started to convert the cellar, either themselves or by employing contractors, but found problems with the infrastructure. There was damage to the party wall. They stopped work and covered up the damage before putting the house on the market. This being the case, I suspect the whole family would be aware. At least, Deepak's father would have to make the decision to move and would be aware of the reason why."

Allen nodded his agreement before drawing the obvious conclusion.

"And when the surveys showed the extent of the damage and meant the house was unsellable without extensive remedial work, Mr Bhatti must have made the decision to demolish the property."
"But what about next door?"
"It was in a similar state with damage to the party wall. They decided to kill two birds with one stone, as it were."

147

"Thanks, Allen."
"Oh, another thing."
"What's that?"
"Post-mortem examinations on both bodies found evidence of recent cannabis use."

****

They took the evidence back to DCI Gardner.

"Evidence suggests that they intended to convert the cellar of number 33 for industrial use. We think a cannabis farm. They then found structural problems which meant the property, and the one next door, were unstable. Both families moved out, but soon found they were unable to sell their houses. They would have needed to spend a large amount to rectify the damage in order to sell them or accept a ridiculously low offer from a developer. The other option, which I believe they took, was to destroy the houses, claiming it was the work of extremists, and collect the insurance pay-out."
"That makes sense."
"I'd like to have a look around the Keighley properties, sir. I've a feeling they may have kept some evidence regarding cannabis cultivation."
"And your reasoning?"
"Having begun to fit out the cellar of number 33 and finding severe problems, they moved to Keighley. They decided to destroy evidence at the Girlington properties. If we assume they intended to continue their foray into farming, the Keighley property would have to be regarded as suitable, which suggests they would take the kit they'd bought for Girlington with them."
"So, you're asking for a Search Warrant?"
"Yes, sir. For both Keighley properties."
"I'll see what I can do. I presume you would want to raid both properties at the same time."
"Yes, sir."
"Leave it with me. Well done, you two."
"Thank you, sir."

****

They got the go-ahead from DCI Gardner the following morning.

"I've got your Search Warrants. Liaise with Forensics to ensure you hit both properties simultaneously. I've notified Keighley that we'll need some Uniforms to assist. Confirm arrangements with them when you're ready to go."
"Thank you, sir."

The two groups were in position by noon. At the signal, both groups pulled up outside the target houses and served the warrants. Lynn and Andy, with staff from Forensics, entered the Bhatti's house, while uniformed officers guarded exits and outbuildings. The second team, led by Jo-Jo and Louise, performed the same exercise at the home of the Patels, watched by curious neighbours. The two groups kept in touch with each other via frequent phone calls and messages as discoveries were made which verified their suspicions. Cannabis farms had been established in the attic and cellar spaces in both premises, and the garages used for storage of packaging materials. Soon, a police van arrived to take the occupants away for questioning while evidence was removed and taken back to the lab for analysis.

Two hours later, the premises were secured before the police and Forensics team left in buoyant mood.

Questioning of the two families took place in Interview Rooms 1 and 2 concurrently, the Bhattis in turn being questioned by Lynn and Andy, while Jo-Jo and Louise handled the Patels. However, little progress was being made. Both families argued that the materials were there when they moved in. They didn't know what it was. They didn't touch it. They just expected the previous owners to come back and collect it.

Meanwhile, their phones were being analysed, and eventually all the calls had been traced and categorized. They found calls to people they knew were drug dealers and brought them in for questioning and eventually, in return for promising leniency regarding some of their activities, they received sworn statements that both the Bhatti and the Patel family were involved in the production and sale of cannabis.

The detectives were ecstatic and formally charged the two families in front of their solicitors. Eventually, they were also charged with conspiracy to defraud their insurance companies by making false claims. They left it in the hands of the Crown Prosecution Service to determine what charges they would face concerning the possession and use of an Improvised Explosive Device with intent to cause damage to property. The CPS acknowledged their willingness to consider options in return for information regarding the purchase of the IED. The families agreed to co-operate and provided details of the site from which they purchased the explosive device on the Dark Web, and instructions regarding access to it, which were passed to the NCA to action.

Between them, the team closed the case, writing up the files, and completing the paperwork, relishing the fact that another crime had been solved. One of the team suggested going to celebrate in the pub but the prospect wasn't generally accepted. Lynn spoke up.

"If it's all the same with the rest of you, I don't feel it's appropriate to celebrate our success when our boss is suffering so much. I'd rather put my time to helping him catch a killer."

There were nods of agreement and the idea was dropped.

****

Lynn was at HQ early the next morning, but instead of going straight to her desk, she called into the canteen for a coffee. She was surprised to see Gary there and joined him at the table.

"Morning, Gary. How's it going?"

She was taken aback by his response.

"To tell you the truth, I'm sick to death of having all this work to do and the responsibilities I've got on my shoulders. I'm at the end of my tether. I need a holiday, a break. I just can't keep going like this."

Lynn's response was immediate and ferocious.

"Get a grip, Gary! What about me? I've lost my mother. What about Brian, who's lost his family? Brian's under tremendous strain. We should be backing him up, not moaning about our own workload. Why do you think we were both promoted to Detective Sergeant? It was to prove whether we could learn to accept responsibility, cope with stress and be good enough at our job to inspire those

150

beneath us. You need to get a grip, Gary! Prove you're good enough to do your job! And never forget how Brian's coping, at least on the outside. It's because he's a professional. You need to learn from him. Look at him and try to imagine how he must feel inside. Think about what he's lost and just bear in mind that he's still here, leading his team. He inspires confidence in others. That's the role model you should learn from. If he can do it, with all he's suffered, why can't you?"

With that, she walked away, leaving Gary open-mouthed and speechless, her coffee untouched on the table.

****

Progress on capturing Abadi was almost non-existent and all those involved in the case were becoming frustrated. Teresa's partner, Nikki, was still in hiding in a safe house out of the county. Finally, Teresa sensed a breakthrough and called Brian and Scoffer to the Conference Room.

"Sorry, Don's not with us today, Teresa, but if you've some news, let's hear it."
"OK. I've been wondering why we've had so few definite sightings of Abadi. We've had lots of potential sightings, but the descriptions we got varied to a great degree, so they weren't taken seriously. Anyway, I asked around and was able to get access to the facial recognition software that the Border Force uses. I ran thousands of images through it, using only the criterion of height, and guess what?"
"Go on."
"The system found over twenty images which were more than 80% matches to Abadi's passport photo. And each image was significantly different from the others."
"What exactly are you getting at, Teresa?"
"He's a master of disguise. Look at these two images on the desk. One of them is the one we captured from the Zoom call when we hacked Youssef's computer. The other was taken by a member of the public who thought he was acting suspiciously. They look like two different people. Moustache, no moustache. Dark hair, fair hair. Uneven teeth, perfect teeth. Mole on right cheek, no mole, etc. He's also a master of make-up, using different skin tones to make his face look slimmer and tricks like that. He's like a chameleon. He's a real expert at changing his appearance."

"Christ! I should have guessed."

"He's fooled more people than us, Brian. He comes and goes, knowing that if he's seen, whoever's seen him can only give a description of what they saw at that particular time. So, the posters we've put out are irrelevant. On any given day, he will bear little resemblance to who he really is."

"So, what do we do?"

"Don't rule out any sightings based on descriptions, unless they're significantly shorter than our man, and put out a new Identikit image based simply on generic factors, such as facial structure."

"Fair enough. We'd better look back through our records. Thanks, Teresa."

"There's another thing I'd like to do."

"What's that?"

"Well, we've got all these potential images of Abadi, all different. How about I run them all against the Passport databases? My guess is, we'll turn up a few more aliases."

"Ok. Get on it."

It took two days, but eventually Teresa had a list of eight aliases used by Abadi, along with the image in the relevant passport. She circulated them to NCA and all UK forces, as well as border passport controls, along with a note explaining what to do if he is recognised.

One of the copies landed on the desk of Allison Wardle, an administrative assistant working in Passport Control at Manchester Airport. She surreptitiously photocopied it and slipped the copy into her handbag. Then, at home, that evening, she plugged in her laptop and sent a private message.

Allison had met Abadi twelve years previously when she holidayed in Jordan. They had a fling, but she didn't realise she was pregnant until after she arrived back home. She contacted him. He wasn't interested but she decided to keep the baby anyway. Some years later he tracked her down and asked to see his child. She allowed it and they bonded to the extent that he called on her every time he was in the UK.

****

Teresa spent her time digging up further information about Abadi's aliases and put together a folder for each one. Brian and Scoffer, (and occasionally Don), went to the addresses they contained to interview all who would have known him.

Eventually, Brian and Scoffer arrived at the home of Allison Wardle. She invited them in out of curiosity and listened incredulously as Brian laid out the full extent of his criminal activities. She was horrified.

"I'm sorry. I find it hard to believe. He's such a gentle man. My daughter Carla adores him. He's such a generous, warm-hearted man. He wouldn't harm a fly! You've made a terrible mistake."
"I can assure you he's solely responsible for a number of vicious murders in Yorkshire, including my wife and our two children. So, please excuse me if I disagree with your opinion of him. He's a ruthless killer, I assure you. Now, can you help us find him?"
"I don't know."
"Then perhaps these will help persuade you."

He opened his briefcase and took out a pile of photographs, laying them out on the table in front of her. They were crime scene photographs. She looked at them in horror.

"This is what a gentle man he is. These people, innocent people, were all murdered by this warm-hearted man, as you call him. Their only crime was that they were family of the police officers who were at the scene when his girlfriend died in the process of detonating a bomb with the intention of killing hundreds of innocent bystanders. This was his revenge! This young child. Her name is Samantha. She wasn't even born when his girlfriend died. How could he hold her responsible? Just an innocent little girl, who was murdered along with her brother and mother, who happened to be my wife. Now, I'll ask you again. Can you help us find him?"

Allison burst into tears.

"I can't believe this."
"It's the truth. You don't know him as well as you think you do. He's a cold-blooded murderer. There are still people on his list. You have to help us stop him."

She sighed, dried her eyes, and whispered.

"I'm sorry, I've already sent a message to him."

"What?"

"This information, this passport photo, I've already seen it. I work at Manchester Airport, in Passport Control. I didn't believe it. I thought he was being set up. So, I warned him."

"He's a mass murderer, for Christ's sake!"

"He's also the father of my daughter."

"And he's the killer of *my* daughter, and my son. And my wife, for Christ's sake."

She was silent for a moment, still stunned by what she'd heard.

"What do you want me to do?"

"Help us find him before he kills again."

There was silence in the room while Allison thought over her options.

"I don't have an address for him, but I do have an email address and a mobile number."

"Write them down for us, please."

She did as requested, passing them to Brian. He stepped away and called Teresa.

"Hi Teresa, I'm sending you an email address and a mobile number for Abadi. See if you can do anything with them, please."

"I'm on it."

He turned back to Allison.

"What exactly did you tell him when you tipped him off?"

"Just that the police were looking for him."

"How did he react?"

"He just said he knew. And that he was going to make things worse for you."

"Did he say what he meant by that?"

"No."

"That's OK. I know exactly what he meant. Thanks for your time. And if he makes contact again, don't mention you've spoken to us. Just try to arrange to meet him somewhere and let us know immediately."

Allison hesitated for a few moments, before agreeing.

****

Abadi was seated in his car, parked at the roadside fifty yards from the house he had been watching through his side mirrors for around an hour, waiting for a sight of his target. He pulled down the sun visor above the windscreen so he could admire his latest incarnation. Ginger-grey wavy hair, skin tone much lighter than usual, glasses and a short grey moustache and beard. He made himself as comfortable as possible in the old Ford Focus and waited.

Eventually, in his mirror, he saw Mrs Lee's car, or rather *two* cars. He cursed silently. She was still being guarded by the police. He watched patiently as another car drew up a few minutes later. Three men got out and approached the car in which his target sat. They took the house keys and went in through the front door as the target watched while her chaperones in the other car concentrated on any movement in the surrounding area.

There was a sudden flash followed immediately by the sound of the explosion as the windows blew out, scattering shards of glass in all directions. Adabi cursed under his breath. They'd tripped the switch on the explosive device he'd hidden in a drawer! He hadn't expected them to perform such a detailed inspection. He thought they'd simply search for a hidden murderer with a knife, rather than a booby trap bomb. That wasn't his normal modus operandi and one of the officers had paid with his life for his attention to detail.

One of the officers in the car outside ran towards the house while the other jumped into Mrs Lee's car and drove her away at high speed. Abadi started his engine and pulled away in the opposite direction, thinking there would always be another opportunity.

****

The news quickly reached CID HQ and Brian was informed. He set off immediately to be with his ex-partner's mother who was being accommodated under close guard in a hotel near a slip road to the M62. Of the officers who had entered the house, one had been killed immediately in the blast, a second had suffered minor injuries from flying debris and the third was unharmed physically but severely traumatised by what had occurred.

The other members of CID were called into HQ for a conference. The mood was one of anger, understandably, as one of their own was personally involved. The outcome was that details should be released to the media without delay. They wanted blanket coverage and DCI Gardner organised a press conference so that the Six o'clock News could lead with the story.

Within twenty-four hours, every media outlet in England had featured the story. The T & A front page headline read:

HELP US CATCH 'THE CHAMELEON'

Underneath and inside were pictures of the various known disguises of the criminal, along with pictures of his victims, and details of his background. The police, however, had kept back some details so as not to jeopardise their investigations.

****

Back at his flat, Abadi washed and changed, donning the make-up he used at home in case anyone visited unexpectedly. It took around 30 minutes but was worth it. When he'd finished, he could easily pass for a man in his 70's like the rest of the pensioners who lived there. His flat, on the ground floor, was next to a fire escape door which he used to leave the building unseen. A few yards further down there was an exit gate leading to a row of lock-up garages in one of which he kept whichever vehicle he had at the time. It was ideal and had served its purpose. Soon, he would be moving on.

After a light meal, Abadi read the story in the Telegraph & Argus, smiling at the press's adoption of the soubriquet 'The Chameleon'. He put down the paper and turned his attention to his next victim, opening a file on his laptop where the names of his remaining intended targets were listed. He knew that each killing would bring the police one step closer to catching him. Ideally, he would kill them all, but he had to be pragmatic and draw the line before he was caught. He considered each target in turn, weighing up the risks, before making his decision. He would go for the man who had played a pivotal role in the hunt for his lover Amy Winston. He took a can of beer from the fridge, opened it, and sipped slowly as he plotted his operation.

CHAPTER 13

From the bottom of the wardrobe, Sayid Abadi took out a wooden two-tier cantilever box and opened it out on the table. In the top tier were several compartments, each storing contact lenses of different shades and colours. He picked out one pair and checked how he looked in the mirror. The bottom tier held spectacles, each a different style, some shaded. He carefully selected the ones he wanted, checked them in the mirror and put them on. He replaced the box in the wardrobe.

He put on his overcoat and black woollen cap with ear flaps and walked up a flight of steps to the door of Mrs Coombs, the wheelchair-bound widow with whom he'd become friendly. He knocked on her door and heard the high-pitched bark of the little chihuahua which was her pet, and which he regularly took for a walk in the evening.

Once outside, he was confident he was safe. He'd even once walked past Brian Peters in the street with the 'borrowed' dog on a leash, without drawing a second glance from the great detective. Now, he intended once again to reconnoitre the area where Brian lived.

He walked the dog for five minutes in the local area before putting it in the back of the car from where it could watch the world go by. He drove through Idle village and up Westfield Lane, passing the road where Brian lived and pulling up at the kerb a hundred yards further along. He got out and let the dog out, keeping it close on a short lead as he walked back to the junction and turned right. The road was quiet as the light was starting to fade, but he could see a car parked ahead facing him, with two people inside, the passenger on his phone. Confidently, he continued walking towards them, paying them no attention as he stopped occasionally while the dog had a pee. Eyes fixed straight ahead and heart pounding, he continued at the same pace, passing the car without giving it a glance. He continued until he was outside Brian's house, where he paused while the dog sniffed the low wall. Then, having snatched a quick sideways look at the house, he continued until he reached the end of the road and turned the corner out of sight, and only then let out a long breath. Brian was home. He had seen him through the window walking back and forth across the front room, a phone to his ear. He hadn't seen anyone else, nor were there any other cars on the drive. He continued to the next junction where he again turned right and walked on until he ended back on Westfield Lane just a short distance from his car. He put the dog in the back, turned the car, and headed back towards Idle, passing the road where Brian lived and where the observation car was still parked. He smiled as he drove home, constantly checking his rear mirror and certain nobody was following him. He garaged the car and returned the dog to its grateful owner.

****

Sheepishly, Gary approached Lynn at her desk the following morning.

"I'm sorry, Lynn. You're right. I'm sorry."
"And I'm sorry for reacting the way I did. Let's forget it. We were both having a bad day."
"Thanks. But I take on board your comments. I'm just struggling to cope. It'll get better."
"It will. You've got a good role model to follow."

****

Brian had been engaged in a long call to Don, who had updated him on his situation after spending most of the previous afternoon at the hospital having yet another scan and further tests. Regardless of what Don said, his tone of voice was enough to convince Brian the situation was serious. At one point he'd asked Don to give him the truth.

"How long have you got?"
"Long enough, Brian. I'll be hanging on until we catch the bastard. The net's closing in. We'll get a break soon with all the publicity it's getting. Someone's bound to spot him."
"What if he's skipped the country?"
"He won't do that. He wants to finish it."
"Not as much as *I* want to finish it. Don't forget this is personal."
"I'll never forget that, Brian. You know that."
"I know. Let's just keep at it. He'll make a wrong move eventually and we'll have him."
"I believe that, Brian. That's the only thing that keeps me going at the moment. We'll catch him. And we'll make him pay."

"We will."
"Any luck tracing his email or mobile number yet?"
"Teresa's still on it."
"I didn't expect it to take so long. Give her a call after lunch."
"I will. Thanks, Don."
"Take care."
"You too."

Brian was glad he hadn't mentioned his own health problems during the conversation. That very morning he'd attended an appointment with his doctor who had an update on his hospital examination.

"It's diverticulosis, which in itself isn't necessarily a major problem. The real issue is that the examination discovered two sessile polyps which may have become cancerous. These have been excised and will be examined in the hospital lab. All being well, they've been removed before any further damage has been caused."
"When will I know?"
"When the results came back from the lab, they'll know whether they were cancerous before they were removed. If not, you should be OK."
"And if they were?"
"If they *were*, they'll need to take you back in for a scan and further treatment."

****

Teresa was full of apologies when Brian asked for a progress report.

"Sorry, Brian. I've got nothing. The email should have been easy. It's a relatively simple process, but for some reason it fails to find anything. All I can think is that it's got some added protection to cause it to fail. It's possible he's using a VPN, so a Court Order has been served on various Internet Service Providers to hand over connection and usage logs. But we've got nothing of any use. I'll need to talk to someone at the NCA to see if they can help."
"What about the phone number?"
"Same. The standard method fails. The provider of the network is unable to find any information about it. It's somehow piggy-backing on a network proxy server but nobody knows the name or address

of the user. I'm looking through the Dark Web for clues. This has beaten me, I'm afraid, Brian."
"OK, Teresa. Thanks."

He turned to Scoffer.

"Any ideas, Scoffer?"
"Nothing, boss. Don is out of ideas as well. Basically, we're waiting for some help from the public or for him to make a mistake."
"Is there any way we can encourage him to make a mistake?"
"What are you thinking of?"
"Making him angry. Forcing his hand. Setting him up so he takes unreasonable chances."
"Like what?"
"I don't know. But there must be some way we can get his back up and bring him out into the open."
"Maybe we can get the T & A to print something which really annoys him."
"That might work. Let's think about that. He must have a weakness we can exploit."

It wasn't long before Scoffer had a brainwave and approached Brian at his desk.

"I've had an idea, boss. It might just unsettle Abadi and force him to take chances. It might just turn things in our favour by making him lose his cool."
"I'm interested. Tell me more."
"We feed a false story to the T & A. One that really riles him. This is my idea. We pretend we've been researching his background and found some of his contemporaries at Hull University. They invariably describe him as a loser. Some regarded him as a latent homosexual, whose relationships invariably failed. He was branded as narcissistic. He was what they would call nowadays an 'Incel', an involuntary celibate."
"I like that, Scoffer. Incels are in the news often these days. Usually when they've committed a crime. These people obsess over their own unattractiveness. Incels place the blame on women for their misery. Basically, Incels can't get laid and they hate anyone who can. This could work, Scoffer. Let's give it a try. I'll call Helen at the T & A. Well done, Scoffer."

****

The Telegraph ran the story the following day, including comments from fellow students during his time at Hull. These people were not identified, and the comments were in fact concocted and intended to anger Abadi. It worked. When he read the article, he was seething! It was all lies! He wanted revenge on the man who'd released the information to the press, DI Brian Peters, and from now, his top priority was to murder those who hunted down Amy Winston, rather than their families. Brian Peters was top of the list. He started to write his 'shopping list'.

Over the course of the next few days, he collected the items he needed. Some he bought online, others from hardware shops and gardening centres, ensuring he only bought one item at a time so nobody would guess his purpose. He spent hours in his flat assembling the parts until he was satisfied that he had built an effective IED. Carefully, he placed it in an Amazon box he kept for just such a purpose, attaching the trigger to the lid so that it would explode on opening. Next, he wrote an address label and attached it to the box which he placed in the centre of the table while he prepared and ate a light meal, then sat quietly, waiting until the light faded.

He chose his disguise carefully before slipping out to his lock-up garage, the box clutched tight against his chest. He placed it in the passenger's footwell and drove carefully up to Five Lane Ends and down Wrose Road before turning right on to Westfield Lane. He slowed as he passed the junction with the road where Brian lived, checking the cars he passed were all unoccupied and once satisfied, he parked up and walked back towards the house. There were no lights showing, and no car in the drive. He walked to the rear of the house and left the package by the steps to the back door before walking back and pushing a note through the front door stating that a parcel had been left. He had taken great care to make the note look genuine, having painstakingly erased the incorrect information from a used note and replacing it with new data, and was satisfied with his work. He smiled to himself and returned to his car to drive home. Once inside, he switched on his laptop to check the local news at regular intervals for a report of an explosion.

****

161

Brian had spent the evening visiting Don, whose health was deteriorating. Nonetheless, Don was focused on the task in hand – catching the Chameleon – and brushed aside any concerns about his health.

"When it's time for me to die, then I'll die. But before that happens, we've a killer to catch. So, bring me up to date on what's happening."

Brian informed him about the fake story they'd planted in the T & A.

"We're going on the front foot. It's time we dictated what happens. We want to lure him out, make him angry, and hope he makes a mistake. We know he'll come for us now, and we're ready for it."
"It's a risky strategy, Brian, but I think you're right. Just be careful. Too many good people, innocent people, have already died."
"I know. That's why I'm prepared to risk my own life so that nobody else gets murdered."
"Well, all being well, and depending on what they've found from the tests they've done today, I'll be let out in the morning. If so, keep me posted."
"Will do. We'll make sure someone's keeping an eye on you."

Brian drove straight home. It occurred to him he hadn't eaten since lunch but resisted the temptation to get a takeaway. He'd make do with a sandwich and a cup of tea. He was pleased with the way he was resisting the lure of the whisky bottle, though he knew the fight wasn't over. He was taking it one day at a time.

He parked the car on the drive and walked to the front door. He hesitated and walked round the outside of the house, peering in through the windows, checking for anything out of place, any signs of disturbance. It was then he noticed the package by the back steps. Resisting the desire to pick it up, he bent down and inspected the label. It was handwritten. He was immediately suspicious. An Amazon box with a handwritten label was unusual and was highly unlikely to have been sent by Amazon. Nor was he expecting a parcel delivery from any other source. He took out his phone and called the bomb squad, then got back in his car, reversed it on to the road, got out and knocked on the doors of the nearby houses, telling them little, but advising them to stay indoors until they were told it was safe. He returned to his car and waited until the DAF bomb disposal truck pulled up behind him. The six officers jumped out, had a quick briefing from Brian before commencing work, then got to it. Each officer knew his role perfectly and approached the task professionally, quickly deploying a remote-controlled robot to x-ray the suspect package in order to ascertain the composition of the bomb and its likely potential. From the information gathered, the leader manipulated the robot arm to lift the box carefully from its position, placing it inside a heavy-duty steel casing so that it could be transported to a nearby field to be safely defused. The entire operation was concluded within an hour and neighbours were informed the crisis was over. The leader of the bomb disposal team discussed the situation with Brian before they left.

"We've been right through the house and garden, and it's clean. You can sleep soundly tonight."
"Was it a home-made device?"
"Yes. Of the type terrorists use. Very common in places like Syria, Iraq and the like."
"I thought as much. I know exactly who is responsible."
"I'm not being funny, but people who receive this sort of thing generally *do* know who's responsible. I assume it's connected to a case you're working?"
"Correct. I'm glad you didn't have to detonate it. Our friends in Forensics will be able to confirm who built it."
"Once we've made it safe, we'll drop it off there, then."
"Thanks. I appreciate your help."
"All part of the service."

Brian sat in the house, thinking. So much had happened in the past few months. His life had been turned upside down. It would never be the same. He had lost what he loved the most. There were times when he felt there was no point in carrying on, times when he was at his lowest ebb. Times like now. But he'd become accustomed to feeling that way and had developed a strategy to keep him going. He took out his phone and opened the app, scrolling down for the song. The one which meant so much. He found it and pressed 'play'. Springsteen's 'I'll Stand By You'. Sarah's song. He closed his eyes and let the tears well up.

"A story of heroes that fight on at any cost, of a kingdom of love to be won or lost

We'll fight here together 'til victory is won, come take my hand 'til the morning comes
Just close your eyes..."

It had become his mantra. Listening to the song reminded him there *was* a point in carrying on. It was his duty to continue, to do his utmost, until he'd gained retribution for the pain Abadi had inflicted on him. He had to avenge the murder of his wife and kids. He would not stop until he'd accomplished that task. Or else died in the attempt.

****

The following morning, he was in a meeting with DCI Gardner in his office with Scoffer, while Don took part via video link.

"So, we've got his attention. We've got him angry, and his bombing attempt failed. So, what next?"
"We keep up the campaign. Try to get him even more angry. Then he'll make a mistake."
"Any luck yet in finding his lair?"
"Unfortunately, no. Teresa's still on it."
"I assume you've spoken to all your neighbours?"
"Yes. The only lead we got was from a pensioner who lives on Westfield Lane. He told us he'd seen an old man walking a dog in the area recently. He's lived there for more than thirty years and never seen the man before. He said he found it odd that someone would drive somewhere just to walk a dog along the streets. There are some lovely countryside walks in the area for someone with a car. He's got a point."
"One of Abadi's disguises?"
"We think so."
"Did he identify the make of car?"
"Unfortunately, no. Just a dark-coloured, small hatchback."
"So, what's your next move?"
"Give the T & A another story designed to anger him. A psychological report stating he's an inadequate human being, craving attention because he's a nobody. Something like that. I want him taking chances to see me face to face. It's coming down to me and him. I'd like your permission to carry a firearm."
"You know I can't do that unless we have a scenario where there's no danger to the public."

"I'd like a gun to keep in the house. I've a feeling he'll come for me."
"Sorry, Brian."
"OK."
"Run your story and see how he reacts."

The meeting ended. Brian was unhappy that the DCI had refused him permission to carry a firearm. He already had the one Don had given him. He would just have felt better if his DCI had given his approval. No matter. If there were consequences, he would accept them. He felt safer with the Glock in his house.

Brian and Teresa between them concocted a bogus profile of the killer designed to belittle him and fuel his anger. It was a dangerous ploy but, unless they could locate him by other means, it was all they had. The T & A were happy to print it.

****

Abadi read the story online, in his flat, growing more and more angry as he read. He knew who was responsible for the bogus profile and he also knew its purpose. But it hurt and angered him all the same. He vowed to kill his tormentors, Brian Peters being at the top of his list. And this time, no bombs. It would be face to face, him and Peters. He wanted to see the pain in his eyes, the anguish on his face. He wanted to watch him die. He wanted to gloat. He started planning.

****

Teresa had been making little progress on tracing Abadi's location. She had spoken to utility suppliers, asking for his home address, and providing a variety of aliases, but they were reluctant to comply, indicating that only a Court Order would allow them to release the information. She'd been waiting now for a week for permission to be granted. And even if they granted permission, there was no way of knowing which name he had used to purchase the service. He might have other aliases unknown to CID. He was also probably using a VPN – a Virtual Private Network, which hides his real location. She decided to try different means and phoned the NCA again.

"Alex, I need a favour."

"How can I help you, Teresa?"
"If I can get the IP address that Abadi's computer is using, can you help me trace the real physical address?"

There was silence for a few seconds before Alex replied.

"As long as it remains between you and me, I can help you."
"I promise I won't tell a soul."
"OK. I'm sending you a link to a database. As soon as you have the information you need, get rid of the link. This is a one-off."
"Thanks, Alex. It's a long shot, but it might just work."

Teresa checked the link to ensure it worked before making the next phone call. Northern Powergrid.

"Could you tell me if you have any planned maintenance in the near future, please?"
"Why exactly do you wish to know?"
"Well, I'm fed up with wasting time waiting for the Court Order to come through, so, I thought, perhaps if there were a sudden unexpected outage where the power went down just for a second or two...."
"What exactly do you expect that to achieve?"
"Well, when I'm working at home, I find it really annoying when my computer goes down. And then, of course, there's another short delay after it powers back up when my IP address is public until my VPN software loads and becomes active again."
"Ah, I understand. You want us to suffer a quick outage so you can trace someone? Which area?"
"Bradford."
"That's a wide area."
"Yes. Look, this is really important. We're doing all we can to capture a mass murderer and would really appreciate a little help from you."
"I'll talk to my boss. I'll get straight back to you."
"Thanks. We really do appreciate it. You'd be doing a great public service, helping to catch a mass murderer."

She got the call an hour later.

"We're expecting a problem tomorrow morning at 10am. It's possible our customers in the local area will suffer a loss of service for a few minutes when their power goes off due to an unexpected problem. Good luck."

With a big smile on her face, she passed on the news to Brian.

"We've got a break, Brian. At ten in the morning, our target's internet service is going down. We need to be ready. Let's just hope he gets his electric from Northern Powergrid."

****

CID's HQ had switched to emergency generator power in preparation. Teresa sat at her PC, Brian on one side, Scoffer on the other, all of them with eyes fixed on Teresa's PC, where the clock in the bottom right-hand corner showed 09:59.

"Any second now."

As the clock changed to 10:00, the display on the screen came alive when the algorithm which Teresa initiated attempted to locate the IP address from a phishing email she had sent to Abadi's account. They knew they probably had only about a minute from the time Abadi's PC restarted to the time it then took for his VPN program to become active again. In that time, the email would have to be delivered so that Teresa could note the physical IP address it was delivered to, before it was disguised again by his VPN. Once they had the physical IP address, tracing its physical location would be simple.

"Come on. Come on!... Yes! That's it! We've got the IP address. Just let me run it through this program and we'll get the actual home address."
"Hope it's not a mobile phone."
"It's not. I've already ruled that out. It might be a laptop, though, which means it could be on the move."

When the trace finished, the physical address was displayed.

"It's static. It's a flat in Greengates."

She wrote down the address and passed it to Brian.

"Go get him."

"Let's pay him a visit, Scoffer. Get your stab jacket on."

****

Seated in front of his screen, Abadi initially had been merely annoyed when his power went down. It was one of those things which only seemed to happen when he was doing something important online. He noticed the amber light blinking on the router and realised it was restarting, so he went to make a cup of coffee. There was nothing he could do until service was re-established.

He'd returned to his laptop and noticed that his email program had restarted now that his internet was active again after the temporary 'blip' when his router went offline. He noticed a new email from a company he'd never heard of. He opened it, quickly reading the text. It was market research, asking if he'd take part in a survey. He typed 'no' and pressed 'enter'. Then, he saw the message appear in the corner of the screen stating that his VPN was now active again.

Immediately, he realised the implications. His real IP address had been briefly exposed. He couldn't rule out the possibility that someone had acquired his location. He went quickly from room to room stuffing clothing and other items, including his laptop, into a suitcase until he was confident he had everything he needed to continue his work. He locked the door and ran to the lock-up.

Shortly afterwards, two police cars arrived outside the flats, the occupants jumped out and broke down the door of Abadi's flat. Finding it empty, Brian called Forensics to collect any evidence which may be available. He was clearly frustrated. While there, he and Scoffer spoke to his neighbours who were unable to tell him anything he didn't already know. They all seemed to agree on the fact that he was 'rather a strange man' who didn't interact with them to any extent. Nobody had seen him leave in a hurry. Nobody had any idea where he might have gone. A few of them mentioned that he occasionally visited a pub just up the road from there and it was generally known that he shopped in the area. Brian and his team, therefore, had no other option but to check out these local establishments. They learnt nothing new.

****

Having finished work for the day, Brian drove home, until, passing the Idle Draper, he decided to call in for a pint. It had been a while since he'd been in – in fact, it was not long after Sarah and the kids were murdered – but he simply fancied a pint. He parked in the public car park and crossed the road. The pub was quiet, which pleased him as he wanted peace to gather his thoughts. Any hopes of peace were shattered as he saw Scouse Billy approach him.

"Hello, Brian. How are you?"
"OK, Billy. Yourself?"
"Fine. Listen, we were all really shocked to hear about your wife and that. Terrible thing. Anywhere near catching the bastard?"
"Ongoing case, Billy."
"Well, there was a woman in here earlier, looking for you. Well, I say 'woman', but she was a bit masculine. You know what I mean? A bit tranny-like."
"What did she want with me?"
"She just asked if you'd been in recently. I said I hadn't seen you for a while. Then she said, or *he* said, 'shame about your family'. Then he said, 'if you see him, tell him I was asking after him'. Then he just walked out."
"Did he leave on foot? Did he have a car outside?"
"I don't know, Brian. I didn't think much of it. Just thought he was a bit of a weirdo."
"If you see him again, Billy, let me know, please. Take my number. I want to know *immediately* if you see him. OK?"
"Aye."
"Jim's not in, is he?"
"I think he's out the back, in the Brewery Yard."

Brian went straight out of the back door and into the Brewery, where Jim, the owner, was cleaning up before the evening crowd arrived.

"Hello, Brian. Good to see you. How are you?"
"I'm OK, Jim. I need a favour."
"Just ask."
"Can I see your CCTV from this afternoon? The bar area."
"Course you can. Follow me."

They went up to the private top floor, where the monitoring system was located. Brian stood behind Jim as he keyed in the required parameters to fast-forward through the day's recording until the approximate time Scouse Billy had indicated. Then, Jim moved the recording slowly, frame by frame until their target came into view. He could be seen clearly staring straight at the camera. Smiling. Gloating!

"He's mocking me. Can you get me a copy of that, Jim?"
"Certainly. Just take half an hour while I find a disc. I've got some somewhere."
"Thanks. I'll get someone to pick it up if you'll leave it behind the bar."
"OK."
"See you later."

He left without having a drink and went back to his car.

****

Abadi was in the flat in Heaton. It was a long-term rental, but he rarely used it. It was his bolthole, somewhere to hide when his back was against the wall. He knew this time would come eventually and he was prepared. Everything he needed for his final assault was here, and he had time to plan carefully before the final battle. In sha'Allah, he would prevail and avenge his lover's death.

He laid out the photographs and maps on the kitchen table and pondered over his plan, pacing the room occasionally as he weighed up his options. He knew he would have to act soon. They were closing in. Yet he had no fear. It was he who was in the right. He would prevail against these infidels. He took out his well-thumbed copy of the Quran and read quietly.

****

A series of images of Abadi taken in the Draper had been circulated to all officers with an addendum to report any sightings, keep in sight and call for backup. It was stressed: Armed and dangerous. Do not approach.

Brian was in his kitchen, seated at the table with a mug of coffee while communicating with Scoffer and Don via Zoom. He voiced his concerns.

"It looks to me as if we're at the endgame. So, ideas, please. How do you want to proceed?"

"I'm betting you're his prime target now, Brian. You're the one who's led the pursuit. He'll come for you."

"I agree, Don. I think we should all get over to the boss's house and take our stand together there."

"I'm happy to face him alone. There's no reason why you should be dragged in, Scoffer."

"We're in it together. You're not leaving me out, boss."

"OK, Scoffer. I appreciate it. You're in. But I think maybe you should stay home, Don. You're ill enough without this."

"No chance. Don't forget I still hold a firearms licence, and still have a handgun in the safe at home. Besides, I'm responding to treatment and having a good day. I don't want to waste it sitting at home worrying about you."

"OK. Make your way over here when it gets dark. Go round the back, up the alley and in the back gate. Text me when you're here and I'll let you in."

"We'll come together. I'll pick you up, Don."

"OK, it's settled. I'll see you later. Thanks, both of you."

He closed the call and set about preparing for the assault, whenever it may come. He had some surprises in store for his would-be assailant.

****

Don and Scoffer arrived together, parking some distance away and walking down the lane at the back to be let in the back door. After a quick discussion, they sat in the lounge and waited. Half an hour passed before Don spoke.

"Anyone fancy a small whisky?"

He was walking towards the kitchen when the back door was blown off its hinges by an explosion. Before the dust had settled and Don had regained his wits, Abadi had jumped over the shattered door, and disarmed Don who had hardly had time to draw the gun from his shoulder holster. He pulled Don to his feet, and, with the gun at his head, marched him into the lounge as Brian and Scoffer got to their feet to investigate the cause of the rumpus. Instantly, Abadi pointed the gun at Scoffer and pushed Don towards Brian.

"Sit down all of you, or he dies."

They complied.

"Throw your weapons on to the floor in front of me."
"We're unarmed. Only Don had a gun. Scoffer's not authorised."
"I don't believe you. Throw your weapons on the floor or I kill him."

Brian was ready for this moment.

"My gun's in that drawer."

He nodded in the direction of the Welsh Dresser.

"Left hand drawer."

With the gun still pointing at Scoffer's head, Abadi moved slowly and carefully towards the dresser, never taking his eyes off his captives. He put his hand on the handle and pulled the drawer open.

There was a sudden explosion as the drawer was opened, tripping the switch and causing a jet of thick, sticky liquid to be ejected, temporarily blinding Abadi as he instinctively turned to face the source of the noise. In the confusion, Brian and Scoffer overpowered him and held him down on his knees, taking the gun from him as well as the knife hidden inside his jacket. Brian recognised the knife. It matched the description of the one used to kill Sarah and the kids. Curved, approximately seven inches long. He held it to Abadi's throat.

"Say your prayers, pal. Make it quick. My patience is running out."

Scoffer realised what was about to happen and shouted to Brian.

"Reinforcements are on the way, boss. Just hold him there. Don't do anything you'll regret."

Abadi glared defiantly at Brian.

"Kill me. I dare you!"
"Don't worry. I'll kill you with the greatest of pleasure. I'm just wondering how much pain I can inflict on you first."

Suddenly, without warning, Brian plunged the knife deep into Abadi's stomach and held it there as his victim lurched forwards, clinging onto Brian's arm, a despairing, pleading look on his face as he slid sideways to the floor, blood pouring from his wound when Brian slowly withdrew the knife. None of the team moved to help him, nor made any attempt to save his life. They were relieved and glad to watch him die. Brian smiled as soon as he realised his enemy was finally dead. He turned to the others.

"You'd better call it in and arrest me."

Scoffer was first to answer.

"No chance. He killed himself. We all saw him stick the knife in his own stomach."

There was silence for a few seconds while they mulled over Scoffer's suggestion. Then Don spoke.

"No. I killed him. There was a scuffle and we overpowered him. The knife hidden inside his coat fell to the floor. I picked it up and stuck it in his stomach. I killed him."

Again, there was silence before Brian shook his head.

"You can't do this, Don. I have to take responsibility. And I'm not ashamed of what I did. He deserved it. And I thank the Lord I had the opportunity and the courage to avenge the murder of my family. I'll take my punishment with the greatest of pleasure."
"No, you won't, Brian. I haven't been totally honest with you. My time is nearly up. By the time it comes to trial, I'll be dead."
"No. You can't take the blame for my action. Neither of you can."
"Listen to me, Brian. You have a life in front of you. You've already suffered enough for this man's crimes. You've got your revenge. You shouldn't be punished for what's happened here. Scoffer and I won't let you."
"He's right, boss. If you won't let Don carry the can, I'll own up to it. You don't deserve any further punishment. You deserve a medal."
"There you are, Brian. Go upstairs and get changed. Get rid of those bloody clothes. Hide them, burn them, whatever. Just make sure they never get found. Give me the knife so I can wipe your prints off and get mine all over it. That's an order!"

Without further argument, Brian did as Don had ordered. Don turned to Scoffer.

"OK, Scoffer. Call the fuzz. Then we sit down, open a bottle of malt and agree on the story we're going to tell them when they arrive."

They all sat in the lounge, ignoring the corpse, and toasted their success with a couple of large whiskies. Scoffer was still obviously reliving the scene in his mind.

"How did you feel when he had the gun to your head, Don? I'd probably have crapped my pants."
"It's frightening, Scoffer, but it's not the first time it's happened."
"Really?"
"Really. And the first time, I wasn't even in the police force. Christ, I must have been so naïve in those days."
"I find that hard to believe."
"Well, I'll tell you, then you can make up your own mind. I'm not ashamed of it. I just put it down to experience. So, anyway, it happened a long time ago."
"I can't wait to hear this, boss."
"OK. Well, when I left school after my 'A' levels, I didn't want to go to university. I'd had enough of education for the time being. I just wanted to get a job and earn some money so I could enjoy myself. So, a teacher got me an interview with an insurance company which had a main office in the city centre, but after less than a year working there, I was fed up. I couldn't envisage staying in that business for the rest of my life. I'd met up with friends from school who'd gone to university and were having a whale of a time, so I quit my job, and then found I was too late to apply for university for that year. So, I switched to plan B. I got a job with a builder as a labourer. I worked hard, did overtime whenever it was offered, and I saved all I could. Then, one day I decided to go travelling. I quit the job, got a passport, changed all my savings into French francs and packed a rucksack and off I went to hitch-hike around France. I'd always fancied visiting Paris, Dijon, Lyon, Marseilles, Cannes, Nice, Monte Carlo and the like, so I planned my route accordingly, hitch-hiking all day, then spending the night at a campsite or in a cheap back-street hotel, before a bit of sightseeing and then back on the road. Occasionally, if I really liked a place, I'd book in at a campsite for a few days and have a good look around. I loved Lyon and stayed for a week at a campsite a few miles out of town. I made friends with a group of Algerian workers who had a caravan

on the site while they were contracted in the area, and each evening I was invited to join them for a meal and drinks. We'd play cards for hours. It was all going to plan until I left Marseilles, travelling east. I was offered a lift, but the driver explained he was only delivering to an address not far from St. Tropez. I accepted anyway and ended up in the middle of nowhere. Once I'd left the main trunk road, traffic was much lighter, a lift became more difficult, and I had to walk a fair distance. Eventually, though, a car stopped and offered me a lift into St. Tropez. I was so grateful. The driver was a slim, casually dressed man in his early forties, I guess. We talked in French about all sorts until we arrived in St. Tropez. He dropped me in the centre, explaining he had business to attend to. He pointed the way to a campsite and was off. The trouble was, when I got there, I found the campsite was closed for the winter, and I had no option but to walk all the way back to the town centre to try to find a hotel room. The first two were full, but as I trudged to the next, a car horn sounded. I turned to find the man who'd given me a lift earlier. He explained he'd now finished for the day and was on his way home. He invited me to join him for a meal. I accepted, of course. He had a nice flat just on the outskirts of town and quickly prepared a meal as we talked. He was good company. Funny, easy-going, intelligent, and knowledgeable on any number of subjects. Honestly, I was enjoying his company and lost track of time until I realised how late it was and told him I'd have to leave to find a hotel. Without hesitation, he invited me to stay the night. I accepted, only realising after that it was a one-bedroom flat."

Don took a deep breath, looking around at his eager audience, before continuing.

"I'd been set up, and there was no way I was having sex with this man. Any man, for that matter. I told him so, but he said it wasn't a problem. I was still welcome to share his bed. So, there we were. He was reading a gay magazine while I tried desperately to stay awake. But eventually I must have dozed off."

He looked around, embarrassed.

"Suddenly, I woke. He had his hand on my dick. I backed away, shouting at him to pack it in but he persisted. I gave him a slap which stopped him in his tracks. He apologised. I got out of bed, taking a pillow and a blanket, and sat in an armchair in the living

room, tired as hell but frightened to fall asleep in case he tried again. But eventually, I nodded off. When I awoke, he was making breakfast and laid a plate for me. I told him I wasn't hungry and was leaving. He promised he'd give me a lift to Fréjus, so that I could get back to the main road, the A8, towards Cannes. I accepted. He seemed to have forgotten the previous night and was chatty as he drove along a quiet country lane. And then he stopped. I could see in the distance a junction. He explained that I should turn right at the junction, then the next left, which would take me into Fréjus. He, unfortunately, would be going in the opposite direction. Then he said, 'It has been nice knowing you.' And then he pulled out a gun and held it to my temple. I almost crapped my pants. He said, calmly, 'Say nothing about last night to anyone. Promise, or I will kill you.'
Naturally, I promised. He told me to get out, still pointing the gun at my face. I got out with my rucksack and walked towards the junction, not daring to look back. A minute later, he sped past me, and I watched him turn left at the junction. I sat on my rucksack at the side of the road and cried before finally getting up and walking to the junction and from there to Fréjus, where I went into the first bar I came to and ordered a large whisky. It was only 10am!"

"Did you tell the police?"
"No. I thought about it, but homosexual acts between consensual adults were legal in France at that time. I would have had to convince the police I was not a willing participant, which might have been difficult since I was naked in bed with him. I had to put it down to experience."
"And did you really think he was going to kill you?"
"At the time, yes. Thinking about it since, the gun was probably a starting pistol or an airgun. But I didn't know it at the time. I knew nothing about guns. Anyway, I just look upon it as a coming-of-age ritual. I don't think anything has frightened me so much, since. I guess that's why I joined the Army. I wanted to be the one with the gun in his hand."

Brian shook his head in amazement.

"I take my hat off to you, boss. I guess that's why you've always seemed so calm when we worked in the CTU."
"I might have looked calm but maybe I just learnt how to hide my fear."

CHAPTER 14

Brian and Scoffer were in DCI Gardner's office. Don was unwell and dialled in to join the meeting. Gardner wanted the truth, no matter how unsavoury it may be.

"I've been in this game for a long time. Sometimes, things happen unintentionally. Sometimes things happen which are right, but unjustifiable in law. So, tell me what happened, each of you, one at a time. Brian, you're first, please."

Brian took a deep breath, hoping he'd rehearsed what he was going to say well enough to sound convincing, and spoke clearly and without hesitation.

"We were expecting him. I'd seen a CCTV image of him in the Idle Draper earlier. He *knew* there was CCTV. He was staring straight at the camera. He was looking for trouble. I discussed it with Don and Scoffer. We came to the conclusion that he was going to come for me because I was the one hounding him. So, we were in the house waiting for him. Don got up to go to the kitchen for a drink when the back door blew open. Abadi burst in and disarmed Don. He brought him into the lounge with Don's gun to his head and then pointed it at Scoffer and told us all to sit down. He asked me where my gun was. He didn't know, but I'd booby-trapped a drawer in the dresser, and I told him my gun was in it. When he opened the drawer, there was a loud bang and a jet of sticky liquid shot out. He was temporarily blinded and disorientated. He dropped the gun. Scoffer and I jumped on him and overpowered him. In the skirmish, Abadi's knife fell to the floor. None of us knew whether he was carrying any other weapons, but we guessed he would be as he was trying to get his arms free. For all we knew, he might have had an explosive device. It was then that he got stabbed."
"Who by?"
"I couldn't be sure, sir. It was quite chaotic."
"Thank you, Brian. Would either of you two like to take up the story?"

Before Scoffer could speak, Don took up the narrative.

"I could see Brian and Scoffer were having difficulties subduing Abadi, sir, so I picked up the knife so that there was no possibility of Abadi getting hold of it. But he was still flailing around and at one point it looked as if he might be getting the advantage in the contest. Just for a second, it looked like he might get a hand free and not knowing whether he was carrying any other weapon, or an explosive device even, I took no chances. I stabbed him in the stomach. I admit it, sir. I killed him. I believed all our lives were in danger and so I killed him. End of story."

Scoffer backed him up.

"That's how I saw it, sir, Don had no choice but to kill him. He couldn't take the chance he had another weapon or an IED strapped to his body."
"Did none of you think about picking up the gun he'd dropped?"
"No, sir. We found it later under the sofa. One of us must have accidentally kicked it away during the skirmish."

Gardner considered the situation for a moment before giving his verdict.

"Since you're all adamant that what you've just described is what actually happened, because you feared what might ensue if you failed to take the appropriate action, I accept your story and will forward your version of events to Professional Standards, just as a matter of procedure. If it's any consolation, I believe you."
"Thank you, sir."
"And well done to all of you. You've put an end to a reign of terror, which caused so much misery to so many people, including some of our own. Abadi got what he deserved."

They filed out of the office, pleased with Gardner's acceptance of their version of events. Their only worry was whether the Professional Standards committee would take the same view. Brian decided to call on Forensics to see if they had any evidence to counter their version. He made an appointment to see Allen Greaves after lunch. But first, he made a point of thanking Scoffer.

"I guess you're free to go back to your unit now, Scoffer. Thank you for all your help with this case. You were invaluable. Assuming I still have my job after Professional Standards have looked at the evidence, I'll be lobbying hard to get you with us permanently, as long as that's what you want."
"Absolutely, boss. There's nothing I'd like more. It's been a real pleasure working with you on this."

They shook hands and Brian left him to say his goodbyes to the rest of the team. Scoffer grinned and reminded him.

"Sorry to disappoint you, boss, but actually there are still two weeks left of my secondment to your team. Unless you don't want me for two more weeks?"
"'Course I do. Let's go arrest someone."
"Let's wait until after a crime's been committed, eh?"

After lunch, Brian and Scoffer went to the Lab where Allen was waiting. He shook Brian's hand.

"Well done, Brian. Well done, Scoffer. You've taken a dangerous man off the streets. You should be proud."
"We will be, as long as you have no evidence of any wrongdoing on our part."
"The evidence backs up the incident report, Brian. The only prints found on the murder weapon belonged to Abadi and Don McArthur. It's a straightforward conclusion. There's nothing more to add, unless someone comes up with a totally different theory, which we'd have to investigate. And I don't expect that to happen. According to our findings, you have no case to answer, and that's what goes into my report."
"Thanks, Allen."

****

It took a further week before Professional Standards issued their verdict: Abadi was killed by Don McArthur who stabbed him in the stomach to prevent him from killing or seriously injuring the other officers. No charges would be made against any of the officers who were present at the incident. The investigation was closed.

After work, a party was held in the Draper to celebrate the end of the hunt for Abadi. It would have been a riotous affair but for the absence of Don McArthur who had been taken into hospital the previous day as his cancer entered its final phase. Brian could be seen anxiously checking his phone at regular intervals during the course of the party. Although he took part in the celebrations, he was obviously distracted. Understandably, his thoughts were elsewhere.

His phone buzzed. He knew who the caller would be and moved away from the group and into a quiet corner to take the call.

"Brian Peters."
"Mr Peters, I'm sorry to have to tell you over the phone, but your friend, Mr McArthur, is close to the end. You asked to be kept informed. I'm sorry, there's nothing we can do...."
"Can you keep him alive for just a little while? I can be there in half an hour or so."
"We'll do all we can."

Teresa, watching from across the room, could tell from his expression what the call was about, and walked over to him.

"Was that the hospital, Brian?"
"Yes. I need to get there before...."
"I'll give you a lift."
"Thank you."

Teresa had a quick word with DCI Gardner, who nodded his agreement to her request before she and Brian hurried to her car.

"What was that about, Teresa?"
"I told the DCI the situation. He's going to put the word out to make sure we don't get stopped for speeding on our way to Wakefield."

He managed a weak smile.

"You think of everything."

****

They were soon at the hospital and running towards the ICU unit. As they reached the entrance, Teresa took Brian's arm.

"This is going to be hard for you, Brian. Please don't feel as if you have to hide your emotions. I'm here for you."
"Thank you."

Tears were already welling up in his eyes as they approached the bed where Don McArthur lay, hooked up to breathing apparatus, tubes snaking from his body to various machines, a screen displaying his vital signs. His eyes were closed until Brian squeezed his hand gently and spoke quietly.

"I'm here, boss. Teresa's with me, too."

Don responded by moving his fingers just a little but enough to reassure Brian he knew they were there.

No words were required. They sat in silence until Don's eyes opened briefly and closed again. Tears fell from Brian's eyes when Don's lips moved slightly as he took his final breath, and the machine sounded its alarm as the display changed to show what they already knew. His life had ended. Brian burst into tears, still gripping Don's hand as if he was trying to will the life back into him until Teresa placed her hand gently on top of his and whispered.

"I'm so sorry, Brian. Do you want to be alone with him for a moment?"

Brian nodded, unable to speak. Teresa stood and walked slowly out into the corridor, wiping away her tears.

As the medical staff switched off the monitoring apparatus and disconnected the various tubes, Brian sat silently at his dead friend's side for a few minutes, thinking back through some of the cases they'd solved together before focusing on the one where it all started – the terrorist bombing in Bradford City Centre in 2017. He remembered it so clearly. He still had nightmares about it. He would never forget that day.

Suddenly, a thought snapped into his head. He couldn't make sense of it. He was certain that when Don's lips moved for the final time, he'd heard him say 'This isn't over'. He knew that wasn't possible, but the thought wouldn't leave his mind.

Once the paperwork had been completed, they were leaving the ward when a nurse stopped them.

"Mr McArthur asked me to give you this. He borrowed some paper from me to leave a note for you."

She passed him a folded sheet of A4 on which were scrawled the words:

"Brian, sorry I can't say goodbye. I have to go now. At least I have the satisfaction of knowing it wasn't Abadi that killed me. I'll be watching out for you. This isn't over."

It brought tears to his eyes again. He thanked the nurse, put the note in his pocket and walked with Teresa back to her car. She called DCI Gardner with the news, receiving his condolences in return, along with a request for Brian to take time off on compassionate leave.

They drove in silence back to Brian's house, which, thankfully, had been cleaned up after Forensics had collected their evidence following the skirmish with Abadi. Teresa fetched the bottle of Knockando and two tumblers from the kitchen and poured two glasses, one large, one small, as they sat on the settee. It was obvious that something, not just Don's death, was troubling Brian.

"Talk to me about it, Brian, please."
"About what?"
"What's bothering you? Apart from Don, that is."

He took a drink, pondering his options, before his response poured out.

"I killed Abadi."
"No. Don killed him. He confessed."
"He confessed because he was dying. He'd nothing to lose. He wanted to give me another chance."
"If that's true, you did the right thing."
"No! I'm a police officer. I'm supposed to stop crime, not commit it."
"Listen, Brian. You did the right thing. You brought a killer to justice."
"Justice? He never got to trial."
"He was guilty! That was plain for all to see. If you hadn't killed him, he would have killed you. And others. You did the right thing. Anyone would understand that."
"I took a life. How can I live with myself?"
"It's your job to bring criminals to justice for Christ's sake."
"Bring them to trial, yes. But I'm not the judge, jury and executioner."
"Stop now! And listen. If you hadn't killed him, what would have happened? He would have continued his murderous spree, that's what. How would you have felt if he'd killed Don, and Scoffer? How

would you have felt if he'd gone on and killed me? Just stop and think how many lives you've saved. Don was a hero, but he knew he was dying. He had nothing to lose. He's given you the chance to continue doing what you're good at. Don't you dare throw it all away after he's given you another chance."
"How can I live with it?"
"Listen. How many people have a friend like Don to get them out of scrapes? He did it because he valued you. He had nothing to lose, but *you* have. He's given you another chance to carry on doing what you're good at – catching criminals. Not many people get a second chance. Don't let that chance slip through your fingers. You deserve it. Is that clear?"

There was silence, then Brian turned to Teresa, kissed her on the cheek and said softly.

"Thank you. I don't know what I would have done without friends like you and Don."
"There are more than me and Don. We're all here for you."
"Thank you. I knew you were special the first time I saw you."
"You were only the second person in my life who made me feel that way."
"I wish sometimes I'd been the first."
"Me too, sometimes. But there are some things we just can't change."
"I know. We can still work together though?"
"Absolutely."
"Let's have another drink."

But Teresa wasn't finished. She knew there was something else on Brian's mind.

"So, come on. What is it?"
"What?"
"What else is bothering you?"

There was a moment's silence as Brian pondered over whether to tell her.

"You'll think I'm mad."
"Tell me. I'm your friend. If something's bothering you, I'm here. Tell me."

He took a breath before it all poured out.

"Just before Don passed away, as I sat there, thinking about the cases we'd dealt with together, I found myself thinking back to my first major case with him, when we were in the Counter Terrorist Unit. I was thinking about the Bradford Bombing, and I swear I heard Don say, 'This isn't over'. It was so clear. I know it's not possible, but it was as if he was passing on his final orders to me. Then the nurse handed me a note he'd written for me earlier. That said the same thing – it's not over. He was telling me there's something we haven't turned up yet. Something we need to dig into before we close this case. I *know* it. It was Don's final message to me. I have to keep digging for the truth so that Don can rest in peace."

Teresa held his hand gently.

"I believe you. I'll start on it tomorrow. Are you going to tell the DCI?"
"Only that I believe there are loose ends to tie up and ask for his permission to keep the case open."
"Well, if he doesn't, we'll do it on the quiet."
"Thank you."

Teresa suddenly realised they were staring into each other's eyes. She dropped her head and spoke softly.

"I'm sorry, Brian. I have to go."
"Yes…. Of course. I'll see you out."

He got her coat and walked her to her car.

"Are you coming in to work tomorrow, Brian."
"Yes."
"Good. I'll see you there. Goodnight."
"Goodnight, Teresa. Drive safely."

She started the engine, smiled, and drove away. He watched until she was out of sight, then returned to his whisky. He downed it in one and went to bed.

****

The alarm clock woke him at 06.00, as he'd planned. For the first time in many days, his head was clear, and he felt refreshed. He showered and dressed, gulping his coffee so that he could be on the road early to beat the worst of the rush. By 07.30, he was walking up the steep incline to his destination, the Cow and Calf rocks, and sat on a blanket he'd brought. He played the song on his phone, deep in thought, transmitting silently his message to Sarah.

"Now I know it can feel like you're slipping away, at night you'll get lost in that deep dark place
We'll let the night come and do what it may, together we'll find the courage, we'll find faith
Until you awake…."

There were tears in his eyes when he turned off the music before reaffirming silently for Sarah's benefit.

"I got your murderer, darling. I've got revenge on the man who took your life and killed our kids too. But there's someone else. This isn't over. Yet. Kiss the kids for me. I'll be with you soon, when I've closed this case."

He stood up, walked back to his car and was at his desk by 08.30. DCI Gardner had expected him, regardless of his instruction to take time off.

"Morning, Brian. Are you OK?"
"Fine, thanks, sir."
"I thought I told you to take compassionate leave."
"You did, sir. Thank you, but I have an outstanding case to solve."
"Is it really that important, Brian?"
"I believe so, sir. I won't rest until I've got to the bottom of it."
"Then you'd better come into the office and tell me the full story."

****

DCI Gardner was sympathetic, but unconvinced. Nevertheless, he permitted Brian to investigate further, with the proviso that he would not divert Teresa from her key duties to the rest of the team. He agreed, left the office, and went straight to Teresa's desk where she was printing some documents.

"Morning, Brian. I didn't expect you in yet."
"I was up early. Things to do."
"Me too. I've been looking into Abadi's history. Europol have sent me some information and promised more when I give them a more focused remit. This is just basic history. It's a start."
"Thanks. Is that copy for me?"
"Yes. I'll work from the online info."

He took the documents back to his desk, and began working through them, all the time making copious notes and cross-referencing other information relating to some of the incidents noted in the file. He pulled over a whiteboard, scrubbed it clean and started noting key facts. One point stood out. Far from being a 'lone wolf' intent on avenging the death of Amy Winston, Abadi also had a record as a hitman, taking on assignments for the Italian mob and warring factions in the East Adriatic countries. He was a mercenary! A gun for hire. He called Teresa.

"Teresa, I've found an interesting fact. We've established Abadi was a mercenary. What's the chance of getting hold of a record of his finances?"
"I'm sorry, Brian. I tried some time ago when you first asked me. Then I got side-tracked by other work. I'll try again. I'll talk to Europol. I'll get back to you as soon as I hear something. This could be a breakthrough."

Brian started thinking. If Abadi was active in Albania and its neighbouring countries, is it possible he could at some point in his career have met Hardcastle? That would explain a lot.

He called Alex Sinclair at the NCA.

"Hi Alex. I'm looking for a favour."
"Go on, Brian. You know we'll help if we can."
"Thanks. I assume you're aware that Abadi is dead."
"Yes, Congratulations on wrapping that one up."
"That's the point, Alex. I'm not entirely convinced we've wrapped it up yet."
"Has something come up?"
"Yes. Teresa's been working on it with Europol. We've unearthed the fact that, apart from having a vested interest in murdering relatives of the officers who were involved in investigating the

Bradford Bombing, he made a living as a hitman. He was a mercenary."

"You think he was paid to kill your family and all those other innocent people?"

"I think it's entirely plausible. And I think I know who might have employed him."

"OK. What help do you want from us?"

"I want to prove there's a link between Abadi and ex-DI Hardcastle."

"Wow! Now I understand. I can see the motive."

"I want to know everything about Abadi's history. Anything at all you turn up might be enough to link him with Hardcastle."

"We'll do all we can to help, Brian. I promise."

"Thank you. I need closure on this."

"Of course. We're on it. I'll ask around."

****

Brian faced a moral dilemma. If his theory that Hardcastle hired Abadi to kill Sarah and their kids simply as an act of revenge on Brian for being the key man in putting him in jail, then why would the families of other officers be on the hitlist? Was it his revenge on the entire team? If so, Brian would have to bear the weight of guilt for all the murders as he was the one who led the initial investigation which put Hardcastle in prison. He would have to redeem himself by proving Hardcastle was as responsible for the murders as the actual killer, Abadi. He felt he had to do everything in his power to close this case. He arranged for Scoffer's secondment to be extended.

****

Over the next few days, communications flew rapidly back and forth between Europol, Teresa and NCA. Brian constantly updated his whiteboard with key facts as they emerged. A major victory for NCA was in persuading the Maltese bank where Hardcastle had an account to allow them access to details of all his transactions since 2017. The result left them deflated. The account was closed by HMRC when Hardcastle was jailed, and all his known assets were seized by HMRC.

Nevertheless, Teresa was not to be defeated and dug deeper in her attempt to unearth something significant. And then, she made a massive breakthrough. Less than two hours later, she burst into the Conference Room waving a printout.

"This is it! This is the gamechanger! Since the beginning of the year, a regular amount of money has been transferred into a shell company account, to be later transferred to an account held by Abadi, and guess where it came from? No prizes. As we half expected, Hardcastle has been paying from an offshore account for services rendered, or to be rendered. It's all here. And I'm just waiting for Abadi's account details to arrive so we can match them."

"Well done, Teresa. Pass the info to Europol. It might be enough for them to see if they can trace other transactions. I think we'll find he has more than one account abroad."

Later the same day, the team had access to Abadi's UK account, which showed he made payments for air travel to the UK the day before Brian's tragedy and for a return flight to Tel Aviv the day after. Similar payments for the next incident followed the same pattern. After that, he applied for a flat belonging to a housing association and began paying for his tenancy. Teresa set about contacting the recipients of his payments and matching the dates with Brian's assistance. They were able to see the pattern of further payments made from a shell account being forwarded to Abadi's UK account after each murder incident and other payments tallying with his expenses. It was evident Hardcastle was the source of his income.

"Well done, Teresa. I bet all this information was encrypted."
"Of course, but that's never stopped me deciphering data in the past. As we discovered, when Hardcastle was found guilty of running a drugs empire, and murdering his partner, his Maltese account was closed, and his assets seized by HMRC. So, on a hunch, I checked his visitor log at HMP Manchester and discovered that his accountant had visited him a few times in the early weeks. So, I looked into *his* business finances. He received significant amounts of money on a regular basis from a company called DP Global, based in Albania. Thing is, they don't appear to exist. Their business address is a fast-food takeaway! DP could be Daniel Patrick – Hardcastle's forenames. He's not widely known for his inventiveness. Anyway, it appears to me that Hardcastle's income from his criminal activities is now being paid into DP

Global, which is then making payments for other criminal activities."

"How do you fancy tracing every single transaction Hardcastle's made since he's been in chokey? I'm betting there's a lot more criminal activity to uncover. Keep digging."
"I'll get on it."

Teresa started her research into DP Global and laboriously followed up every lead until she struck gold on the Dark Web. She called Brian, asking if she could speak to him in private. They agreed to meet in a coffee shop in the Broadway Centre. Brian was intrigued and was waiting when she arrived, looking over her shoulder occasionally. She was acting nervously.

"What's wrong, Teresa? You seem on edge."

"I'm sorry for all the secrecy, Brian, but I've discovered things I didn't want to make public until I've completed my investigation and had the results corroborated."
"This sounds serious, Teresa."
"Potentially, it is."
"OK. Try to relax. I'll get you a coffee. You keep an eye on the door."

He returned with her coffee. And sat facing her. She was still nervous. He put his hand on hers and squeezed it gently.

"Try to relax, Teresa, and tell me what you've found."
"Well, I discovered the physical location of DP Global is actually in London and please forgive me for this, I hacked their server."
"That's not a problem, Teresa. What did you find?"
"A number of payments, regular payments, to someone in HMRC. I don't mean tax payments to the Tax Office; I mean payments to one particular person who's employed there. You'll never guess who!"
"Why don't you just try to calm down and tell me?"
"The Chief Finance Officer! James Lloyd."
"What?"
"It's not that much of a surprise, surely? In the last decade when he was Permanent Secretary for Tax, a man called Dave Hartnett set a precedent by being supposedly complicit in corporate tax avoidance deals by the likes of Vodafone and HSBC."

"Why would the Chief Finance Officer receive payments from Hardcastle?"

"I can't work that out. I've tried to figure where they might have met but can't find a connection. I'll keep working on it."

"You realise if this gets out, all hell will be let loose?"

"That's why I need to find the connection; the reason for these payments."

"How would you feel about me informing the NCA?"

"I'd rather you gave me a little time to present a feasible case. I don't want to make a mistake on this. If I do, my career is over. I'll be drummed out of the Force. You, too."

"I'm prepared to take the chance. How can I help you?"

"Cover up my activities. Justify to the DCI the amount of time I'm going to have to spend on this. Tell him I'm investigating Hardcastle's cashflow to see who he was importing the drugs from and who was buying them from him."

"No problem. Can I get Louise to help you?"

"No disrespect, Brian. It's not that I don't trust her, because I do, but I don't want to get anyone else in trouble if I'm wrong."

"Apart from me."

"Sorry, yes. But you wouldn't let me proceed with this unless you had faith in me, would you?"

"You're right, of course. OK, get to it."

After the rest of the team had finished for the day, Brian remained at his desk, gathering background information on James Lloyd, when he came across an interesting article first printed in Private Eye. It exposed Lloyd as a hypocrite for doing a deal with a multinational company over unpaid tax, while pursuing a prosecution against the husband of one of his female office staff who occasionally did cash-in-hand jobs without declaring them in his income tax return.

Brian thought over the implications of what he'd read. Lloyd was on Hardcastle's payroll too. By the time he switched off his PC and pulled on his jacket, he was convinced.

The following morning, he headed straight for Teresa's desk.

"We can't deal with this, Teresa, regardless of how much I'd like to. This is a job for the NCA. Let me set up a meeting. Don't mention this to anybody. We don't know how many people are involved. For the moment, it stays between you and me and the NCA."

"Agreed."

The case was duly passed to the NCA who were delighted. Brian reminded them, though, that although they were now investigating a case which involved Hardcastle, they were not allowed to mention any other charges against him without prior agreement with Bradford CID as they were still pursuing other allegations against him and others.

CHAPTER 15

Brian and Teresa continued their investigations regarding Hardcastle. They examined every transaction on a monthly statement Teresa had copied from an email query to DP Global she'd found online. Interestingly, the email contained the number of a mobile phone. The text of the email itself was encrypted and it took a while before Teresa was able to decipher it. It was simply a query regarding an underpayment for 'services rendered' to someone who called himself 'Shifty'.

They pondered the relevance of the mobile number but were unable to find out who it belonged to until Brian made a suggestion.

"Whoever it belongs to has made certain it can't be traced by the usual methods. Therefore, they've something to hide. Now, let's assume it's being used covertly, for illegal purposes. It's on correspondence relating to DP Global, so it in effect belongs to Hardcastle. What if he's using it covertly while he's in prison? In effect, he's still running the business, but by phone. It's possible a member of staff is aware and is turning a blind eye in return for money. I think it's worth trying out this theory. Fancy a trip to HMP Manchester with me and Scoffer?"

"Yeah. I like field work."

"OK. Find out how the wardens' shift patterns work, please. We may have to spend quite a long time there."

"Sounds like we might have to take sandwiches."

"I wouldn't recommend the prison food. You never know what they might put in it when they realise they might be serving it to police officers."

Teresa established that if they were there continuously between the hours of 11.30am and 9pm they would have the opportunity to see every prison officer on shift that day. They would have to take the chance that there may be personnel off sick while they were there, but Brian thought it was worth the visit anyway. As they would have a lot of ground to cover, they agreed to restrict their visit to the wing where Hardcastle was resident and the areas where he worked. Teresa duly made the arrangements with the Prison Governor, asking also that they should be escorted only by two of his most trusted prison officers.

****

They arrived at the expected time and were escorted around the building by the Assistant Governor and a senior prison officer. They had a map of the establishment and had their route worked out to include each area. They moved from one area to the next, stopping in each one just long enough for Teresa to press the button on the phone in her pocket and listen for the subsequent response. If none was heard, they would move on to the next designated area.

Fifteen minutes later, they found themselves in the laundry, where a group of prisoners were working. Normally, Hardcastle would be among them, but Brian had requested he be confined to his cell during their visit. It turned out to be a good hunch, as, when Teresa pressed the call button, they could hear a faint ringing response. They split up in an effort to trace the source. Brian found it. In the toilets, wrapped in a waterproof sealed bag in a cistern, the phone had been carefully placed so it could be removed for use without anyone noticing. Brian took it out of the bag and connected it to his portable device to copy its data. Then, he replaced the phone as he'd found it before the team filed back to the Governor's office.

The Governor listened intently as Brian explained the relevance of what he'd found and explained his next step – linking it to Hardcastle. Although it rarely happened while he was on duty, the Governor allowed himself a smile on hearing the plan. On his order, Hardcastle was allowed out of his cell to join the other prisoners on work detail in the laundry. Unknown to him, the man introduced to the prisoners as a Social Worker on assignment was in fact a police officer, Scoffer. Less than half an hour later, Hardcastle sought permission to go to the toilet. Permission was granted and when he returned, Scoffer sent a text to Teresa which simply consisted of the single word 'CALL'. Seconds later, he could clearly hear the ring tone emanating from Hardcastle's direction. Scoffer texted again 'YES!'. He made sure not to make eye contact with Hardcastle who seemed annoyed that his concealed phone had rung. His face dropped the moment Brian and Teresa, accompanied by the Governor, appeared with two guards who led Hardcastle to a private room and ordered him to sit and empty his pockets. When nothing suspicious appeared, Teresa took her phone out of her pocket and pressed 'CALL' again. The ringtone on Hardcastle's phone was clear and a guard patted him down, locating the phone in a makeshift pocket sewn inside Hardcastle's overall.

"Put it on the table."

Reluctantly, Hardcastle complied, glaring at Brian, who picked up the phone and scanned through the contacts list matching many of the names against a second list which Teresa took from her pocket, a list she'd copied from the Dark Web when scanning DP Global's files. Although Brian had already copied the data when the phone had initially been located, he wanted Hardcastle to see him scanning it so he could gauge his reaction. Hardcastle's glare spoke volumes.

"So, you have use of this phone to conduct your business. Tell me how it got in the toilet cistern in the first place."
"No idea."
"Look, Hardcastle, you know the drill. If you cooperate, you might just get out of jail before you start drawing your pension."
"No idea."
"OK. Take him back to his cell."

Hardcastle was taken away, issuing threats as he left. Brian was unmoved, thinking out loud.

"What I want to know is who put the phone there. Who brought it in? Who keeps it charged up? And, who removes it before the scheduled deep searches which are carried out at regular intervals in prisons?"

He looked straight at the Governor who sighed, evidently embarrassed.

"Deep searches are only notified to staff the day before they take place. The staff involved are told which areas are to be searched."
"So, a member of staff would have time to remove anything which should not be there?"
"Yes."
"What would happen if you ordered a snap search immediately?"
"Prisoners would be ordered back to their cells and a search carried out."

"Would it be possible to order your staff on duty to carry out a search in one hour's time?"
"For what purpose."
"I suspect one of your officers is complicit. I'm hoping to panic him into removing the phone from its hiding place so we can catch him red-handed."
"How do you know that officer is even on duty at the moment?"
"I don't, but we're prepared to stay all day and run the charade for each shift."
"OK. I'll organise it."
"Will you get someone to escort Scoffer to the laundry so he can put the phone back?"
"One of my officers will see to that."
"Thank you."

Once he had placed the phone back in the cistern, Scoffer called Brian who asked the Governor to organise another spot search. Brian's hunch proved correct. The first search yielded a dividend. The moment after the toilets in the laundry had been searched and no phone was found, the search was halted, and the prison officers lined up. Teresa took out her phone and pressed 'CALL'. The ringtone could be clearly heard. All eyes were on the same prison officer, who sighed and was clearly embarrassed. Brian approached him.

"Empty your pockets. All of them. NOW!"

He simply put one hand in his inside breast pocket and brought out the phone he'd taken, handing it over with the excuse,

"I just found it in the toilets. I was going to find out who it belongs to. I was going to take it to the Governor."
"When we examine it, I'm sure we'll find some reference to you. We're taking you back to Bradford with us. We'll let you clock out first. We don't want them paying you when you're not on duty. That would be criminal!"

They were in high spirits on the journey back to Bradford, following the van with their prisoners, the prison warder and Hardcastle, inside. As soon as they were booked in and left to wait for Hardcastle's legal counsel, Brian and his team set to work on analysing the contents of the phone's memory, writing relevant details on the whiteboard. The search threw up some surprising results after Teresa had cracked the passcodes and accessed the files, one of which was laid out like a shopping list, as she explained to Brian,

"The first two characters are the initials of the purchaser, the third is the wing he's on, the fourth and fifth is the cell number and after that is the product and the price. For example: MDG07SK20 would be for Mark Dawson, G wing, cell 7, Skunk cannabis, £20, which buys probably one eighth of an ounce."
"So, where is the order sent?"
"To someone on the outside who deals. I'll be able to get their names and locations in a while."
"And how do they get them to the users?"
"Some of the guards act as mules. Hardcastle gives them the address to pick them up from and supplies the cash that prisoners have paid to him. They bring them in when they come on shift. They've obviously found a way of bypassing the body search which takes place when they report for duty."
"Can you get me the names of the mules?"
"I'll have them by the end of the day."
"Good work, Teresa. If you find anything unexpected, let me know."
"In this game, nothing is unexpected."
"You're getting cynical."
"I had a good teacher."

He called at DCI Gardner's office and informed him of their progress before organising interviews with his prisoners, whose legal representatives were beginning to complain about the delay. Gary and Louise were assigned to the prison officer, Michael Harper, while Brian and Scoffer took Hardcastle.

****

Gary and Louise entered the Interview Room, apologising for the delay before getting down to business.

"So, Mr Harper, how long has this been going on?"
"I don't know what you're talking about."
"Let's not piss about. We know you're taking orders for drugs from Hardcastle, going out and procuring them, bringing them to work so Hardcastle could sell them to his customers, and receiving payments from Hardcastle as a result. We have hard evidence of

that. And, in addition, we've got Hardcastle's statement implicating you."
"He wouldn't do that."
"Well, he has done. We've got a list of his customers as well. You were also responsible for taking the mobile out of Strangeways so it wouldn't be found during spot searches. You just brought it in when Hardcastle asked for it so he could process orders and check his bank account to make sure you were paying in the full amount you received from sales – less your wages, of course. Isn't that true, Mr Harper, or should I call you 'Shifty'?"
"No! You've got it all wrong. I'm not 'Shifty'."
"So, who is?"
"I don't know."
"OK. I believe you for now, but unless I get a full confession regarding your other activities, I won't let it drop. Talk it over with your legal representative. We'll be back later."

In the corridor outside, Louise and Gary had a coffee and chatted.

"So, he says he's not 'Shifty'. Do you believe him?"
"Yes. I just asked the question to get his reaction, and I got the feeling that whoever 'Shifty' is, he's higher up the ladder than Harper."
"Maybe the boss will have more luck with Hardcastle."
"You ready to go back in for Round 2?"
"Yep."

After a quick conversation with Brian and Scoffer, they returned to question Harper again.

****

In the other Interview Room, Hardcastle was in a defiant mood.

"Your stooge next door, Mr Harper, has told us all about your operation."
"You don't need to ask me, then, do you?"
"We'd like you to clear up a few things."
"Such as?"
"Who's Shifty?"
"Never heard of him."
"You should have. You've underpaid him. He wants more money from you."

"Oh, right. In that case it will be one of the prisoners. I lost at cards the other night. Couldn't pay my losses. People think I'm made of money."

"You must be really crap at cards, Hardcastle. You're paying Shifty every week. Don't you ever win?"

"Like you say, I'm crap at cards."

"So, who's Shifty?"

"I'm saying nothing."

"Please yourself. We'll find out soon enough. We'll be able to track every call you've made, every account you've paid money into and every account you've received money from."

"I doubt that very much. As you know, CID officers aren't famous for their intelligence."

"But we've got a winner. What you poker players call an 'ace in the hole'. We've got Teresa Shackleton."

"Her? What can she do?"

"She can unlock all your secrets. You just never realised how skilled she is. You treated her badly, Hardcastle, and now the tables are turned, she wants retribution. And she'll get it. She's working her way through all your financial records as we speak. Your house of cards is on the verge of collapse."

He paused for a moment, looking straight into Hardcastle's eyes.

"We know all about your dealings with James Lloyd."

Hardcastle's face showed a momentary sign of panic before he composed himself.

"I don't know anyone of that name."

"No? You're paying him a lot of money. Why don't you save us a lot of effort and tell us all about it? And it might even knock some years off your sentence. Think about it, eh?"

Before leaving, Brian couldn't resist one last dig.

"I really can't believe you were stupid enough to leave your phone switched on while it was hidden in the laundry toilets. God, you're such a numpty!"

CHAPTER 16

Gary took a call from Teresa the moment he arrived at his desk in the morning.

"Another arson attack for you to look into, Gary. Girlington again. I'm sending you the address."
"Thanks. Any free officers available to join me?"
"Louise will be with you in a minute."
"OK."

They drove in silence to the address, an end of terrace house not far from one of the previous incidents. Parking up behind the SOCO van, Gary could see Allen Greaves in discussion with Fire Brigade officers, so made his way towards them.

"Morning, Allen. What have you got for us?"
"Same M.O. as before. Petrol poured through the letter box and set alight. Windows broken by firebombs. No casualties, thankfully. They all escaped through the back door. Luckily, the kids were staying with friends. There were only adults on the premises, man and wife, and her mother."
"Lucky coincidence the kids were out?"
"Possibly. I'll let you talk to them."

Gary held a lengthy conversation with Mr and Mrs Hussain as a result of which he had more questions than answers. He was not yet allowed into the premises but looked in the back yard where the Fire Brigade had thrown items of fire-damaged furniture. He was struck by how little there was, and by the lack of large items. He walked over to Allen Greaves.

"Allen, I've a few questions you may be able to answer."
"Fire away. Oops! No pun intended. What can I help you with?"
"The stuff in the back yard. Is that all the furniture that was damaged?"
"I was wondering about that myself. I asked the Fire Officers. That's the lot. I thought it was a bit odd. There was only one double bed and one single. Where did the kids sleep? There's no cooker, or fridge either. I'm sure you can guess what I'm thinking."
"Insurance scam."
"Precisely."
"Did they own the house, do you know?"

"They rented it. From a company with a premises in Manningham."
"Called?"
"Let me check my notes. Here we are. J & L Estate Agents. Premises on Oak Lane."
"Thanks, Allen. We'll leave you to it."

There was still one question in Gary's mind which needed an answer. He walked over to the Chief Fire Officer.

"Could you tell me, please, when you arrived on site, where were the occupants?"
"They were on the pavement, on the other side of the road."
"How were they dressed?"
"As they are now."
"Fully clothed?"
"Yes. I thought maybe their neighbours had lent them something to change into."
"Perfect fit. Coincidence?"
"Maybe they'd stayed up late."
"My report says the fire started at about 3am. A bit late to be watching TV, don't you think? More likely they stayed awake waiting for the fire to start. Or, more likely, to be *started*."
"I suppose that would explain why there was so little furniture in the house. They had it removed before the fire started."
"That's exactly what I'm thinking."

****

Gary and Louise returned to HQ where they both gathered information regarding the recent arson attacks in the Girlington area. They also noted addresses which were currently unoccupied and those available to rent. By lunchtime, Gary had the information he needed, and asked DCI Gardner if he could hold a meeting for all the team so he could test a theory and get opinions. The DCI agreed.

Once everyone was assembled, Gary pointed to a whiteboard where he had pinned an enlarged aerial view of the area affected.

"Louise, will you please read out the addresses of the houses which have been subjected to arson attacks while I mark them on the map."

A red X was placed over the properties, one at a time, as Louise read them out.

"Now, can you give me the addresses of properties which are rented through agencies."

Louise read them out as Gary marked them on the map.

"And now, the addresses of any empty properties, please."

Again, Louise complied, and it wasn't long before the pattern became clear.

"Someone's clearing a site for redevelopment, I think."
"You think they may be underinsured, so someone's picking them up on the cheap, with a view to demolishing them, and just holding on to the land?"
"It's possible."
"What about the properties still standing? It's not a total clearance."
"No, but it's possible that the properties undamaged might already be in the hands of a developer. Think about it. Say someone wanted a large area of land, for some big scheme. So, he tries to buy up the properties in his way. Then word gets around and the owners of those properties raise their prices until the buyer refuses to buy. Instead, he burns them out and buys the land on the cheap."
"So, you think he already owns the houses still standing?"
"Possibly. It's possible he's been buying them as they became vacant over the years. He may be renting them out until he's ready to redevelop. It's a valid theory."

Brian spoke up.

"Well done, Gary. It's definitely worth following up. Find out who owns the properties still standing in that area, and when they were bought. If you find they're rented, then you've definitely got the answer. If they're still privately owned, then I think we can expect more arson attacks. Another thing which would be worthwhile would be to check with City Planning. There may have been a previous proposal to redevelop thrown out. Find out if that's the case. Maybe someone's clearing more of the site to resubmit the proposal. And if anyone has any free time, I'd be grateful if you could help Gary with this. It's all yours, Gary. Get to the bottom of it."

Afterwards, Brian took Gary aside.

"Well done, Gary. That's good work. Pass on my thanks to Louise, too, please."
"Thanks, boss. I will."
"One thing I'd like you to do is bring the Hussains in for questioning. Find out who was responsible for the arson attack. Threaten them with a charge of conspiracy to commit arson, or fraudulently claiming on insurance. Anything. Just frighten them. I want to know who's behind this. I've got complete faith in you on this one, Gary. Crack the case for me."
"I'll do my best, boss."
"I know. You always do."

Gary walked away, beaming with pride. He stood in front of the whiteboard, looking at the area covered by the 'X's. It was large enough for a variety of uses. A supermarket, maybe? Maybe not, since Morrison's was just down the road, but a mosque would be an appropriate addition to the area. Or a school, a Muslim faith school. He made a mental note to look into that when he discussed the area with the City Planning Department.

****

They sat patiently in Reception, thumbing idly through magazines until the meeting in progress ended. Shortly after, they were approached by a short, balding man in his fifties wearing an ill-fitting suit who introduced himself as Head of Planning, George Cavendish. They followed him into his office and sat patiently while he checked his emails.

"Sorry about that. I always seem to get emails when I'm in a meeting, and they're always urgent."
"We do understand, sir. We tend to get urgent business to attend to as well."
"Yes, of course. So, what can I do for you?"
"We'd like to know if there are any planning applications for the Girlington area."
"There are always applications. Can you be more specific? Attic conversions? Conservatories?"

"We're thinking larger scale. Supermarkets, mosques. the sort of thing which requires extensive demolition and groundwork."
"Well, there's nothing current, I can tell you that much. If there were, it would be in the T & A already."
"What about if we go back a few years?"
"Off the cuff, I can't give you an answer. I've only been in this position for about eighteen months. We'd have to do a search of the archives for anything further back."
"Surely, everything is computerised now?"
"To an extent. The computers will tell us where to find the actual original documents, but they're kept in secure storage offsite."
"If I show you an aerial shot of the site we're looking at, will it help you locate the documents more quickly?"
"I doubt it. If you could tell me the date the application was *submitted*, I could locate them in a flash."
"Thank you for your time. We won't bother you any further."

They left the office and made their way back to Reception. Gary approached the Receptionist.

"Excuse me, but Mr Cavendish couldn't really help us with our enquiries. Is there anyone else who could help us locate a particular planning application?"
"Do you have a date?"
"If you're free, today would be good."
"Sorry, I meant do you have the date of the planning application?"
"Unfortunately, no."
"How about the road or street name?"
"I have a plan of the area we're interested in, if that would help."
"Let me have a look."

Gary took out the printout and passed it to the Receptionist, who studied it for a moment.

"I remember this. It's going back maybe five years or more. Mr Cavendish's predecessor cursed about it for ages. It kept being dismissed and resubmitted with a few small changes, then dismissed again, then resubmitted. Finally, it was thrown out. Between you and me, a few of the councillors at the time were unhappy about the decision."
"Why was that?"

"There were rumours that money changed hands. They were never proved, but the rumours never went away until the councillors lost their posts."
"I don't remember seeing anything about it in the papers."
"It was kept very quiet. All the staff had to sign confidentiality agreements."
"Including you?"
"Let's say, mine's just expired."

She smiled and winked at Gary. He smiled in return.

"I understand. Thank you. Could I put in an official request to have all the relevant documents unearthed? It's really important."
"Give me an address to send them to, and I'll see what I can do. It may take a while."
"As soon as you can, eh?"
"Of course. Can I have your name again, please?"
"DS Ryan. Call me Gary."

He winked at her and waved as they walked out of Reception.

"I didn't realise you were such a charmer, Gary."
"It was just an act. I'm not usually like that. Not with women, anyway."

****

The following week, two large cardboard storage boxes were delivered to CID HQ, for the attention of DS Gary Ryan. Eagerly, he opened the first box. On top was a note, which read.

'The files herein are stored in date order, with the newest on top. Please replace them in the same order. Thank you.'

Each file was bound by elastic bands with the reference number and contents briefly described on the cover page. Gary removed the files carefully, examining each one until he found what he was looking for. It was a submission for the construction of a mosque. He took it to a spare table, where he went through the file, page by page. He was looking for details of the company which submitted it. When he found it, it was a company he'd never heard of. So, he Googled it.

"Well, well, well. That's a bit of a surprise."

The company name sounded innocent enough – "M & H Architects Ltd" – it was the names of the directors which caught his attention. They included ex-DCI Moseley and Danny Hardcastle and a name they weren't familiar with, David Patterson. Gary Googled him, was directed to his Facebook page and discovered he was currently a student of Economics at Salford University. After passing on the information to Teresa, he called Louise.

"Get your coat on, Louise. We're off to Salford."
"Oh, how lovely!"

Gary and Louise drove to Salford University, parking outside the Main Building. They made their way to Reception, from where they were directed to the Administration department who would be better placed to find the student they wished to talk to. It took a while but, eventually, it was established that he had no lectures to attend that day, but if it was any help, they could give his registered address. They took it and went back to the car to work out their journey to the address they had been given. They were surprised to find it was a modern apartment on Salford Quays.

"He must be top of his Economics course if he can afford one of these! The rent's over a grand a month. How the hell does a student afford one of these?"
"Let's go and ask him. See if we can pick up some money-making tips."

They buzzed the number, held up their IDs to the camera and were admitted. The lift was facing them. Gary looked puzzled.

"Where's the graffiti? I've never been in a high-rise which didn't have graffiti on the lift doors."

Louise smiled.

"Never been anywhere this posh, eh?"
"This is out of my league."
"Shall we go back to Girlington, then?
"Nah. Let's see how the other half live."

David Patterson, a tall, casually dressed, wild-haired young man, admitted them into a spacious, well-kept apartment which must have seemed palatial to a student. Gary couldn't help asking.

"I'm sure you've been asked this a million times, but how on earth does a student manage to pay for a flat like this?"
"Actually, I won the money on the lottery."
"You're kidding! How much did you win?"
"I don't remember the exact amount. Quite a lot."
"You don't remember how much? If *I'd* won the lottery, I'd be able to tell you the amount down to the last penny."
"Well, sorry, but I can't remember. It was a lot."
"So, where's the framed photo of you receiving the cheque? Where's the framed report from the local paper?"
"I didn't want any publicity. You know what students are like. They'd have been queuing at the door."
"So, when did you win?"
"About a year ago."
"And as soon as you banked the cheque, you bought this?"
"More or less."
"So, how much did it cost?"
"I can't remember exactly."
"A life-changing event, and you hardly remember any detail about it. I think you're telling porkies. What do you think, Louise?"
"I think he's a very modest, sensible young man. I also think he's an outright liar. So, come on, tell us the truth. Where did you get the money from for all this?"

He hesitated as both officers glared at him.

"My parents."
"Liar. We've already spoken to them. They hardly see you these days since you've become a millionaire. You've disowned them."
"That's not true!"
"So, tell us the real story."

Patterson sighed, considering his options. Realising they were few, he opted to tell the truth.

"You're right. I used to be a hard-up student, living in a rented hovel with three other students. I had a part-time job working behind a bar to pay the bills. Then one day I saw an ad on WhatsApp. It looked like easy money. Hours to suit, etc. So, I

206

followed it up and met this bloke in a boozer. He was a bit flash, and kept buying me drinks, asking all about me, like a proper interview. And at the end he told me I'd impressed him, and he wanted to give me a job, but I'd have to be vetted by his associates first. I agreed and we all met in a Wetherspoons in town the next night. Again, all my drinks were paid for, and I got a meal as well. Then they told me what I had to do. It was money for nothing! They wanted me to be in charge of a company who were proposing to develop a site on the quays. I was nominally in charge, but I had nothing to do with it, except put my name to some documents. What was there not to like? So, I agreed, and straightaway they brought me to this apartment and asked if I liked it. Then they said it was mine. All I had to do was sign documents and keep my mouth shut. I couldn't say 'no'."

"Didn't you realise they were crooks?"
"Not at first. I just thought they preferred to do business while keeping a low profile. I thought it was probably a tax dodge or something. Anyway. I'm not a millionaire. They give me a wage to keep me going, and they pay for the flat. I have no legal right to it. If I don't carry on doing what they tell me to do, I get kicked out onto the street."
"So, who are these people?"
"I only know their first names."
"Addresses?"
"No."
"So, how do you contact them?"
"They message me. Tell me where and when to meet them."
"Then what happens?"
"I sign some papers, they give me some money, and that's it."
"You don't have any contact numbers for them?"
"No."
"OK. Write down the names for us. You don't have any photos on your phone by any chance?"
"No."
"OK. Don't go anywhere. We'll be in touch. And don't tell your business associates you've been talking to us."
"OK."

As soon as they left the flat, Gary called Brian to request permission to borrow his gizmo for copying data stored on a mobile phone. He planned to return to Patterson's flat to collect contact information regarding his business associates. He looked at the list of first names Patterson had given him. There was nothing which struck a chord, but he would write the names on a whiteboard at HQ in the hope that perhaps someone could make a connection.

****

The following morning Gary and Louise set off again for Salford, this time with the intention of copying all the data from Patterson's phone for analysis at HQ. When they arrived, Patterson had already left. They spoke to his neighbours who informed them he'd been seen the previous evening carrying suitcases down to the car park where they were loaded into a dark-coloured SUV which then drove off with Patterson in the passenger seat. Nobody could give a description of the driver, apart from the fact he was male, and nor did anyone note the number plate.

Fortunately, there were CCTV cameras in the car park, monitored, he guessed, by the company which owned the car park. He Googled it and called the number. Soon, they were on their way to the company's local office to view CCTV footage.

****

They approached the Reception desk, described the car and asked who was driving it the previous day.

"Mm, not sure really. What time was it?"
"Evening. I'm not sure of the time."
"Registration?"
"Don't know."
"I don't know. If you can give me the time, I might be able to find out. It might be a pool car."
"I'd like to see CCTV coverage of the car park over on Salford Quays."
"Which one? We have three."
"Look, this is a serious investigation. If you don't comply, I'll have you arrested for whatever reason I can think of. So, think about it."
"I'll just get the supervisor. Just take a seat."
"Thank you."

They sat and waited. Louise whispered to Gary.

"You're beginning to act more like Brian every day."
"I'll take that as a compliment."
"It is a compliment."

They were soon scanning CCTV images, looking for a dark SUV. Gary spotted it being loaded with suitcases.

"Stop! Stop it there. That's it. Can you zoom in on the driver?"

The supervisor did all he could to improve the quality of the image, but it remained indistinct. He did, however, confirm it was a pool car and looked up the log for the previous day which gave the name of the employee who was the nominated driver. Gary thanked him and took a copy of the CCTV image to take to the lab for enhancement. At the same time an alert was sent to all northern forces to be on the lookout for David Patterson, whose image had been circulated.

****

Gary was looking at the list of names he'd put on the whiteboard. It was untouched. They were common enough names, James, Eric, Paul, Dan and Douglas, yet no-one had made any suggestions. Until Brian walked in, took one look at the board, and wrote 'Muesli' after 'Douglas' and 'Hardcastle' after 'Dan'. He looked at Gary.

"It's possible."
"Why the hell didn't I think of that? It's logical. We know Hardcastle's at the centre of much of our investigation, and he's tied to ex-DCI Moseley. But what about the others?"
"If you look closely into Hardcastle's recent business dealings, I guess you'll find them. Ask Teresa to run the names through one of her programs."
"Thanks, boss. I'll do that."
"Where did you get the names from, Gary?"
"I got hold of a load of planning applications from City Hall and I was working my way through them when I came across the name M & H Architects, who'd submitted many of the plans. Among the directors were the names Hardcastle and Moseley, which explains the name of the company. Another name was David Patterson, who turned out to be an Economics student living in a posh apartment on Salford Quays. He was a bit evasive, but I got first

names of the people he dealt with. We were going back to take his phone and grab the data from it, but he's done a runner. Sorry, I never made the link. It's so clear."

"Everything's clear with hindsight, Gary. So, back to the planning applications. I assume you were looking at the Girlington area?"

"Yes, boss. This company, M & H Architects, submitted several plans over the years, but it sounds as if Patterson was just used as a conduit for money laundering. He didn't actual do any work for them, which is why I wanted his phone. An APB's been issued for him."

"OK. Let me know if you match any other names."

"OK, boss. I don't expect Hardcastle will help us on this. And Moseley's in the USA, I believe."

"I believe so. But it's worth checking if he's been over on holiday or some other reason. Ask Teresa to check with Immigration."

"OK."

"And Gary, well done. That's good work."

"But I missed the most obvious connection."

"It happens. Nobody's perfect. Between you and Louise, you've uncovered some good leads."

"Thanks, boss."

"The other thing you could check is the data we grabbed from the phone Hardcastle used in Strangeways. That might help you identify some of the other directors of M & H."

"Of course! I'll get straight on it."

****

Gary and Louise spent hours going through the data pulled from the phone Hardcastle used in prison. He evidently conducted his core business from it. One of the first names of any great significance appeared almost daily – Hardcastle's solicitor, a man named Wainwright. *Eric* Wainwright, which just left 'James' and 'Paul' to identify. Gary recognised the importance of Wainwright, who was not only a solicitor, but also a consultant property-broker and financial wizard whose name was listed in an advisory capacity in documents concerning corporate buyouts and mergers. He also did consultancy work for M & H Architects! Gary immediately alerted Brian.

"So, it's obvious Hardcastle's not just sitting on his ill-gotten gains while he's in chokey. He's putting it to good use via Wainwright. It seems we might need assistance in unravelling this lot. I'll inform the NCA. Well done once again, Gary."

"Thanks, boss."

"By the way, Teresa just got back to me about Moseley. He's no longer in the USA. He flew into Manchester Airport a week ago. We're trying to trace him now. I'd like a nice friendly chat with my old boss."

****

Louise continued to work on the information they'd gathered concerning M & H Architects. She logged her findings meticulously, cross-referencing them to other names they'd uncovered, constantly connecting the dots until the full picture became clear. Excited by her finds, she asked Gary and Brian to comment on her conclusion. Slightly nervous, she handed them each a printed report before working through it, page by page.

"Three years ago, you may remember a former mill in the Wapping area, which had been left unused for many years while there was a dispute about its future. There was talk about it being restored to its former glory and re-opened as an Industrial Museum and craft workshop units. Other interested parties wanted to change its use to residential flats and plans had been submitted to that effect. So, there was this battle between developers and those who were trying to have the building listed as having historical and cultural value, and they'd reached a stalemate. Then, the problem solved itself when the building mysteriously caught fire and burned to the ground. The council sold the land for redevelopment as housing and quickly approved the plans, and now the site is full of not-so-affordable housing. The land was bought by a company called Future Bradford. Guess whose names are among the owners? A man called James Ratcliffe, and another called Paul Ratcliffe. They are father and son and used to run a demolition firm. In case you haven't made the connection, the names 'James' and 'Paul' were both on Hardcastle's contact list pulled from his phone and were also among Patterson's contacts."

Louise sat back with a smile of satisfaction on her face. Brian congratulated her.

"This is good work, Louise. Did they ever prove it was arson?"
"No. It was strongly suspected, but not proven."

211

"OK. We're not finished yet. See if you can find any other potentially dodgy dealings concerning Future Bradford. I've a feeling we've opened another can of worms."
"OK, boss."
"When you've done, pass it to me for a final read, and then it goes to the NCA. It's too big for us, but they'll bring us in for the kill. And I'll make sure you get due credit for the work you've done. Both of you."

****

Gary and Louise called unannounced at the Hussains' newly-rented house in Manningham. Mr Hussain reluctantly agreed to speak to them, on the understanding that he and his family would be protected if his collaboration were to become public knowledge. With Gary's promise of confidentiality, he confessed to being complicit in the arson attack and gave a full account.

"They told me I would be able to claim on my insurance, then they would buy the house from me and compensate me for the inconvenience. Then they told me when the attack would take place so we could make ourselves safe. We decided to move out most of our furniture and store it, and make sure the children stayed with relatives. Then, we got a phone call telling us to get out of the house, and minutes later it was set on fire."
"And who were these people who arranged all this?"
They were called Ratcliffe. They were father and son, James and Paul."

****

The Ratcliffes were arrested late that afternoon on a building site in Yeadon, and when questioned, both admitted they were responsible for organising the Girlington arson attacks and recruiting kids to carry out the attacks. They were adamant they were working on instructions from Danny Hardcastle.

CHAPTER 17

Teresa used a disguised phone number to call Moseley's home phone on the remote chance he was there. She was rewarded when he answered, and hurriedly made up the reason for her call.

"Oh, good morning, sir. I'm calling to ask if you would be prepared to answer a few questions for the opportunity to win a brand-new Mercedes car? It will only take a few moments."
"I'm not interested."

He put down the phone, but Teresa had been able to recognise his voice from the few words he'd spoken, and informed Brian immediately.

"Moseley's at home, Brian."
"Thanks. We'll set off straight away. Could you ask the Harrogate lads to keep an eye on the place to check if he moves before we get there?"
"I can ask."

DCI Gardner drove, happy to get out of the office, and was in good spirits throughout the journey. Neither man had much idea how the meeting would go but were prepared to play it by ear.

They pulled up outside a large, detached house with a brand-new Lexus on the drive.

"Looks like he's done well out of his severance pay, boss."
"More likely, it's a bonus for extra-curricular activities. Let's have a word. You do the talking, Brian. It's your case."
"Thank you, sir. It will be a pleasure."

He rang the bell and waited. They could hear the sound of a vacuum cleaner from inside the house. He rang again. This time the vacuum cleaner switched off and the door opened seconds later. It was Moseley.

"Sorry to bother you while you were cleaning, Mr Moseley. We'd like a few words if you can spare the time."
"What do you want?"
"We'd prefer to talk inside if that's OK with you."

Moseley turned to Gardner, looking him up and down.

"And who the hell are you?"
"I'm DCI Gardner, sir. I took over at Bradford after you were thrown out."
"I *retired*. Not that it's any business of yours."
"Can we come in, sir?"
"If you must."

He showed them into a large lounge and motioned for them to sit.

"So, what's all this about?"
"Your name has come up in one of our ongoing inquiries, Mr Moseley. An inquiry into some dodgy business activities."
"Surely, you don't think I'm involved in anything criminal?"
"Of course not, sir. But I'm sure you can help us with our inquiries, as they say."
"Well, get on with it, then. I haven't got all day."
"Neither have we, sir. So, just answer our questions, eh?"
"Go ahead. But I must warn you that I have the right to refuse to answer certain questions unless my lawyer is present."
"I'm sure that won't be necessary, sir."
"Very well. Ask your damned questions."
"Thank you. Can you tell us, please, why you receive a monthly payment from your ex-employee, Daniel Hardcastle?"
"That's a personal matter. None of your business."
"If you are on his payroll, it's certainly our business. I'm sure the Tax Office would be interested too."
"That's enough! I'm calling my lawyer!"
"OK. Tell him to meet us at Bradford HQ."
"I'm not leaving this house until he arrives."
"You don't have a choice. I'm arresting you."
"On what charge?"
"On the charge of being a crooked little bastard."

Gardner stepped in at that point.

"Just a second, Brian. I'd like a quiet word with this gentleman."
"Yes, sir. I'll just stand in the garden and piss on his nice flowers."

Gardner struggled to stifle a laugh as Brian walked out of the house. He turned back to Moseley.

"I hope you'll forgive my colleague. He can be a bit hot-headed."
"That sort of conduct is inexcusable from a police officer. I will be reporting him."
"Really. Well, perhaps you should just stop and think before you do. How's your wife, by the way?"
"She's fine. What's that got to do with it?"
"I was just wondering how you would feel if someone walked into your house while you were here talking to me and stabbed her to death. If someone smashed her skull with an iron bar. And you were here, talking to me, and there was nothing you could do about it. How would you feel? Why would anyone do such a thing? And then, later, you found out it was because you were present when somebody was killed while trying to detonate a bomb in the centre of Bradford. How would you feel?"
"I can't possibly answer that."
"No. I bet you can't. Because you would make sure you never were put in that position. I don't think you care much about what's right and what's wrong. I believe you are the sort of man who is always on the side of whoever is winning."
"How dare you!"
"You don't give a shit about what's right and what's wrong, as long as you get paid. You're exactly what Brian just described. A crooked little bastard."
"How dare you! Get out of my house at once!"
"I'm leaving now. But you're coming with me. Put your hands behind your back while I cuff you. And don't resist, or else I'll call Brian back in to subdue you."
"And what's the charge?"
"Being a crooked little bastard."

He marched Moseley outside where Brian was waiting.

"Put him in the car, please, Brian. I'll lock up. Don't want anyone to enter the house and steal anything, do we? That would be against the law."

Brian grabbed Moseley by the arm and pushed him roughly into the back of the car, making sure his head made contact with the top of the door frame.

"Mind your head, sir. We don't want you to come to any harm, do we? We want to make sure that if anything happens to your wife while you're in our custody, you get to know about it. You know, like, if anyone breaks into your house and stabs her and smashes her skull...."

"I get the message. What do you want?"

"We want your full cooperation. We want you to tell us everything you know about Hardcastle's business. Exactly who's on his payroll and what they're involved in. In return, we promise you we'll be lenient. You'll go into the Witness Protection Scheme. You and your wife will be safe. You'll be given new identities. You know the score. Your choice. We're taking you to HQ. You'll have time to think about it while you sit alone in your cell waiting for your lawyer. The offer's on the table for a limited time only, and the clock is ticking. You only get this offer once. Your choice."

They drove in silence to HQ and parked in the space allocated to the DCI. Brian felt compelled to comment.

"I bet this takes you back, Muesli. You had your own parking space! All that power. And respect. Well, that's all gone out of the window now. You're just another criminal we've brought in. You'll sit in a cell and everyone who passes will stare at you, wondering what you've been up to. Some of them will remember you, no doubt. And, no doubt, they'll laugh at you. I bet it's hard for you to remember way back when people used to respect you. Well, those days are over. Now, you're just another criminal. And the only way you'll get any respect, or self-respect, back, is if you cooperate fully. Think about it, eh?"

They left him in a cell, alone, for an hour until his lawyer turned up, demanding his immediate release. DCI Gardner quickly put him in his place, explaining they would be interviewing him in relation to some very serious offences, and he would only be considered for release once he had satisfied the police that he had cooperated fully and honestly, and wasn't considered a flight risk. The DCI let the two men talk in private while he went to the canteen with a grin on his face.

In the meantime, the DCI's request for a warrant to search Moseley's house had been granted and Forensics were already on their way, accompanied by Scoffer and Louise.

****

Finally, ex-DCI Moseley was ready to be interviewed and was accompanied by his lawyer as Gardner and Peters got to work.

"We know you flew to the UK alone, therefore it's safe to assume you're here on business. We know your wife is at home. We have people watching her due to the friendship between our respective forces. Now, just because I've said that, please don't assume she's safe. Her guards can be persuaded to look the other way if we don't get total cooperation from you. So, please don't attempt to contact anyone after you leave here, and instruct your lawyer likewise, because if we so much as suspect you've told anyone we're investigating, it will just take one phone call and a man will go to your home and murder your wife."

Both Moseley and his lawyer looked horrified, but Gardner added his own comments before either of them could speak.

"DI Peters is speaking metaphorically, of course. What he meant to say is that your wife will have her hand spanked with a wet lettuce. So, how about telling us the full story?"
"I want protection for myself and my wife."
"You'll get it."

Moseley looked at his lawyer who nodded. He continued.

"Years ago, I happened to mention in conversation with Hardcastle that I'd been ripped off by a cowboy builder who'd left me having to pay another builder to rectify the damage caused when I had an extension built on the back of the house. Hardcastle told me not to worry about it. He said he'd have a quiet word with the cowboy builder. A week later, he gave me ten thousand pounds to cover the damage which he said the builder had agreed to. I took it at face value. But from then on, Hardcastle kept reminding me I owed him a favour. And every now and then, he'd commit a small indiscretion and I'd look the other way. Of course, it escalated to the point where I 'looked the other way' while fully aware Hardcastle was involved in criminal activities. At that point, he started paying me regular small amounts to keep my mouth shut. I learnt also that some officers in his team were in on it too. To be honest, I'm glad it's all come out into the open. I was complicit, I admit it. I'll happily tell you all I know as long as you'll protect me."
"We promise. Carry on."

The interview went on late into the afternoon before it was concluded. Moseley was sent back to a cell 'to rest', while Gardner and the team worked out their strategy.

****

The entire team worked late into the evening, until Gardner himself called a halt to proceedings.

"Go home, please. All of you. It's been a long day but enough is enough. Thank you all for your efforts. I *do* appreciate what you've all put into this case. When we're done, we'll celebrate, but until that point it's all hard work. It will be worth it; I can assure you. Now, go home."

Brian listened and watched with pride as the team reluctantly put down their work and prepared to leave. He smiled and whispered quietly to Teresa.

"Don would be proud of him, Teresa."
"He's like Don in many ways. He leads by example. He gets stuck in and acts like he's a part of the team, not just the leader. I like him."
"Me too. And I respect him."
"I think everyone here feels the same."
"You should have seen him in the Interview Room. He's a real pro. I can't wait to see him in action tomorrow."

****

Next morning, Brian was called to Gardner's office before the interview continued.

"You'll be conducting the interview today, Brian. I have other things to do, unfortunately. Take whoever you wish along with you."
"I think it would be useful for Joe Schofield to get the experience if that's OK with you, sir. I know he would like to join us permanently, so the experience will stand him in good stead if he gets considered for a post with us."
"Very well, Brian. I'm sure he'll learn from you."
"I was just thinking he'd learn a lot by sitting in on a session like yesterday with you conducting it."

"I have every confidence he'll learn from you, Brian. He respects you."
"I'm happy to teach him what I can, sir."
"OK. Get to it then."

Moseley, along with his lawyer, was waiting impatiently in the Interview Room when Brian and Scoffer entered.

"Sorry we're a little late, gentlemen."

Moseley expressed his anger despite his lawyer's attempt to calm him.

"You've kept us waiting nearly half an hour."
"Eighteen minutes actually, which isn't long really, considering you could spend the rest of your life in prison. Now, shall we continue? Good. First, I'd like to talk about a company called M & H Architects."

Moseley sighed. The police obviously had done their homework.

"What do you want to know?"
"Let's start with your plans for a mosque in Girlington. Your name appears on the plans."
"First of all, I have nothing to do with the company, apart from being a director."
"Along with our old friend Daniel Hardcastle."
"Yes. He made me a director though I never did any work for them. It was just a vehicle through which he could pay me for 'services rendered'."
"Like paying you for turning a blind eye."
"More or less, yes."
"Were you aware that, for that project to go ahead, it would mean demolishing several occupied houses."
"Danny told me he was in the process of buying the required land."
"Actually, he was paying someone to burn them down. Some residents were killed in the process."
"I wasn't aware of that."
"OK, next. So, you're telling me that you had nothing to do with M & H Architects, apart from being a director?"
"That's right."
"Did you ever meet the other directors?"
"No."

"Never?"
"No."
"That's odd. You're sitting next to one of them."

Brian turned his gaze on Moseley's lawyer, who suddenly looked very uncomfortable. Brian continued.

"Isn't that right, Mr Wainwright?"
"It's true I've done some advisory work for them in the past, yes."
"Like advising which houses need to be demolished for building plans to be approved?"
"I have no comment to make."
"No? I expected you to say, 'I want to see my lawyer'. This is farcical, don't you think?"
"I'm not answering any of your questions. I'm merely here to support my client."
"And is he paying you for this 'support'? Or is Hardcastle footing the bill?"
"I'm not answering your questions. I'm not the one who's been arrested."
"Your turn will come."

They eventually took a break for lunch. Sandwiches and coffee were provided for Moseley and Wainwright, who were made to stay in the Interview Room and only allowed to use the toilet if accompanied by an officer. Quite discreetly, Brian made sure they had to wait for this privilege.

After lunch Brian brought up the subject of the company Future Bradford.

"They built that substandard estate in the Wapping area and pocketed a fortune before the company was liquidated. We're still chasing the owners, James and Paul Ratcliffe. Your company, I believe, worked on their behalf on the scheme."
"My client has no comment to make."
"I thought not. How about you, Mr Wainwright? You worked on this scheme too. Do you have a comment to make?"
"No."
"OK. Let's move on. Your house in Harrogate, Mr Muesli. Sorry, slip of the tongue, Mr *Moseley*. I noticed it's still furnished although nobody lives there, and it's not for sale. Can I assume, you keep it available for your frequent visits to the UK?"

"We haven't yet decided whether to sell it. I just check it whenever I'm here. Pick up any post and that sort of thing."
"You don't actually stay there?"
"Not overnight, no."
"Well, perhaps when you get your new identity to start your new life, you'll be able to sell it. You'll get a decent price for it. Good condition, nice furniture. Don't you agree, PC Schofield?"
"Yeah. Very nice. And don't worry. We left it as we found it."

Moseley was enraged.

"You've been snooping round my house? How dare you!"
"I wasn't snooping, sir. I just accompanied Forensics when they did a full search of the property. It was surprising what they turned up."

Moseley was restrained from commenting further by his solicitor, and simply sat, seething in silence. Brian continued.

"Right. Time to get down to business. Tell me everything you know about Hardcastle's enterprises while he's been in chokey."
"I don't know anything."
"Do you actually want to spend the rest of your life looking over your shoulder? Expecting to be murdered at any moment? And what about your wife? We made you an offer. Take it and talk. Or suffer the consequences. And if you refuse, what do you think your wife will say when we tell her she will be murdered, brutally?"
"OK, OK. What do you want to know?"
"Let's start with the role of Hardcastle. He's the kingpin. Correct?"
"Yes."
"We know he was active in the sale and supply of drugs while he was a serving officer. What else was he up to before he was arrested?"
"I really don't know."
"You turned a blind eye?"
"Yes. I suspected he was importing hard drugs but didn't pursue it."
"Did you know the officers in his team were involved in his illegal activities."
"Not until it became public knowledge, no."
"For a DCI, you really weren't on the ball, were you?"
"Look! I was not far short of retiring. I'd had a long career. I'd worked hard and was a model officer until I made the mistake of

allowing Hardcastle to corrupt me. I admit it. It was the money. Once I took the money, it was downhill all the way."

"You never thought about reporting him?"

"Of course, I did! But it was too late by then. I was in it up to my neck. I couldn't wait to get out of the country. I just hoped it would all blow over when Hardcastle was arrested, but the payments kept coming, and I couldn't bring myself to come clean."

"Then I've absolutely no sympathy for you, but you've got one last chance of redemption. We're going to leave you while you write a statement. Tell us everything! I want to know everything you know about Hardcastle, his friends, his business associates. Anything you tell us will help keep him in prison for the rest of his life. Do that, and I don't care what misdemeanours you've committed, you won't be held to account. And, so that your solicitor can't influence what you write, he won't be with you because we're taking him into another room where he'll face similar questions. I'll say this just one more time. You're just small fry, but if you don't cooperate, you'll be charged with everything I can think of. If you *do* cooperate, you'll be allowed to start afresh with a new identity and a clean slate. Your choice, and the offer won't stay on the table for long. Do yourself a favour and help us put the real villain away for the rest of his life."

****

Once Moseley's statement had been photocopied and passed around the team, Brian held a meeting at which each member of the team was given a specific course of investigation to undertake. Where there were overlaps, officers would collaborate. All progress reports were typed up daily and passed to the rest of the group so that everyone knew the status of every phase of the operation. Every member of the team worked late every evening, and they were all at their desks at weekends. The only member of the team who was allowed time off work – one afternoon - was Brian who represented Bradford CID at a special service in Don McArthur's honour. There, with his head bowed in silence, he made a vow to bring the case against Hardcastle to the conclusion Don would have demanded. Then, and only then, would his boss rest in peace.

As he walked back to his car, he pulled out his phone, switched it back on and checked his messages. There was only one voicemail, from Teresa. He listened.

"Don't make any concessions to Muesli until you talk to me. I've found something important."

He checked his watch and called her back. He was astounded at what he heard and raced back to HQ.

CHAPTER 18

Teresa was on the phone when he reached her desk. She acknowledged him but put a finger to her lips to indicate he should remain silent until she finished her call. He sat impatiently until she closed the call and turned to him with a huge grin.

"You'll love this, Brian."
"It must be important, so let's hear it."
"Well, I started to wonder why Muesli would decide to decamp to the USA when he left the force. I mean, it seemed an odd choice. To my knowledge he has no family in the States and all the time he worked here I never heard him express any affection for the USA. He always seemed to me the sort of person who would retire to the seaside, Bridlington, maybe, or the Isle of Wight. But not the USA. So, out of curiosity, I found his USA address among some of the papers Forensics took from his Harrogate house. I looked on Google maps and found it. It's huge! I did a bit more research and discovered it's a very upmarket in-high-demand area. So, I called one of my contacts in the FBI and he sent me some surprising details. Listen to this. The property now owned by Muesli cost him the small matter of 4.5 million dollars! Imagine that! The area is taking over from the Hamptons, which apparently is becoming a little passé. It's a massive house in acres of grounds. Believe me, even if Muesli had been allowed to take his full pension, there is no way he would be able to afford the bills to run the house, never mind buy it."
"So, he's got another source of income?"
"Yep. And we both know where from. He's not been honest with you, Brian. These are not just small amounts he's taking from Hardcastle. This is a partner's share. He needs to be brought back down to earth."
"Thanks, Teresa. You've stopped me making an arse of myself once more. We'll keep this between ourselves for now, until we've got all we can out of Muesli, and then I'll renege on my promise of protection. It'll serve the bugger right."
"I agree with you entirely, Brian. But I thought you'd already promised him witness protection, with his lawyer present?"
"I did, but his lawyer's crooked too. So, any promise I made, as far as I'm concerned, is void. They can argue it out between them."
"I'd love to see his face when you tell him."
"Me too. I'll sort it."

****

By the time he was ready to leave HQ, Teresa's sealed file regarding Muesli's financial affairs was on his desk. He put it in his briefcase and took it home.

He sat at the kitchen table until midnight, reading the file, making notes. He was taken aback by the epic scale of the financial figures involved. It was bigger than anyone imagined. He finally put the file aside and went to bed, determined to raise the matter with the DCI as soon as possible.

He hadn't slept well and during the drive to work the next morning, he'd wrestled with the options. Finally, he decided to tell DCI Gardner the facts and let him make the decision. Teresa joined him in the DCI's office where Brian laid out the known facts before adding his hypothesis.

"We've always assumed Hardcastle was the man behind the drugs business, and that he involved others when it suited him, paying them according to their role in each transaction. But what if they were all part of a consortium where Hardcastle was the nominal leader, but the rest of his team were all willing conspirators?"
"What exactly is the point you're trying to make, Brian?"
"We've assumed that the likes of Tarkovics and his fellow officers just took back-handers for playing minor roles in the transactions. Turning a blind eye, etc. But what if it was a team effort? We've seen how rich Muesli has become; surely it's worth looking into his team's finances."

There was silence while Gardner thought it over before he gave his decision.

"While it pains me to even consider the possibility that a team of CID officers could work together willingly to carry out serious criminal offences for financial gain, I have to say it's not impossible. Therefore, you have my permission to investigate further. Use as many members of the team as you need on this. That is, if you can trust them."
"That's a valid point, sir. But, believe me, of the current staff, I trust them all."
"Then go to it. If you need anything, just ask."
"Thank you, sir."

Brian gathered his team in the Conference Room and laid out his theory, adding for the benefit of all present:

"I have a strong suspicion that the officers I've named were corrupt. Please rest assured that I do NOT include any of the personnel who currently work with me. The officers named were all here when I joined. In fact, the only personnel working here at that time who are still with us, apart from myself, of course, are Gary, Lynn and Teresa. I have no doubts whatsoever regarding their honesty. So, put aside your current investigations although you may find they overlap with what I'm asking you to look into. So, work in twos. Take a folder and check thoroughly the finances of the officers in Hardcastle's team. Teresa and I will be looking at payments made by Hardcastle's shell company in the hope that we can link the named recipients to the officers under suspicion. Anything you come across which seems in any way suspicious, flag it up. OK, let's get to it."

Gradually, over the course of the next week, details began to emerge of regular unexplained payments to the CID officers, all for amounts over £10,000, all from the same company, registered as DH Logistics. The only officer who did not receive such sums was DS Barlow. Brian believed he had the answer to that.

"Barlow acted as an occasional driver, and so would probably be paid in cash in smaller amounts. I have no doubt the others would have received cash payments too, in addition to their 'salary' from DH Logistics, Hardcastle's drugs import business."

Over the days, a further pattern emerged. Regular transfers of several thousand pounds were made from each officer's account. They were made to various companies in sequence. They all appeared to be 'shell' companies, which automatically transferred the deposits immediately to other accounts. One by one, they identified the holders of many of those accounts which were offshore. They were all ex-officers. Their money was simply being 'washed'. Among them were the members of Hardcastle's CID team, and another name they hadn't expected – McGuire, the Lottery winner and ex- prison officer at Strangeways.

"Come on, Scoffer. Let's go and have another word with him."

The last time Don had spoken to McGuire, he'd left convinced that McGuire's extravagant lifestyle was due to a Lottery win. He'd had it checked; McGuire had indeed won close to five million pounds, had a house built and then packed in his job. It had now become apparent, though, that he still had a regular income which could be traced back to Hardcastle.

He allowed them into his house. To describe it as 'opulent' would be an understatement. They sat down on a huge black leather settee. Concealing his envy, Brian got straight to the point.

"The last time one of my officers spoke to you, you told him you'd bought the house with the proceeds of a Lottery win."
"That's correct."
"I know. We checked."
"So, why are you back?"
"You left something out."
"What?"
"Your other source of income. From Hardcastle, a prisoner you did business with."
"You can't prove any of that!"
"We can. We've looked into your finances. You receive a five-figure sum every month from an offshore account. It's paid into one of your many offshore accounts. You've long since spent your lottery winnings, but you still have bills to pay. Don't worry, Hardcastle's looked after you. There's more in one of your offshore accounts than the amount you won on the lottery, which tells me you're still working for him. So, would you like to tell us about it before we have your account frozen?"

McGuire looked stunned. He was dumbstruck; his world was on the brink of collapsing. He put his head in his hands and sighed.

"OK. It's true. He's paying me but let me explain. When I worked at Strangeways, he was admitted and had a hard time from some of the old lags initially. We turned a blind eye. He deserved it. A bent cop. But it wasn't long before he started offering money to some guards for protection. Some of us took it. Then he started asking for other favours, like access to a phone. Everything has a price, and we didn't think there was much harm in it. Then I won the lottery and packed my job in. I was glad, really. I could see where it was going. He was asking for more 'favours' and getting them as long as he paid. Then, one day I got a call from him at home. He warned me that he'd make public the fact I'd been on his payroll unless I kept my mouth shut. He said he still had friends in the Force who'd make life difficult for me. When I agreed to stay silent, he asked me to launder money for him through my account. He said because I was a millionaire, nobody would query the large amounts passing through it. He said I'd get a decent percentage. So, stupidly, I agreed. But, I promise, I've never spent a penny of it. It's sitting in an account, earning interest till I die. Then, it gets distributed to various charities. Here, let me prove it."

He walked over to a roll-top desk from where he pulled an envelope containing his Will.

"Here, read it. When I die, everything I own goes to charity. There it is, in black and white. Feel free to talk to my solicitor. He'll verify it all."
"You're giving it all away?"
"The lot. What good is it to me when I've gone?"
"OK. Mind if I take a copy on my phone?"
"Be my guest."
"Well, thank you, Mr McGuire. Just one more thing and we'll leave you in peace."
"What's that?"
"I want the names of the other prison warders on Hardcastle's payroll."

McGuire sighed, then complied.

"I'll write them down for you."

****

They drove back to Bradford, Brian driving in silence while Scoffer called Teresa with the new information they'd received so that it could be verified without delay.

When they arrived, Brian called Teresa, asking her to meet him in one of the empty Interview Rooms. He had an overdue apology to make to her.

"I'm sorry to disturb your work, Teresa, but I owe you an apology."
"Whatever for?"

"For taking advantage of your loyalty to me that night at my house."
"You didn't take advantage, Brian. I came to you voluntarily because you needed me. You needed my company. It wasn't as if we had sex."
"But what if Nikki found out?"
"Nikki knows. I told her the following day. She understands, Brian. We're fine. She thought it was a lovely thing for me to do, so don't worry."
"That's a relief! Thank you, Teresa. You're a wonderful woman."
"And you're a wonderful man, and I'll always regard you as my best friend, but, unfortunately, not my lover. It's just how it is."
"I'm so glad you're not angry with me."
"Not at all. You just showed your human side. Anyway, is that it? I've loads to do today."
"Anything we can help you with?"
"If you could spare Louise for a few hours, it would be a great help."
"I'll send her up."
"Thanks, Brian. I need to spend some time getting all our info on Hardcastle ready to pass to the NCA. I really want to nail that bastard."
"Me too. Any progress on evidence against the crook at HMRC?"
"James Lloyd? Nothing, I'm afraid. That's already gone to NCA. They're better positioned to gather evidence on that."
"OK. Thanks again."
"My pleasure."

He winked and replied, smiling.

"The pleasure would have been all mine, *if* it had happened."

There were two letters on the hall floor when Brian arrived home. The first one, from the BRI, he opened immediately and read where he stood. As he'd expected, it was his test results. It was good news; they were all negative. He breathed a huge sigh of relief before moving to the kitchen to read the other letter. It was from the company which administered Sarah's life insurance policy. The pay-out was more than Brian had expected but was still scant consolation for the loss of his wife. Never mind; now he could move on. Taking out a notepad, he made a quick list of things he needed to do. Close Sarah's accounts and have the money transferred to his. The same with the kids' ISAs. Bag up all their clothes and the kids' toys for the charity shops Sarah supported. He would contact a local Estate Agent in the morning with a view to selling his house. That had been the most difficult decision; the house was full of memories. But those memories were now just ghosts. He had to move on. He had to try to take the memories but leave the ghosts. And, after that, what next? A flat somewhere? Or should he move away from the area and try to build a new life somewhere else? Leave it all behind. He could afford it now. And then there was the small matter of his job. A job he used to relish. A job he was good at. A job which now had cost him so much. And if he continued to do it for the rest of his working life, what would he get? A pension. A comfortable pension with which to live out his life... alone. And the memories of the many victories he'd played a part in, but which in the end were outweighed by the one crushing incident which ended his married life, taking away his wife and their family. He sat at the kitchen table, sobbing, his head in his hands.

It was a difficult decision for him to make, but eventually he decided to go in to work next morning. Good news was waiting for him.

"They've got Patterson, Brian. He was picked up in Liverpool last night. Do you want to interview him?"
"No. Let Scoffer do it, with Jo-Jo or Paula alongside him just to keep him within the boundaries of reasonable behaviour. The experience will do him good. I think he's capable of doing a good job."

There were two reasons why Brian had passed up the option of leading the interview. Ostensibly, he was giving Scoffer the opportunity to show how he'd progressed and learnt on the job. The other reason was that Brian wanted nothing more to do with police work and had come in simply to speak with the DCI and hand in his resignation. The ringing of his desk phone interrupted his thoughts.

"Brian, could you please come up to the Conference Room? It's important."
"I'm on my way."

When he walked through the door, he was surprised to find the entire team waiting for him, each with a glass in hand. As he walked in, he was greeted by spontaneous applause.

"What's this about?"

"Come in, Brian. We all decided it would be a good idea to celebrate the fantastic job you've done in leading the team to such a magnificent result. My superiors instructed me to thank all the team for the work they've done, but to reserve special thanks to the man who leads them. Well done, all of you. But above all, special thanks to you, Brian. You've done an outstanding job, in very difficult circumstances. We're all grateful, and, believe me, if I could give you a promotion, I would gladly do so."

"Thank you, sir. But let's not forget I couldn't have done it without the help of every single officer here, but above all, let's not forget the role of my mentor, Don McArthur, who would have loved to have been here today. He taught me everything I know, and still influences my thinking every day. And while I appreciate your thoughts today, I believed Don when he told me this isn't over. However, the entire process we've gone through has worn me out physically and mentally, and enough is enough."

There was silence in the room, until Scoffer spoke up.

"If that's an indication that you're thinking of packing it in, please think again. You're still teaching me the job, and I still have some learning to do. And I guess every other member of the team is of the same opinion."

Gardner immediately endorsed Scoffer's statement.

"Scoffer's right, Brian. I need you to continue to train and encourage the team. They've all improved under your leadership and it's only right they should have the benefit of your wisdom and experience to become the best officers they can be. Do we all agree?"

There was a resounding cheer from the team. Brian put his hand up to silence them before he spoke.

"I came in to work this morning with a letter of resignation in my jacket pocket. I fully intended to hand it to DCI Gardner. I realise now that perhaps now is not the right time. I'm extremely proud of the way my team has progressed while I've been here. But it's not just down to me. DCI Gardner's arrival had a lot to do with it. It's good to have an honest and intelligent man at the head. And let's not forget Don's contribution. We should all be grateful for his input to these complicated cases we've faced recently. But most of all, I have to thank each and every team member for your hard work, perseverance and tenacity. But let's not congratulate ourselves yet. This isn't over. And I'll stay with the team until it is. Thank you all, and cheers."

****

Brian finished work early that day to allow an Estate Agent to view his house and take photographs prior to offering it for sale. The agent gave Brian his valuation and Brian agreed without question. He was more interested in getting out of the house than how much it was worth. By the weekend, he'd had an offer which he accepted. Now, he had to find somewhere else to live, and quickly. He used websites to narrow his search and arranged to look at a few over the weekend.

****

When Brian arrived at work on Monday morning, Teresa couldn't wait to give him the good news.

"The NCA have picked him up, Brian."
"Picked who up?"
"Lloyd. James Lloyd. At the HMRC headquarters. In front of the entire staff! They told me they've got enough to charge him, thanks to some assistance from various members of Hardcastle's consortium, and some of his colleagues at HMRC who've long had suspicions he was bent. In return, he's told the NCA all he knows about Hardcastle, and given us hard evidence. Looks like they've all grassed each other up."
"Thanks for that, Teresa. That's made my day."
"By the way, the NCA discovered the identity of the man who was known as 'Shifty'."
"Surprise me."
"A man named Barry Lloyd, James Lloyd's brother, used to work for Mr Shifter, the removals company. He was sacked after it was discovered he was siphoning money into his own account through some false accounting; hence he was referred to as Mr Shifty. His

brother James used the nickname from then on in his dealings by text with Hardcastle."

He immediately made arrangements to visit Hardcastle at HMP Manchester to congratulate him on his downfall and was delighted to be able to go that afternoon. To his surprise, DCI Gardner asked to accompany him.

They were shown to the Interview Room and made themselves comfortable until Hardcastle was brought in by a burly guard. He sat opposite, scowling. Brian opened the conversation.

"I'm pleased to tell you we won't be harassing you or your accomplices any longer. We're happy you'll all get the sentence you deserve."
"I've been stitched up. I was just a pawn in the game. There are others above me."
"Maybe. But we're happy we've got enough on you to keep you in chokey for a long, long time. It's over."
"I'll appeal. I've got well-paid lawyers."
"I know. I also know where their pay has come from. We've found the money trail. Every branch of it. Believe me, it's not just you that's going to spend the rest of their life in jail."

He paused, smiling, before delivering the coup de grâce.

"And do you know who was responsible for unearthing all this damning evidence against you and all the others in your criminal empire? Teresa, that's who. Surely you remember her. Teresa Shackleton, the clerical officer you despised because she's of Jamaican descent and, dare I say it, a lesbian as well. She's worked hard, using all her undoubted skills and tenacity to put all the evidence together to pass to the Director of Public Prosecutions. They've looked at the evidence and you will be tried. And by the time you have any chance of parole, you'll be an OAP, and all the wealth you had stashed away will have been confiscated. Tough, eh?"
"I'll get even."
"No. All your assets have been frozen. You've no money. Neither have any of your accomplices. There's nobody to help you because you can't pay them. How does that feel?"
"People owe me favours. I'll put the word out and one of them will kill you."

"That won't happen. We both know that. But I'll promise you one thing. If I'm still alive when, if, you get out of prison, I'll be waiting across the road for you. And we'll settle it there and then."
"I'll look forward to that."
"Me too."

The next item on Brian's agenda was to settle up with Muesli. He had him brought to the Interview Room with his solicitor. Brian was not surprised to note that Muesli was now represented by a different lawyer, his previous one having been remanded due to his involvement in criminal activity. Muesli looked pessimistic, wondering if there might be more bad news for his prospects of release. Brian didn't disappoint him.

"I've been looking at your recent financial records."
"And?"
"I notice you seem to be receiving a huge amount of money on a regular basis. What's it for?"
"For consultancy work."
"Consultancy work for a group of criminals?"
"Businessmen."
"OK. *Illegal* businessmen."

Muesli remained silent. Brian continued.

"I previously said you'd be treated leniently if you cooperated with us. Now, I find you've been concealing the fact that you continue to receive huge amounts of money from criminal activities."
"I knew of no such activities."
"Yes, you did! You simply chose to look the other way while they took place. Well, let me tell you this. When you're on trial for your crimes and we get to the bit where the judge gives his guilty verdict and reads out your sentence, *I'll* be looking the other way, so that you don't see me crying with laughter."
"You promised you'd get me a deal for my cooperation!"
"I've changed my mind. Enjoy your years in chokey."

****

Brian was at his desk when Teresa called him.

"Brian, I've just taken a call from Mr Sullivan. You'll remember him - the journalist who gave us the lead on Rose Phelan?"

"Ah, yes. I remember him. What does he want now?"
"Permission to print his novel about Hartley, I think."
"He knows he can't do that until after Hartley's trial."
"I think he may have something up his sleeve to persuade us."
"OK. I'll talk to him."

He drove up to Heaton and parked outside a neat semi. The front door opened as he got out of the car and Sullivan was waiting to greet him.

"Come in, Mr Peters. Thank you for coming to see me. Please follow me into the lounge."

Brian complied but refused the offer of a drink.

"I'm sorry. I don't have time. We're very busy at the moment, so can we please get to the point? Why do you wish to speak to me?"
"A week or so ago, a woman got in touch with me after I wrote a brief outline for my new book, about Simon Hartley, in the Telegraph. She believes she's the one that got away."

Sullivan sat back in the armchair looking smug, expecting Brian to take the bait. Instead, he simply said,

"If that's the case, she needs to present herself at HQ and ask for me or one of my team."
"I get the impression she was hoping to be paid for her story."
"While it's true we have informants who keep us aware of certain criminal activities, we don't make a habit of paying members of the public for information."
"In that case she won't talk to you."
"In that case we could charge you with failing in your public duty to inform the police of her identity, knowing she has evidence pertaining to a crime we're investigating. So, her name and address, please."

Sullivan sighed and wrote the name and address on a notepad, tore the sheet from the pad and handed it to Brian.

"Thank you, Mr Sullivan. I can assure you that when Hartley gets what's coming to him, you'll get my full cooperation regarding details for your book."

****

Brian and Louise parked outside a run-down semi on the Ravenscliffe estate. He made doubly sure the car was locked before they walked to the front door. Their knock was answered by angry barking from within. Louise remarked

"She doesn't sound happy to see us, Brian."
"Don't prejudge, Louise. Perhaps she has a dog."

The door was opened by a scruffily dressed, haggard-looking woman who looked to be in her sixties but who in reality was in her late thirties. The small dog by her feet looked to have had an equally difficult life.

"Miss Watkins? DI Peters and DC Holmes. I believe you have some information for us about Simon Hartley."
"What's it worth?"
"It's worth your freedom from fear that he'll come looking for you, because we want to put him in prison. Your testimony will help."
"I'm not going to court."
"You won't have to. Just tell us your story, then perhaps we can help you."
"With money?"
"We can help you get off drugs. That'll save you a lot of money."

She sighed.

"Come in."

She explained how she was working on Lumb Lane. An addict, she needed money for heroin, so she sold her body. One night, a man picked her up and drove her to Heaton Woods. She had a bad feeling about him and at one point during sex, he tried to strangle her. She fought back and kicked him in the balls, before scrambling out of the car without her shoes, and running away, hiding in the woods. She lay behind some bushes, in the damp grass as rain started to fall and stayed there until, eventually, daylight broke. She made her way home on foot, soaked and shoeless, and found the flat she used was locked and her keys didn't fit. Her neighbour told her the landlord had changed the locks because she was behind with her rent, so she slept on the streets until a man took her in. He gave her drugs and beat her and used her for sex. In time, she escaped and found refuge with the Salvation Army. They helped her get clean and got her the house. Now, she was back on drugs, living off benefits and hoping to sell her story to the papers.

Brian showed her photos of Hartley and she was able to identify him positively as the man who'd tried to kill her in Heaton Woods.

They returned to the car with her signed statement.

"What are you going to do, Brian?"
"I'm not sure. We have to include her statement as evidence, but it's hard to say whether she's telling the truth or just fabricating a story for financial gain. I think at the moment we have to give her the benefit of the doubt. I just hope they don't call her to give evidence in court. And, let's not forget, we still have two bodies, or missing persons, unaccounted for, so the case is still open."

They drove back to HQ, another task completed. Another day over. Brian wondered how many more he could face. Or, more to the point, how many he *wanted* to face.

Tomorrow, he would take the day off and drive to the Cow and Calf to spend time thinking it over in the company of his family.

THE END

Previous novels by Ian McKnight

Premonition (Dec 2017)

A fast-paced crime thriller centred on a terrorist plot to explode a bomb in Bradford City Centre and the CTU's attempt to thwart it.

The Devil Finds Work (Oct 2018)

A routine investigation into a girl's death from a drug overdose escalates into the search for an international drugs smuggler in a fast-moving tale of corruption.

Games People Play (Oct 2019)

DI Peters and his team investigate a series of murders while dealing with cases of missing persons, when they become aware of an international human trafficking ring operating on their patch.

Unfinished Business (Jul 2020)

The discovery of an amputated foot leads DI Peters on a trail of crimes involving Climate Change Activists with a hidden agenda, international drugs smuggling; a serial child abuser; corruption in local government, and a computer hacker terrorising and blackmailing innocent victims.

The Pandora Program (Jun 2021)

The team chase people smugglers enslaving immigrants and uncover a paedophile ring.

The Ray Light trilogy: **(2017)**

Losing Lucy
Light Years On
Light At The End Of The Road

A philandering widower seeks to rebuild his life following the death of his wife. A hilarious trilogy full of twists and turns.

The Forkham Predicament (Nov 2020)

A madcap comedy set against the background of a pandemic.

All available from Amazon, in paperback and Kindle